Isla bristled. "No, I
What are you implying?"

"Anti-plastic garbag
these groups. Lot of ske
that."

She broke into a peal of laughter but looked angry, a dangerous spark in her eyes. "What? That's ridiculous! So, you reckon you didn't manage to convince me with your well-referenced arguments," she said, layering on the sarcasm. "And now, I'm a convenient scapegoat. Maybe you shouldn't have left me in here on my own! Maybe you're the one who's responsible."

Pietro flushed bright red, and his eyes bulged as if he were one of his own safety valves, about to blow.

"Hold on, hold on, Pietro. It's upsetting, but you can't blame the signorina," said Edmondo. It was reassuring that in spite of her injury, Isla was clearly not about to collapse and, in fact, was giving every bit as good as she got. "For a start, I suggested the tour. And she didn't hit herself on the head."

"Yeah—and how well do you know this woman? What if she's working with someone?"

"That's enough! I suggest you apologize now. You have nothing to base this argument on, and you insult Signorina Bruni. And me." He stared hard at the older man. "And that is not a good thing, my friend."

Isla raised her head at the tone of his voice, glimpsing the tough, successful businessman behind the suave exterior.

Then the Earth Moved

by

Mary Georgina de Grey

Then the Earth Moved

Cover Art by *Jennifer Greeff*

The Wild Rose Press, Inc.
PO Box 708
Adams Basin, NY 14410-0708
Visit us at www.thewildrosepress.com

Publishing History
First Edition, 2023
Trade Paperback ISBN 978-1-5092-4699-1
Digital ISBN 978-1-5092-4700-4

Published in the United States of America

Dedication

To Ian who has coaxed and encouraged and never
allowed me to give up.

Chapter 1

Was this the bar she'd meant? This luxurious establishment in one of Milan's most expensive hotels certainly looked the perfect setting for Mariella. Isla hoped she'd got it right. Her legs ached, and she was too tired to walk any farther.

But when she put her head around the door, there was her colleague sitting alone at the counter. Isla almost limped across the room and hitched herself up onto the stool next to her.

"Glad you made it. I thought you were going to stand me up."

"I wouldn't do that when I promised I'd come," she said, trying to hide her grimace. Her toes must be bleeding, they were squeezed so tightly into her smart work shoes. What if she just kicked them off? The marble floor looked deliciously cool and would do wonders for her throbbing soles. No, it couldn't be done, not in this sophisticated place.

"Phew! I can't believe how hot it is," Mariella said.

But not the slightest tinge of pink showed in her perfect complexion. She crossed one slim leg over the other, displaying her black, ankle-tie evening pumps. Isla would love to be able to afford footwear like that. They were Blahniks, of course—and they'd have cost what she herself earned in a week.

But the Italian design conference was over now,

and to be honest, she didn't much care about her image.

She settled more comfortably and closed her eyes. Sleep was an attractive idea, but she wouldn't find time for that for a while yet. Although the air-conditioning whispered in the background, beads of perspiration were gathering on her forehead. She dabbed at them with a limp tissue and pushed the thick curtain of dark, wavy hair back over her shoulders, allowing what little air there was to circulate. Instead of hanging around here any longer, she should throw all her things into the car and head south. She could be well on her way in half an hour.

Then, she forced herself to sit upright, even pasting a smile onto her face. Maybe that way, she'd look as if she wanted to be there.

Isla's drink stood waiting, and Mariella had already begun the important process of rehydrating, sipping enthusiastically from a tall glass that contained something with a deep, orangey-red heart. A tiny pink umbrella lay beside her predatory fingers on the bar. Isla took a cautious drink of her gin and tonic and picked up their conversation where they'd left off a little while earlier.

"I'm not a great fan of the way she put those colors together, not in that sort of building. Green and pink for what's supposed to be an upscale restaurant doesn't work for me."

"I'm surprised you say that. Everyone loved the colors."

"Well, a big-name designer was giving the presentation, so of course, she knew what she was talking about."

In fact, the shades the speaker had chosen had

shown no subtlety, and the combinations harked back to fashions in the far-too-recent past.

Forget the sarcasm, though; Mariella just gave her a blank look. If Isla was hoping for discussion about the session they'd attended, she was out of luck.

"I thought they were okay."

And with that, the woman turned to scrutinize her perfect reflection in the mirror which formed the back wall of the bar. Leaning forward, she pulled at a few loose strands of hair to coax them into hanging artfully around her face, before turning back to her colleague.

"All these hours of glorious freedom. I can think of quite a few ways to fill the time—and they don't include work, Isla." She grinned. "Actually, I have my eye on someone."

Of course she did. If the previous days were anything to go by, the only thing Mariella would be interested in was setting up her evening. God, she was like a child just released from school. Isla wouldn't mind being able to switch off at times herself, but *her* mind was still going over the information they'd been given in that morning's session, which had sparked a lot of new ideas. It would be fantastic to give them a try.

After four days in Mariella's company, Isla was pretty clued in about her fellow delegate. In fact, what was surprising was that she hadn't arrived at the bar with a man in tow.

"Did you hear that?"

What on earth was it? She looked around. A strange rumbling was coming from somewhere nearby. Now, the bottles and glasses began rattling, and even the surface of her drink was trembling in the glass. She remembered her mother's words about earthquake zones. But surely this wasn't one, was it? Then, blue lights flashed in the plate glass window and a fire engine ploughed rapidly past. She smiled—even in this most luxurious of hotels, they weren't entirely shut off from reality.

"Come on! Let's talk about something else, Isla. Sometimes you have to relax, you know."

"Sorry! You were going to tell me about your holiday in Tahiti."

For a while, they discussed the very upmarket destination she was going to, but the way Mariella kept scanning the room made conversation difficult. Isla now looked around, expecting to spot a hopeful male heading in their direction—or rather, in her companion's direction—but they still had the bar to themselves, so she took another tiny sip of gin and studied the beautifully designed surroundings, determined to commit it all to memory—because there was no way she'd be able to afford a stay in a hotel like this again. She wanted to experience all the luxury the inflated prices indicated, remember later what it felt like to spend time in a place like this—the sort of environment she sometimes had a hand in creating.

And its understated elegance was truly worth looking at. Her designer's eye scanned the opposite wall, appreciating the delicacy of the Japanese screening at the lofty windows. She imagined recreating something similar in one of her projects. The square frames of black wood could have looked heavy, but instead, they gave an air of sophistication. Of course, the thickness of each piece contributed to that effect. Pulling out her phone, she took a discreet picture. Her phone gallery was full of design ideas that had caught her eye.

"It's all you do," Richard had said to her more than once. "You have no time for me—or anyone else, for that matter. I don't understand you."

"I have to be focused and work hard. I'll never get enough experience to move my career on otherwise. Don't think I don't care for you, Richard, but other things are important as well. I do intend to start my own company. I have so many ideas I want to explore. Please try to support me in this."

He'd just grunted, maybe recognizing that's how she was and that she was unlikely to change.

Well, their conversations were finished. Richard was out of her life, and a good thing, too. And instead, determined not to compromise, she'd worked even longer hours, trying to avoid her empty flat.

"Don't look around now," said Mariella suddenly, "but two sexy hunks from the conference have just come in, and I really fancy one of them. If they come over, just so you know, I like the blond-haired guy, okay? He's mine."

Isla grinned at her. "The blond? Right, I'll totally ignore him."

They'd got on well together, but the older woman's whole focus was on the next few hours and the most interesting man she could find to share them with. For interesting, read gorgeous. They were having this one drink to celebrate the end of the conference, and then she'd go off with the handsomest man in the room.

And that left Isla free to do whatever she wanted. She could go to bed early and get some much-needed sleep or she could leave. That was appealing, although she'd lose out on the final night in this fabulous hotel.

She shrugged. More important things were driving her than how to spend a night in town.

As Isla wiped more sweat from her brow, the barman apologized for the breakdown of the air-conditioning—which had now stopped its discreet susurration. They'd called the engineer and it would soon be working again, he said. Ignoring this, and looking impossibly cool, Mariella scrolled through her phone.

"Have you heard of Viaggi nel Gusto?" she asked him in English. "Someone recommended it. The food's supposed to be really great."

They began talking restaurants, and Isla tuned out. Now the conference was over, she was heading south into the Abruzzo, where she'd be spending the next six months. The region lay about halfway down the Adriatic coast and stretched back into the Apennine chain of mountains which divided Italy in two. Absolutely everything about it appealed to her. But the tiny hilltop town of Fortezza del Tronto was going to be in great contrast to her London life, and that prospect was just a little scary. Would she settle or would she find it too constricting? The way of life too different? She squared her shoulders, and adrenaline flooded her body. She was up to the challenge and desperate to get started.

The great northern powerhouse that was the city of Milan hummed around her, offering all sorts of wonderful possibilities for her last night, but she wasn't interested. According to her research, Milan to Fortezza was six and a half hours by car. The mountains beckoned to her as she imagined the lower temperatures that might come with the altitude. On this sweltering evening, escaping the humid air of the city would be wonderful. But her eyes felt gritty, and she blinked. It was a stupid idea. She risked being a danger to others and would only end up having to sleep in her car along the way.

Instead, she was going to take full advantage of this experience. If Susan, her boss in London, hadn't had to pull out of the conference very late in the day, she'd probably have been breaking her journey in some scruffy two-star on the edge of town. What was she thinking, leaving early?

"I trust you," Susan had said. "You have a good eye and exquisite taste, so you can replace me at the Milan conference, all expenses paid. All I ask in return is for you to do an afternoon training session with the people in the office—over the internet."

She'd agreed to that like a shot and had already picked up more than enough material for it.

She caught her breath now, excited at what lay ahead. She was participating in an exchange, and by all the signs, the next six months were going to be the most challenging of her life. Christiano from the Italian firm had already arrived at Design 501 near Old Street Station in London, the studio where she'd worked until the previous week. She'd delayed her own departure until the last minute to be sure her mother was going to cope with her absence. Reassured that lots of people around cared about her mother, Isla had finally felt able to leave. They'd been very dependent on each other, possibly too much so, and leaving her mother alone worried her, but she had to do this.

The Abruzzo Design Studio sounded like a much more glamorous proposition than Design 501, and she couldn't help feeling she'd got the better end of the bargain—but people would sacrifice a lot to live in one of the world's most exciting capitals. Reopening her phone, she read through Christiano's most recent post on social media. Proving the point, he'd posted half a dozen photos and an enthusiastic account of his day in the metropolis.

Isla yawned widely, quickly covering her mouth when she saw the barman grinning at her.

"Long day," he said, schooling his expression. "Another gin and tonic, madame?"

"Four very long days, actually, but no more gin for me, thanks. I've hardly started this one. Maybe a little more ice and tonic, though." She took a sip and then pushed the glass across.

"Oh, my God," said Mariella, gripping her arm. "They really are coming over. Oh, I'm in love already."

Isla, whose back was to the advancing Adonis, turned to take her glass. A man now stood a little way down the bar from where she was sitting, but he was separated from her by a noisy group of delegates who'd just arrived. Dark eyes fastened on hers. For a moment, his gaze held her like a physical force and her body was suffused with an unexpected warmth. She tried to move but couldn't, couldn't even look elsewhere, as if she'd been fastened in place like those butterflies staked with a pin that you sometimes see in natural history museums. How dared he intrude into her private world like that?—a world she guarded carefully.

She was being stupid—they didn't know each other, so he couldn't be looking at her. He leaned forward as if about to speak, but one of the delegates got between them. It felt like someone had cut the rope that held her, and she went plummeting down, unable to affect the outcome. She forced herself to look behind for the object of his gaze. But no one stood there, and when she turned back, he'd gone as well.

How could that have happened? The image of his face had been seared into her brain, but even as her heartbeat settled to its normal rate, the picture was blurring, and a moment later, she couldn't have said what he looked like. His eyes, though, she wouldn't forget those—or rather, their impact. Only a moment or two had passed, but her life had changed.

Her hand was shaking as she picked up her glass, and she only just managed not to drop it. She took a long drink, welcoming the cold liquid as it coursed down her parched throat. Could she possibly have imagined the whole thing?

Mariella had not been paying attention and had completely missed what was going on, which was a good thing. She was focusing on the progress of the two men from the conference hall, and her smile widened a moment later. As on every other evening, the arrival of some member of the male species had never been in doubt, given the interest she'd aroused over the past few days. The question was simply who would get there first.

"Ladies," said an American voice.

Isla vaguely recognized the blond man who'd led a group on the latest trends in the States, but she didn't remember much of what he'd said, which probably meant he hadn't greatly added to the sum of her interior design knowledge.

"May we join you?"

He didn't wait for permission but pulled up another

stool. Mariella had been attracted quite simply by the fact that he was very good to look at. But so was his tall, dark-haired companion, who remained standing, looking somewhat reserved, and even as if he'd rather be somewhere else. After several days in the company of the beautiful Mariella, Isla was getting used to being cast into her shadow. Even so, she wasn't exactly flattered that this man virtually ignored her.

Only that wasn't important, was it? She'd just been dismissing thoughts of prolonging the evening, so what was she getting annoyed about? But it was always good to feel appreciated. She was no different in that from anyone else.

The image of the mysterious stranger at the other side of the bar filled her thoughts again, and her heartbeat picked up. No, she mustn't go there. She stabbed an olive from the bowl on the counter and used it to stir her drink. The measure of gin had certainly been over-generous. Isla wouldn't put it past Mariella to have requested double or triple shots, with the idea that she'd get her to relax. But maybe not. Perhaps this was what you got when you stayed in a place frequented by billionaires. She popped the olive into her mouth and chewed slowly. You could probably judge the level of exclusivity of a hotel by the proportion of spirit to mixer.

Whatever the case, she needed to be careful. Too much of this stuff might well give you delusions. In fact, that must be what she was suffering from.

A voice broke in on her thoughts.

"You have been enjoying the conference?" The second man was speaking English, and judging from his accent, he was Italian.

She smiled. "Yes, it's been very interesting. I loved some of the sessions meant specifically for us interior designers. Did you enjoy it?"

"*Sì*, I'm an architect, but some interior design as well. What did you think of the lecture this morning?"

They began to talk about the content and organization. He was attractive, intelligent—and not at all like the stereotypical Italian, the idea of which had somehow lodged itself in her mind, courtesy of her long-absent father.

But this man seemed quite different, and she should not jump to conclusions.

"We're going to dinner," announced Mariella. "Coming?"

She wouldn't want anyone tagging along.

"No, I'll be leaving soon, Mariella. This is where we say good-bye." Isla stood up then and gave her a hug. "Have a lovely evening. Give me a call when you're in London—oh, only not in the next six months because I won't be there."

Isla sank back onto her stool and stared blindly at the woman's voluptuous but perfectly proportioned figure as she walked off, leaning on her escort's arm.

How quickly could she leave without being impolite? After all, she had all that packing to do. She drank a little more gin. Really? Packing? How exciting. Instead, she ought to enjoy this evening because she wasn't going to get many further opportunities.

"I should have introduced myself earlier: Michele Verdino."

He held out his hand. Brown eyes. Nice smile. She'd almost forgotten he was there. Now, they shook hands and she smiled, too.

11

"I'm Isla—Isla Bruni."

"Perhaps you would like dinner also?"

"That's very kind, but I have things I must do—I have a long journey tomorrow."

"But surely you will eat this evening? I would appreciate the company. Maybe here, at the hotel, if you prefer."

She was already weakening. She'd been thinking of something quick, a sandwich in the coffee shop perhaps, although that would be a lost opportunity in this sumptuous place. Remember—no complications, her inner guardian warned. But the man wasn't trying to make it complicated. And it was only dinner. She sighed, knowing she'd already lost the battle—and maybe that was okay.

"Then I accept."

They slowly finished their drinks, discussing the highlights of the week. He was fun to talk to and had clear ideas he wasn't afraid to articulate, even if they didn't agree with hers.

"So, what did you think of the colors in that last session?" she couldn't resist asking.

"Not to my taste," he said.

"Nor mine."

It would hardly be a penance to spend her final evening in Milan with this handsome stranger. What harm could there be? Isla thought of her recent, unsatisfactory history with good-looking, dateable men. This one was undoubtedly very attractive—and not half as dangerous to her peace of mind as the man she'd seen at the other end of the bar.

So much the better.

****

Midnight chimed somewhere close by. They were standing in the corridor outside her room.

"I know you have a long journey tomorrow. Here are my contact details, and you have told me where you will work. Maybe you'll permit me to contact you?"

"That would be good," she said, tucking the card into her pocket and then handing him one of hers.

He smiled down at her. "So, I enjoyed our evening." He leant forward and gave her a peck on the cheek. "Good night, Isla."

"Good night, Michele."

She smiled at him and entered her room, locking the door firmly behind her.

Chapter 2

But thoughts of Michele did not occupy any part of Isla's mind the next morning. Instead, as she came awake, the tail-end of a delightful dream about the dark-eyed stranger floated slowly away. The slightest movement would break the spell, so she lay still a little while longer. One thing was clear: she had to see him again, but exactly how was she going to make that happen?

Maybe try to bump into him at breakfast. She looked at the time and saw that for once, she'd slept quite late. He'd probably already left. What about the internet? She reached across for her laptop and fired it up. People were always talking about how great the internet was for tracing contacts—yes, but you had to have some data to input in the first place. And tracing someone on the internet didn't appeal to her, anyway, seemed like an invasion of privacy. She pushed the idea to one side and considered what else she could do, because she couldn't just let it go—somehow, she had to find him and at least get the chance to meet him properly.

That was an idea. Perhaps she *could* find his name, because he must have been attending the conference. Yes, it would be a good starting point; the organizers would have lists and so forth, and she should be able to work out who he was and maybe trace him from that.

Ready to follow this trail, Isla threw back the covers and went into the bathroom.

Downstairs, she diverted from her search for breakfast and headed instead to the main hall. Stands everywhere were being taken down and tables collapsed, and no one from the organizing body was available to answer her questions. Okay, she'd have to think of some other way. Breakfast first, in that very grand dining room.

Pouring a second cup of coffee a few minutes later, she thought over her actions. What on earth was wrong with her? She didn't have time for this—and how could she be thinking of looking him up, turning into a sort of stalker? That meeting—if you could call it a meeting— had been the matter of a moment, with not a single word exchanged. But the thought of him threatened to overwhelm her if she allowed her mind to dwell on him for even a moment. And yet she wanted to spend every minute doing exactly that.

What was he like? Those gorgeous eyes—were they hazel like hers? Kind or hard? How come she hadn't retained the simplest of information from that brief moment in the bar? These were the important things about a person, and she had no answers. How foolish she was, especially given she'd just sworn to keep away from emotional entanglements. She shook her head. She would forget all about it. She couldn't bear the situation she'd got into and was on the point of leaving the table when the waitress arrived with the eggs and smoked salmon. Okay, she'd eat and then she'd go. With the conference over, all she wanted to do was to start the next phase of her life.

If Richard had shown a little more enthusiasm for

what she did, a little more empathy, they might have been a better match and created a future together. But what he'd said was true—she couldn't wait to move her career forward. And even if it excluded certain things, was that really so bad? If you wanted something enough, you had to be prepared to strive for it, and that's what she was going to do. This next stage would be exciting and challenging.

****

Isla glanced down at the clock on the dashboard: just after one in the afternoon. The autostrada had begun as the E35, but she hadn't bothered to work out how the road numbering worked, guessing she'd find her way easily enough. How breathtaking these roads were, as they ran through the mountains, with long, elevated stretches on elegant viaducts. She was dizzy from the panoramic views of the sea, the road entering dark tunnels which left her fumbling for the lights, and then she emerged onto tree-lined boulevards as she drove through the towns. Fortezza del Tronto was inland, high in the Abruzzo area of the Apennine range and, as she turned away from the coast, the road grew narrower, and the mountains dominated.

When she'd told her mother she'd been offered the exchange there, they'd had a lot of conversation about earthquakes.

"Now, I'll be worrying about you all the time."

"Don't, Mum. The last one happened years ago, and that was much higher up the mountain. Really, I've researched it. As far as I can tell, they haven't had a rumble in the town since 2016—and there was no mention of anything happening in Fortezza itself at that time."

"Hmm! I'm not convinced. You don't know where it might happen next."

This was certainly true, but she didn't want her mother to worry. She was cautious and would have found another matter to fret over if Isla had chosen somewhere completely different to go. Mum could be relied on to discover the flaw in whatever her beloved daughter arranged—if it involved her going away from the capital. In all other matters, she encouraged her—just as long as she didn't leave London. Of course, the capital had to be one of the most dangerous places to live, with its terrorist attacks and random violence—as Isla knew to her cost.

It was simple: Mum loved her. There were just the two of them since Dad had taken off, when Isla's brother, Jack, was killed at the age of seventeen and she was just ten. She easily understood her mother's feelings; with the family reduced to half its original size, Mum had concentrated all her love and care on her daughter.

Anyway, if an earthquake were about to occur, the authorities would give warnings well in advance, allowing lots of time to get away, wouldn't they? These people had experience of how to handle such things.

Tall trees and vineyards rolled by, then green hills and, finally, rocks poked through, and a vista of peaks opened up. Then, she was skirting Arquata del Tronto, with only a short distance to go. The tower of a castle dominated the small town and seemed undamaged, but it made her sit up and take notice, because there were areas of cleared rubble and missing buildings, which had to be victims of the 2016 earthquake. From the road, it looked as if half the town had been destroyed.

Could Fortezza have been similarly impacted, despite not being mentioned in any news reports?

A sign showed "Fortezza del Tronto—8," and she indicated left.

Her heartbeat picked up. Any minute now, she'd arrive at her new place of work and meet her colleagues for the first time. Coming to a new job was always unnerving, and she wondered if she'd be good enough. Would they even like each other? Well, she would soon know.

After the turn, the road narrowed again abruptly, at first rising a little. The contents of her stomach slammed down at a sudden descent, and she slowed. Then she was running on one level around the contour of the mountain, and half an hour later, the first buildings appeared. Okay, that was a bit of a relief—no signs of rubble or broken and cracked walls. It would be good to be able to reassure her mother when she called her this evening, and she wasn't going to lie.

She was driving slowly now, looking for the converted church that housed Abruzzo Design. As she entered the town proper, the tinkling of water filled the car, the sound emanating from a charming fountain, into which a stone figure in a short, pleated dress was pouring water from an urn. The scene could have come straight from a Roman frieze. The sound of running water refreshed her, so much in contrast to the stifling air in the car. Almost immediately, the road broadened to become an elongated piazza, with a half-dozen cars parked at the far end. She pulled up next to them and got out.

Oh, this was really great—what a lovely place! She stood by the car and looked around, enjoying her surroundings as the engine ticked and clicked behind her. Chairs and tables occupied an area outside a bar, spilling out toward the center of the space, while stone buildings containing homes and businesses lined the two long sides of the square. Linked together, the houses were separated in places by arches, narrow entrances to little courtyards.

Well, the façades were smooth, no obvious cracks. She'd be able to report that, and maybe it'd convince her mother she wasn't in immediate danger. There were no engine noises, and it was probably too hot for the birds. For a moment she was entirely alone enjoying the deep quiet, and then two middle-aged women with bulging bags came out of the grocery shop. They stopped to talk in front of the fountain, and a dog slunk along, keeping to the shade. A small town in the early afternoon.

But then a man and a little boy, hand in hand, threaded their way through the tables toward the bar entrance. Her heart kicked into overdrive. It was him! No, that wasn't possible. From where she stood, it was only possible to see his profile, but she could have sworn this was the man who had so affected her the evening before. A moment later, they disappeared inside. She took a few deep breaths, trying to calm the feelings the sight had aroused, convinced she was going mad as her imagination ran riot. How could it possibly be him? She wanted to follow, to see if she was right, and it took a huge effort of will to stay where she was. It was crazy—what would she do if it were the same person? But then, she recalled he'd been holding the hand of a child. This could not be the executive she'd seen back in Milan.

Slowly, Isla turned away and scanned the other side of the square. She remained where she was for a long moment, preparing herself for the coming meeting. Okay, that glass frontage had to be the studio building, the only note of modernity in the centuries-old square. The designer hadn't attempted to hide how the whole wall had been taken out. Had they replaced it because it had cracked in some earthquake experienced hundreds of years earlier? Whatever the reason, they must have some clout to get the planning permission for a change like that. But it was well done; while the glass was in complete contrast to everything around it, it didn't try to impose something ultra-modern onto the medieval scene. Behind it, to the right and left, were the ends of the original walls, and the overall effect was to add interest to the little square.

Isla walked across to where the door stood open, inviting her into a vestibule, which led on the far side into a tented atrium filled with plants. In colder weather, they'd probably shut that off to keep the heat in, but at the moment, a welcome breeze flowed through the space. Several magazines on architecture and interior design lay on a gleaming black coffee table. The brochure next to the perfectly aligned periodicals was like the one that had been sent to Susan Greenslade when the idea of an exchange was first put forward. It looked swish—lots of beautiful photographs with good color, on thick paper, very exclusive.

"*Buongiorno,* signorina." The receptionist smiled and rose to her feet. "You are Isla Bruni? We thought you would soon arrive."

The woman was speaking slowly and carefully. Isla guessed her English was limited, so she smiled and tried a few words of Italian.

"It's good to get here. I've had a lovely drive," she added, "especially coming up this beautiful valley."

Instantly, the woman's expression relaxed, and she introduced herself before leading Isla up elegant metal stairs into a large creative studio. A powerfully built older man was leaning over a workstation on the far side of the room, talking to a young man with a ginger beard.

"Let me introduce you to Tommaso," the receptionist said when he turned to face them. "Miss Bruni just arrived, *signore*."

Tommaso Giordano, Abruzzo Design's owner, rested his gaze on Isla and hit her with the full force of his personality. He had to be about sixty, but the abundant, almost-white hair in which streaks of black still showed helped make him a striking figure. Confidence oozed off him. If she hadn't seen the lines on his face, she might easily have taken him for someone twenty years younger. This dynamism might explain why he was such a successful businessman, despite having located his studio in what was, essentially, the middle of nowhere. Now he ushered her into his office and indicated a chair.

"So," he said finally, having taken all the time he needed to assess her, while she waited for him to speak. It was a little off-putting, but she'd forced herself to sit tranquilly. "I understand we can expect great things from you."

Isla smiled. "Is it my work you're basing that on, *signore*, or are you relying on the kind words of my boss?"

Susan Greenslade had a lot of time for Isla, whose

work for one or two wealthy clients had brought in a string of highly profitable enquiries, based on their recommendations.

He gave a broad smile. "Oh, I would never simply accept someone else's judgment, however respected. I've had a good look at some of your finished projects, and now, I'm picking out a couple on our books, where I think your particular style will be appreciated."

"I'm very keen to get started."

He asked a few questions and then said, "Signora Greenslade told me you would want to get going straight away, but you need time to settle in. Monday will be fine." He got to his feet. "Now, I'll introduce you to Eloisa D'Errico. She'll help you find your way about."

The woman, whose long, dark hair fell down her back in abundant waves, looked younger than Isla had expected. She came out from behind the desk to give her a hug. They'd exchanged one or two emails, and Isla felt as if they already knew each other, at least superficially.

"Great to meet you, Isla. We've all been waiting for you."

Tommaso shook hands again with Isla.

"So, welcome once more. Please take some time to get to know our little town. This is a superb place to work, and I always believe my best designers incorporate something of this *ambientazione*...er, this setting into their work, a quality beyond the usual, although you may not be able to pinpoint what it is. But perhaps you will also bring something to it."

He turned to the other girl. "Take the afternoon off, Eloisa."

And with that he was gone.

"Let's get a coffee, and then we can go over to the apartment. Have you had any lunch?"

"Not yet."

"A panino as well, perhaps?"

Chapter 3

"He's very relaxed about allowing me time. Not having to start until Monday, I mean."

"Take it. After all, it's Saturday tomorrow. Once you have something on, he expects complete dedication. Whole weekends can disappear, and I often find myself working until ten or eleven at night." Eloisa smiled. "It's not so bad, but it's a good thing my boyfriend seems to understand—but then, he's a paramedic, and that really can mean long hours, especially if they have an emergency."

Isla wasn't fazed by this. It was her own method of working. She had to become totally immersed in a project to get the best out of herself.

"Anyway, how come you speak such good Italian?"

"My dad was Italian."

"Was? I'm sorry…?"

"He scarpered when I was ten, and we haven't seen him since. No idea where he is." She tried to keep her tone light, so as not to reveal how deeply his abandonment hurt her, even after so long. "I've kept contact with very few Italians, and Mum and I speak English together, so I expect I sound like a ten-year-old when I open my mouth. I'm a bit rusty."

"I hadn't noticed anything wrong."

"I'm going to have to learn a lot of design-related

words. I'm quite embarrassed about it, actually."

"Useful, though, not to have to start with the basics at this point."

This was certainly true. Had she not possessed the skills, she would have been obliged to do a course before her departure, since a certain level of language had been stipulated.

The young women were standing diagonally opposite the café where they'd just had lunch, and now Eloisa pushed open one side of double doors that were set in a wall along from the studio.

"This is very pretty," she said. "I think you'll like it."

They stepped into an enclosed courtyard. A narrow cloister ran around three sides and large terracotta pots, packed with lavender and red and salmon-pink pelargoniums, lined up either side of another door that was painted dark green. Isla took a deep breath and drank in the scents and the tranquility. This was such a change from her tiny flat in central London. The door appeared to be one of three that led into the buildings, each at the center of a wall. A metal bench, placed in the shade of a small cherry tree, helped turn an ordinary space into a charming haven. The last of its pale pink flowers lay in drifts on the flagstones.

"This is wonderful, Eloisa. Was this Christiano's place?"

"No, he used to live down the valley. But Tommaso knows the woman who owns this building, and the apartment has just become vacant."

Taking a long look around her, Isla followed Eloisa, each of them carrying a heavy bag. She could relax in this shady courtyard after a hard day at work—

if she ever finished early enough to do so, of course. From what her new friend had said, it might not happen that frequently.

Now, Eloisa inserted a large, brass key into the elaborately paneled house door and pushed it open. A dim corridor and a narrow staircase with a thin iron balustrade loomed in the low light. They climbed two long flights of stairs. At each landing, a couple of doors led off into flats. When Isla realized hers must be at the very top of the building, she knew it was going to be a good place to live.

****

"It's lovely, Mum—the town and the flat, both. Look on your phone when we've finished talking. I've WhatsApped you a few photos. I'm really looking forward to working here."

They'd been talking for more than half an hour, and finally, her mother was beginning to sound more comfortable about the idea that her only daughter was too distant for her to protect personally. As far as Isla was concerned, Mum looking at things positively would take the pressure off. Coming to Italy had been a big decision, especially as it meant leaving her behind, even though they lived separately.

"Eloisa's promised to take me around the office tomorrow, to show me what I'll be working on."

"That doesn't sound very Italian to me—working over a weekend."

"Mum! You're letting your prejudices show there. Just because Dad was a lazy sod and decamped when we most needed him…" She heard the bitterness in her own voice and quickly stopped. "Anyway, Eloisa volunteered, and we won't be doing any work. I just want to get a feel for things."

****

"Is it all right to leave you here for a while?" her colleague said the following day. "I want to drop in on my grandad. He's on his own since my *nonna* died last year, so I see him as often as I can."

"Of course. Of course it's okay."

She preferred to be on her own. She'd sit in the office without any distractions and look through the various projects she was to finish off for the absent Christiano. She could hardly wait to get down to work, and this would mean being up to speed when she started on Monday morning.

The younger girl closed the door, and her footsteps rang on the metal stairs as she headed for the exit. Then all was quiet. Isla sat at the desk she'd been given, absorbing the details around her. This was a very good space, shadowy at this time of day, lit in places by slanting rays of sunlight in which each movement she made set dust motes whirling. The studio was modern, functional, and pleasing to her eye; someone had spent a long time thinking about the design, thinking about those who would have to spend their working day in it.

Okay, she'd better make a start. She turned on the computer and typed in the password she'd been given. Then, she opened the first of four folders, the names of which had been written down for her.

Nearly two hours later, Isla had absorbed the details of the jobs that Christiano had been unable to close in time and was therefore handing on to her. Two required very little work—a couple of days each, at most. The third was halfway through but didn't look particularly complicated. Her predecessor was meticulous and had left copious notes. She'd have to thank him for that—transferring projects from one person to another could be a nightmare if not handled correctly. She skimmed through the file for the fourth project. Containing a surprising number of subfolders, it appeared to be a very large building and was ongoing, with the initial work carried out over two years earlier. She emailed him quickly with a couple of questions.

Finally emerging from work mode, Isla checked the time. It had raced by and now, only a quarter of an hour remained until she had to meet Eloisa. She clicked through the folders, closing them down, and then pressed the tiny button under the sleek flat screen, noticing again how quiet everything was—no passing cars, no voices in the street. This was so unlike what she was used to.

She glanced over the open-plan space to the boss's office, which was divided from the rest of the room by a screen of glass over waist-high wooden paneling. She could just go in there and have a quick look around. Her curiosity had got her into trouble before, but it wasn't wrong—it was just curiosity. No, it was a tiny bit more than that; she wanted to discover what the next big job was, so that she could prepare and bid for it, depending how it was introduced to the attention of the staff. She shouldn't. It was a foolish idea—but no matter. Anyway, if the office was locked, that would be an end to it. Cautiously, she turned the handle.

The office wasn't locked.

What excuse would she give if someone came in? Maybe she'd just say she was curious. She took a deep breath and entered the room, leaving the door open.

Bookshelves, cabinets, a parallel-motion drawing

board—old school, but a nice touch—a chest-high, well-tended yucca plant in one corner, and a computer station. The main desk, a vast affair in blond wood occupying the center of the far wall, held piles of papers, a set of plans, and, in the middle, two red cardboard files. Now, that looked interesting—they must be new accounts. He'd left them out as if he'd been studying them when he'd finished for the day, and she knew how it worked. She'd observed how Susan did things often enough.

They'd been placed there ready for the meeting on Monday morning.

She walked around behind, to where his chair had been rolled back and left at an angle as if he'd just got up and stepped outside. Using the tip of her finger, she flipped open the first file.

This was a big project, a new-build factory building in Teramo nearing completion. The owners now required interior design for the reception area and various offices, including the managing director's. A very big scheme. She caught sight of the budget and quickly did a rough conversion of the figures to sterling. Yes, she most certainly did want that job. Sketches, photos. Already, her mind was working on ideas to match what she'd read and seen. She did have some industrial experience, and it would be great to start on something like that. She simply had to persuade him to give it to her.

As she turned to the second folder, she heard a noise. Damn, someone was coming up the stairs. In a moment, she'd pressed the cover closed, and seconds later, she shut the door behind her. She was back at her computer, when Tommaso walked in. She looked up, her breath coming a little more quickly than usual, hoping there was no tell-tale flush on her cheeks to give her away.

"Working already, Isla?"

"Just informing myself, getting ready for Monday. I'm meeting Eloisa now." She picked up her bag. "Sorry, I'm afraid I was just shutting down. I have to go."

She smiled and headed to the stairs, her guilt making her unwilling to stay talking. Her heart was beating fast. She shouldn't have done that. How bad it would have looked to be found snooping in the boss's office before she'd even started work. Now, she tried to remember if she'd shut the door properly, if she'd closed the first red file. The way he'd left them had looked so precise, and she was sure he was the kind of person who'd notice if there was something out of place. But of course, she must have closed it.

What on earth had she thought she was doing? What was wrong with her that she was so greedy for the best jobs, when it could put everything else at risk? She had a nagging feeling it was part of the reason she'd consolidated her position so quickly in the London firm, always ensuring she was informed, working out in advance how to present herself as the best person for whatever interesting job came up. Naturally, she'd never done anything illegal or ferreted into people's personal information. Nor would she. She wouldn't cross that line. But she did like to know exactly what work was coming into the office—so that she could be ready for the next big thing. Preparation was everything in the cutthroat world of interior design. Be ready—and grab it. Knowledge was power if used correctly.

As she stepped into the square, the outer door swished closed behind her. Where had Eloisa got to?

In the past, she'd simply have said she was being prepared, but now, she was questioning her behavior, because maybe, having moved to another country, she needed to rethink. Her early years had not been easy, and she'd learned to look out for herself, but for the first time ever, she was seeing this in a different light—not as go-getting and ambitious but as a bit mean and underhand...grasping, even. Shame caused the hot color to flood her cheeks as she picked up her pace. She was going to change.

Eloisa had pointed out her grandfather's house at the far end of the square, and now she turned in that direction, trying hard not to think about uncomfortable things but without much success. Maybe the time had come to address them, even if it was frustrating to have such a juicy project go to someone else.

Back in London, she'd often had the pick of the projects—rightly so, she believed, but it hadn't always sat well with her colleagues. She could not—must not—risk her relationship with these new people, most of whom she hadn't yet even met. Now, common sense reasserted itself: there was no way she could ask for that project she'd seen—or any other job. She would have to wait to see how the work was distributed. Why would Tommaso give her something like that, over the heads of his trusted employees? She bit her lip. There might be people here who were more talented than she was. As someone who'd always been a top student, this was another hard thought, and one she'd rarely had to face before. She'd have to earn her position in this new office.

Chapter 4

Isla settled quickly into work, tidying up the jobs that Christiano had left unfinished, starting the next phase on the ongoing project. Now, a fortnight into her stay, she was on her way to meet what promised to be an important client. The domain wasn't that far away, but it stood at the end of a hot, steep road exposed to the glaring sun. Isla had wanted to walk, but it wouldn't have been enjoyable at this time of day. The track wound up and up, doubling back on itself frequently, almost dizzying in the way that, at one moment, she was facing a wall of rock, and the next, the valley swung into view. And then back again. Eloisa's advice to take the car had been eminently sensible. Wondering how much longer it was going to take, she negotiated yet another tight bend, and then posts of ancient stone appeared, though no gates were attached.

She needed to bear in mind that these buildings were a work in progress, so probably quite a few things were still unfinished. She drove through and parked on a wide, triangular forecourt, facing a low wall. Damned air con—the mechanism had failed five minutes into the journey and being in the car was a torture, but at least, a good breeze stirred the air up here. She climbed out, and it played pleasantly on her skin, drying the perspiration that had gathered on her brow. She left the windows open and went to the low wall that encircled the property.

Two weeks in this area hadn't been enough to inure her to its beauties, and really, that was never going to happen. This wonderful, rugged terrain was so full of drama, broad sweeps of color, and intricate patterns. Already, she saw how she could use some of this in her designs. She would've liked to stand here a while and slowly take in the whole panorama, but she had a job to do today, and this was not the moment to indulge in contemplation. Something buzzed, and she fished out her phone. Nothing. But time had rushed on, and the meeting was in five minutes.

Reluctantly, she turned her back on the plunging views down the mountain and walked briskly toward a lovely stone house with rows of tall windows, four on each floor. She climbed a short flight of steps, which were paired either side of a wide front door. It was all very gracious—except, in spite of its size and location, the house still managed to look homely and unassuming.

To the right, a tower rose up. This was where her work would be concentrated. The building was square and uncompromising, occupying a large area, and was joined by a glass corridor structure to the main house. Heavy-looking tiles were stacked inside, along with bags of what might be cement, so work had not finished there either. The space in front of the tower was paved in large, rectangular flagstones of varying sizes.

"Signorina! *Per favore.*" A neatly dressed woman in her forties, dark hair pulled back in a loose chignon, was approaching the open door from inside. "*Buongiorno,* signorina. If you would like to come this way, *il conte* will see you as soon as he is free. I am

33

sorry—there will be a slight delay."

She led Isla into a cool, shadowy hallway, also stone-flagged, and then to a sitting room on the right.

Il conte? No one had said anything about a count. Hopefully, he wasn't going to be one of those wealthy aristocrats with so much money they thought everything revolved around them. Working among the rich and the famous in London, Isla had resolved a long time ago that she would not be pushed around by people who showed scant respect for her ideas and thought that money could buy them anything.

True, money could buy you a great deal, but she'd had enough of that sort of behavior with a recent client, a Russian woman. Taking a firm stance had almost lost her the project. But that hadn't happened. Ultimately, they'd established a good working relationship, so she would reserve judgment until she knew more.

"May I offer you coffee?—or a cold drink?"

"Thank you. Coffee would be good."

It came almost immediately. She took grateful sips as she gazed around the room. It was very elegant. Someone had renovated the house with sensitivity, doing the minimum to change the original. The colors were muted, some of the plastered walls painted in an antique cream, others in what looked like earl grey vintage chalk. Both were a good accompaniment to the stone.

Unable to contain her curiosity, she wandered around, peering at books which dealt with the archeology of the area. Alongside them, on the same shelves, objects were displayed—stone pots and other items, some rather broken and cracked but having a certain sculptural look, others almost intact—and she wondered if they'd discovered them when the tower had been taken down. Her surroundings made a fascinating study, and when she glanced at her watch, almost a quarter of an hour had gone by, and the woman was back.

"*Scusi,* signorina. *Il conte* sends his apologies. He has been held up but suggests you may like to begin in his absence. I can show you the rooms you will be working on."

Perfect. She could easily spend the time profitably. Sometimes, at the very beginning of a project, she liked to look around without the client, to absorb what needed to be done.

"That would be very helpful. I can get an idea of the scale of the work."

A lot of the final ideas would come out of discussion with the mysterious count, but a preliminary survey would immediately give her a steer. Owners would often have preferences of their own—but no idea to what extent the physical restraints of the building might prevent their ideas being carried out.

Isla picked up her battered leather satchel in which she kept the tools she needed to do a survey and was pointed in the direction of the tower.

"I have opened the door, signorina. Take care. The staircases have not yet been installed—you will have to use the ladders."

Close to, the beauty of the pale golden limestone was overwhelming. The interior would be little more than a shell, with everything still to be done. What a wonderful opportunity, to have been given this plum project. And to think that she'd wanted the factory. She was a complete idiot.

It had cost her to sit back and say nothing, while Rinaldo settled to work on the scheme she'd seen on the boss's desk, but she'd held to her resolve. Everyone in the office was friendly to her, including Tommaso, and she'd decided if she couldn't land a job commensurate with her abilities, it would be very strange. She smiled as she looked around. How disappointed she would have been to discover later that this had slipped through her fingers. One day, she was going to learn to allow chance to play a part in her life. Perhaps that day had already come.

She'd thought as she got out of the car that it looked very new, and of course, it was.

"It was completely derelict," Tommaso had said when he'd asked her to take on the project. "No way it could have been patched up. So in essence, you have a replica of the original, with a few small changes to accommodate modern requirements."

Apparently, they'd painstakingly taken down every single stone and then constructed an earthquake platform on the footprint of the original tower, before rebuilding, using much of the same stone. On the outside, it looked exactly as it had before, no doubt— except there were no cracks, no holes, no broken pieces, and she guessed that existing windows had been widened and new ones inserted. Already, they'd rehung the original door, its stout oak timbers with the heavy iron bands sending out a message of impregnability.

The man must have a serious amount of money to carry out work like this.

Isla pushed open the door and went in. Wow! She hadn't expected this massive fireplace. It must take up nearly a third of the wall. She crossed the room to stand beside it and stretched out her hand to its huge, carved mantle, smoothing her fingers over ancient stone, blackened in places by long-extinguished fires. It would have come from the original building, probably installed at the same time as the tower was built, over seven hundred years earlier. She liked the fact that they hadn't cleaned the stone.

Fire irons and a fire basket occupied the hearth, everything on a large scale, as if made for a giant. A metal contraption with a winding handle was suspended over the fire grate, stretched across the entire width, and fixed at each side into the walls of the chimney. That would have served for roasting meat—half an ox, maybe, or a whole pig. It was an unbelievable asset.

The projected site of the stairwell was in front of her, farther along on the right. Four walls which soared up through three floors formed the tower, but the two upper floors were already in place. She looked up through the gap where the stairs would eventually be installed. The only way to access those upper areas was via the ladders which had been placed there. Should she go up? The lower ladder showed no sign of having been fixed in place, but it was heavy, simply leaning against the edge of the floor above. She went over and pushed hard against it, but it didn't move. Probably safe enough.

There was plenty she could do down here, however, and maybe the owner would arrive back before she'd finished. She took out her pencil and a notebook, flipped it open at a fresh page and drew a small, rough sketch plan of the ground floor. There would be detailed drawings from the architect, of course, but her goal today was to get a feeling for the place and make a few notes, linked to the plan she'd just drawn. When she returned to the office, this would help her recapture her initial thoughts. First impressions were very telling.

She pulled out her phone and began to take pictures.

****

A noise came from right down in the valley. Maybe it was the count returning. But when she tried to pinpoint the sound, it disappeared. Her notebook was now filled with sketches annotated in her small, spiky handwriting. Already, an hour had passed. Was the client coming, or wasn't he? No matter, there was plenty more to do. Gingerly, she climbed the first ladder. The exact distribution of the rooms at this level was yet to be decided. Her work here would come after they'd built the internal walls. She continued up to the next floor. It was easy enough to climb the ladders, although you had to pay attention as you got off. Getting back on to descend would be a different matter. Carefully pulling herself through the opening at the top floor, she stepped onto bare floorboards. They were cut wide to emulate the originals and spanned the whole room, emitting a pleasing scent of newly sawn wood.

What an extraordinary place! How could the main sitting room be anywhere other than this? Hopefully, the owner wasn't going to disagree with that, because she could see lots of ways to exploit the height and light and make it truly fabulous. At this level, the stairs would come up into the center of the front wall, right over the entrance, and an opening on the right led to a loggia which had not even been visible from the outside, due to the angle of her approach. Lovely, so appropriate. A loggia was thoroughly Italian, Roman even.

From every side, views opened over the mountain, or across the peaks, or down to the red roofs of the little town. Yes, she could already imagine how this could work, though she'd want to see it again in the morning—and probably late in the evening—to check on the light. Quickly, she scribbled down ideas as they occurred to her. She'd have to get the plasterers up here. They wouldn't do too much, just enough to prevent the place from looking too rustic, though the owner might have other ideas about that.

A little embrasure caught her eye. It was so charming, and she photographed it. Then she got down on one knee and began sketching, certain she'd get a better feeling of what to do with it from her drawing than from the photo. It called out for some object—a piece of Murano glass, maybe, or one of those amphora-type stone jars. Yes, she liked that idea better. But either one would set the style for the room.

Isla was deep in her work when, suddenly, the air in the space altered. What was that? It was subtle and she'd heard nothing, but she felt the movement. She sprang up and swung around. A dark head was rising through the hole which would eventually become the stairwell. She dropped her pencil and bent to retrieve it, hastily brushing the dust from the knees of her trousers. The man turned as he reached the top of the ladder, and her body reacted, as if he'd touched her, although he was on the opposite side of the room. Immediately, she recognized the feeling and flashed back to their last meeting. She caught a look of surprise on his face before he said, "I'm sorry. I startled you."

He was speaking English, so someone must have told him it was the Englishwoman coming to do the preliminary assessment of the project.

She was staring. It was rude, but she couldn't help it. This was the man she'd seen in the bar in Milan, the man whose image had filled her mind during the greater part of her journey to Fortezza—and on numerous occasions since. Her heart thudded, and her breath caught. This was him. How could he possibly be here?

He stepped off the ladder and came toward her, holding out his hand. "I am so sorry to be late—we had an emergency at work. I could not leave." His eyes were filled with questions as they swept over her. "This is so strange. I—"

"We've met," she blurted out, unable to understand how this had happened. "Do you remember? Not a real meeting, but—"

"The mysterious girl in blue with the blonde friend? Of course, I remember. Two beautiful women. How could I forget?" He smiled, and electricity sizzled between them. "I just didn't realize that it would be you—here—today. This is amazing. I didn't think I'd ever see you again."

How could this have come about? What had he been doing in Milan? And what business was it of hers? The last thing she needed right now was a man to distract her.

They shook hands. A warmth sprang from his touch and spilled over, filling her entire body. Nerve endings pinged all along her arm, as if she were being given a thousand tiny shocks, and she lowered her eyes, unable to hold his gaze. She wanted him, needed to get close to him, to know him. And, perversely, she felt angry and somewhat shocked by the intensity of her desire. This was a new sensation, and it was wreaking havoc on her body and in her mind. She couldn't have this…this ridiculous feeling interfering in her working life. What on earth was happening to her?

How could she possibly hope to set up in business on her own and behave appropriately, if she reacted to her clients like this?

What had happened to the cool, professional woman she knew herself to be?

Chapter 5

Isla took a few deep breaths and smoothed down her hair, trying to gain time before she spoke. How had this come about? Her usual calm deserted her, and she kept quiet, unwilling to reveal her state of confusion.

"I asked for you—no, no, not you specifically," he added hastily, seeing her look of alarm. "I asked for a designer who would be able to handle this building the way it deserves. Tommaso is my good friend. We often meet in the bar across the square. So, knowing that I would require the services of an interior designer, he talked to me about some of your projects—once it was settled you would be coming to Fortezza, of course. He thought we would share an approach."

Somehow, she found her voice. "Yes, he told me when I arrived that he had a possible project lined up for me. Was that yours?"

"Please don't be offended because we discussed you. He knows how much I care for these buildings, and he was sure you would be the best suited to doing the interior. When I saw the pictures of your work, how sensitive you are to the structures you work on, I agreed with him."

She warmed at the praise, of course she did. "I'm flattered. I'll do my best to—"

"Please do. This project means a lot to me."

She'd got her breath under control now and

managed a faint smile. "I still don't understand how we happened to be in Milan at the same time."

"Exactly that—we both happened to be there. A coincidence, not so strange. I too attended the conference. I had a call from Tommaso on another matter, and he mentioned that his new designer would be there, said maybe I'd bump into you. And I very nearly did, but I didn't realize then who you were. You know, I almost came over to talk to you in the bar, but I could see you and your friend were meeting up with other delegates, so I let it be."

So, it was as simple as that.

"It matters to me that I have the right person to do this project, someone who shares my ideas—or at least, understands them. And that means someone with whom I can work. The chemistry has to be right."

Of course, she understood his desire to check things for himself, even though his friend was recommending her. If she had a building she really loved, especially as gorgeous as this one, she wouldn't just hand it over to a stranger without a few enquiries. He possessed both the house and also this extraordinary tower. Waiting in the sitting room, drinking her coffee, she'd begun to appreciate how subtle the house restoration was. Not that there was anything more to do there, but it set the standard he would want to achieve.

"Yes," she said, "the client and designer have to be able to work together, share a vision."

It sounded as if he was a designer, too. Counter-intuitively, that could make a working relationship quite difficult because the client might expect input from her but then seek to change it. Hopefully, that wouldn't happen, but she'd handle it if it did.

A much more serious matter was how was she going to get any work done at all, if he had this effect on her every time they met. She'd just have to ensure it didn't happen too often—keep their meetings to a minimum and communicate online. Professionally.

"And is it?" she asked boldly, hardly daring to risk the question but determined to present herself as cool and in control. "Is the chemistry right?"

"I think so, don't you?"

Once again, she looked down, unable to stop the heat rising up her cheeks. She couldn't help thinking that *some* sort of chemistry was at work, but maybe not the kind he meant. All she said was, "Yes, I believe so. Are you a designer yourself?"

"Of a kind. I'm an engineer. My factory designs plastic parts used in earthquake proofing and other such mundane items. Some of the pieces I have designed myself, and I like to keep abreast of the new developments—hence the conference."

That would explain why he'd been there. It hadn't been restricted to interiors. But now, it was obvious he was done with the explanations. This was a man who did not waste his time.

"Very well," he said. "Tell me what you think of the tower."

"Of course, but usually, I start with a few questions. I like to get a feeling for the client's requirements before I plunge in."

"No, Signorina Bruni. I really would like to have your first impressions. I'm an engineer, and we're renowned for being too wedded to practical solutions at the expense of any esthetic sense—not that I accept that, of course. But this is your expertise. I would like to hear what you would do with this space."

Well, if that's what he wanted, Isla was happy to accommodate him. She'd already seen enough to have some strong ideas. The thought came that he might have delayed his arrival intentionally, to give her time to look around so that they could have this discussion.

"All right," she said, switching to Italian, "but these are just my first impressions. I'm assuming this will be the sitting room, a place to relax in, listen to music." She walked over to a window. "Read, maybe, and enjoy these views. Perhaps not for entertaining other people. It'll be a private space. But you need to tell me if I've got that wrong."

In the main house, there were perfectly good entertainment areas that would be more convenient for guests than to bring them up here. But the position of the house and the desire to respect the original design made those rooms relatively dark. Light streamed in here, so that the golden stone glowed, a living material that transformed the space. This was where one would want to spend time. She walked him around, pointing out things that had caught her attention. He listened intently.

"You're right to assume this will be a place for relaxation. I like your ideas, but I don't want to create a museum to show off objects. Do you think those things you mention would fit with comfortable furniture?"

"Oh, definitely. The choice of seating, for instance, is enormous—and comfortable doesn't have to mean traditional. The beauty of stone like this is that you can put all sorts of modern materials against it, and it still works. I'm sure you can find something to your taste that allows a room that is both elegant and inviting."

"I love the big space, you see. I think I'd want to set the sofas back, so the room continues to feel spacious."

"Yes, but it's very large, and doing that might not look as you imagine. In a room this size, you can be creative with the location of furniture, in order to get certain effects." She looked across the room. "That window, for instance—you can see the architect has placed it to draw the attention to that particular view. It's acting like a picture frame, and we need to respect that. You can do it by organizing the circulation space, so that the eye is drawn to it as you exit the stairwell, before you move farther into the room. Which means the seating will probably not be placed back against the walls." She paused for a moment, but he didn't say anything. "Maybe you could let me have a list of things that are important to you, and I'll try to work them in— or come back to you to clarify."

She was into her stride and had spoken calmly, the professional designer explaining her reasons. With one part of her mind, she registered he was no pushover and she'd have to justify her decisions. But all the time, her pulse was racing and, when she backed away from a window and accidentally brushed against him, the words stuck in her throat, and she had to swallow before being able to continue her sentence.

Eventually, she came to a halt and forced herself to wait. If he didn't like what she'd said, if he decided she wasn't the right person for the job, he could still request another designer. But he'd be wrong to do that. She was already investing too much of herself in the project to take rejection easily.

"So," he said, pausing for a moment.

Her heartbeat picked up. She didn't know how she'd take it if he ended it here. She only knew how bereft she would feel; she had to have this project. The more she'd talked through it, the more she'd wanted to be the one to carry it out.

"So," he repeated, "I think we can work together."

Isla let out her breath.

"I would like you to put together a scheme and come back to me. How long will you need? I shall be very busy for about three weeks, with little time to consider this. Would you be able to present your first ideas then?'

"That would be fine. I need to consider materials, the configuration of the two lower floors as well. But," she added, "the design can be so much more, if you give me some sense of your own preferences. You haven't indicated whether your taste runs to very modern and sophisticated or something more traditional—we've been generalizing so far. Could you give me an idea of what you like?"

"I like what I've heard, but I'd probably go with a traditional approach in terms of materials—wood, natural fabrics, subtle colors, and I guess this space could take some large pieces of furniture. I prefer to keep the metal and hard surfaces for the kitchen and bathroom."

Of course, she could make that work, but she'd been hoping for something more modern and had already regretted that the architectural design was complete and built. She would have liked to create a staircase using fine oak treads and a glass balustrade, which would be so delicate that it would allow the beauty of the stone behind it to show through, but the position of the stairwell was fixed, and that might not be possible. It would depend on how the architect, Leonardo, had interpreted the client's wishes. But it didn't mean she couldn't do a fabulous scheme. Even with such restrictions in place, she was sure she could come up with an innovative design.

"I wonder if you have any artifacts or memorabilia, you'd like me to use."

"How do you mean?"

"Well, when you use an interior designer, you get something very personal, very tailored to your requirements—otherwise you could just use someone with a flair for color and the ability to search out suitable pieces of furniture. If you have any objects that mean something to you, maybe some framed photographs, something that's been in the family for a long while, we could incorporate them."

"Okay, I'll give some thought to that."

"And I can start by picking out materials and furniture, try out a few color schemes, and email you for initial comments."

She'd do two schemes, one that could be called traditional and one much more modern but subtly so, and then he could choose.

"Excellent. Tommaso will give you the plans for the floor below, and I'll respond to anything you send me and then contact you at the end of the month to see where we've got to."

The time allocation was more than generous for this first phase. And it was unusual to have a client who really did appear to put the quality of the design ahead of the budget. There *would* be a budget already discussed with Tommaso, of course, but he hadn't once mentioned money.

"I'll give you my card." He took one from his wallet and scribbled on it. "If you need to come back to look again, to check on anything, just ring Carlotta Forni, my housekeeper. I've written down her number here. Arrange it with her."

He must be anxious to bring the meeting to a close, already heading for the ladder as he spoke. "Will you go first? Let me help you. Or do you need more time up here?"

"No, I'm ready to leave."

Getting onto the ladder was the difficult part. He grasped her arm and steadied her while she engaged on the first rungs. They repeated the process at the next level, each contact sending her heart rate up, but by the time he stepped off the lowest rung of the ladder on the ground floor, she was able to present her professional self.

"Ask Tommaso to show you the proposed staircase," he said. "They start manufacture soon, and it will be installed at the end of next month. Adjustments will have to be made this week."

Of course, she'd have to consult him but doubted major changes could be made at this stage.

They walked out onto the forecourt and shook hands.

"It has been a pleasure, Signorina Bruni. I am sure we shall work well together."

A moment later, he strode off and disappeared into the house, calling to his housekeeper.

Deprived of his presence, the space around her was empty. Slowly getting her wits together, Isla watched a cloud that was traveling across the sun, casting the forecourt momentarily into shade. This wouldn't do. This was work, nothing else.

She sighed. Suddenly, the dream job had become complicated; it was looking less attractive—and more attractive at the same time. She took a deep breath and drew herself up to her full height. When she'd stood beside him her head had come up to the level of his shoulder. He was tall…but what had that got to do with anything? She had to get herself together.

She got into the car but waited a moment longer, her gaze fixed unseeingly on the distant plain that had drawn her so powerfully a couple of hours earlier. Then, she started the engine and reversed, before heading toward the gateway.

Chapter 6

Edmondo Benedetti left his factory in Teramo and turned the Ferrari toward Rome. Thank goodness the meeting with the supply company had been quickly sorted out, given how tight he was for time. He was having to juggle a whole lot of things, all equally important. Even so, his mind was no longer on the work problem, nor on the factory, nor even on the fact that it would take him about another two hours to get to the capital. Instead, he was thinking about Isla Bruni.

He'd had that peculiar jolt of recognition when he'd first seen her in Milan. He'd persuaded himself that he'd misread the situation and was suffering from exhaustion after several sleepless nights. It had worked—more or less—until he'd met her again today. Those long hours where he'd lain wide awake trying to find a way to make things work had been the result of learning that his ex-wife and her new partner were taking off to the United States—today, as it happened.

"A week, Edmondo," she'd said, "and then we're off. You'll have to pick him up before we go. I can't just leave him with Paola."

He didn't like the way she was talking about Adriano as if he were an inconvenient parcel and not their son. And she was right: she couldn't just leave him with her sister.

Not that he didn't want Adriano to live with him—

of course, he did—but the news had hit him quite suddenly when he was in the middle of complicated business negotiations. Then, there'd been the conference to fit in. And as he'd been invited to run a small workshop on plastics and ecology, he hadn't been able to drop out.

But he'd got it wrong—he hadn't misread anything.

His feelings on meeting Isla again had been totally unexpected, and now he was having difficulty understanding his own thoughts and reactions. How, at the top of the tower, had he almost allowed himself to put out his hand to smooth down her glossy, brown hair? And why had he hated to bring the meeting to a close so quickly? He pictured her standing at the top of stairwell, explaining about the framed view the architect had created, and he heard her voice again.

Of course, what he really wanted to do was to spend time learning more about her ideas, while listening to the utterly charming way she spoke Italian. There was no trace of a foreign accent, yet there was something slightly odd about it, as if she'd learned it down in the south, perhaps even in Sicily. Then, she'd gone away to a lot of other places which had softened it and produced something all her own. It sounded wonderful.

But picking up Adriano couldn't be delayed any longer. The boy's mother, Bianca—Edmondo's ex-wife—and her new man, the TV journalist Basilio Protti, would be flying out from Fiumicino this evening at ten, heading ultimately to Los Angeles. Therefore, Edmondo was driving carefully, unwilling to risk any incidents. He needed to get there in time to pick up his son, and then to leave as quickly as possible.

He rounded a bend and saw a road sign: another twenty-five kilometers. His heart lifted at the thought of seeing his boy.

What a pity that things had gone so wrong. These days, he scarcely gave any thought to what had happened to his marriage, but when Bianca had told him she'd met someone else and was moving out of their home and taking their child with her, he'd been deeply hurt—and then just plain angry. All the effort he'd been making to build his business, to secure their future together, was being thrown away and it felt insulting—though not as upsetting as the idea of being separated from Adriano. He'd been very distressed and had thrown himself into work to stop himself from thinking about it all the time.

For Adriano's sake, he'd tried to keep things civilized.

"I need to be able to visit, have him stay with me. I'll try to fit around your timetable to make that happen."

"A pity you couldn't have managed that while we were together," she'd said, only digging deeper into the wound.

Bianca and he hadn't married in church, which had been shocking to both families, each steeped in the Catholic tradition. Edmondo had never succeeded in finding his faith, and Bianca had rejected it years before she met him, so to them, a civil marriage had been logical. Of course, when they parted, it had given members of both families a reason to say their criticisms of such a marriage had been justified. More rifts, more reasons to feel guilty. He gave a deep sigh.

Red lights flashed ahead of him, and he brought his foot down on the brake, hoping the driver behind was alert because he didn't want a holdup at this stage in the journey. But the car responded beautifully, and no one crashed into the rear. A few moments later, they were on the move again.

Anyway, all that was past, and now, he had to concentrate. This was no time for daydreaming about the beautiful, sexy designer and the tantalizing ideas she had for the tower. Adriano deserved his full attention, and he intended to make sure he got it.

He passed a small school in an outlying district, where children played within an enclosure, and it reminded him he'd have to arrange for his son to attend the local school. Life in Fortezza was surely going to be better for him than on the fifth floor of the expensive block where the couple lived. He glanced around as buildings began to close in, but this part of Rome was not very smart, unlike the apartment just off Via dei Condotti in the Monti district. Bianca had always rejected the idea of the boy living with his father and had been largely unwelcoming when he'd wanted to visit, so he'd had to go carefully to ensure continued access to his son. Suddenly, all that had changed.

A rise in the road gave him a wide view of Rome and, far beyond, the sea. He glanced at the analogue clock on the dashboard. He'd be there in a few minutes, and he couldn't wait. He wanted to envelop the child in a big hug again. And then get him home. It would take him time to settle in, of course, poor lad. Thank God for Carlotta, his housekeeper. He was counting on her help, and he didn't think he'd misjudged her. When he'd told her he planned to bring Adriano home, she hadn't hesitated.

"It would be a pleasure to have him here, Edmondo. There's no need to get anyone else to look after him."

It wasn't going to be easy living together, not at first. Adriano was just a child, and he'd probably take time to get used to being in such a different place and no longer having his mother close at hand. How would it feel to have your mother say she wasn't going to be around anymore? It couldn't be good. The poor boy was going to miss her.

Now he left the autostrada and engaged in the constricted streets of the center. The traffic was intense, and he was getting too close to his deadline for comfort. Ah, there it was, around that corner.

Via Della Cappella was a narrow street close to the Vatican Museum, the apartment building sandwiched between two hotels. And there was the *gelateria* that occupied the ground floor. Probably that was a place that Adriano knew well—how the boy had loved going for an ice cream at the bar in Fortezza last summer, when he'd come to stay. It was a treat they'd repeated just a couple of weeks ago. Well, he couldn't offer him an ice cream shop on the ground floor of their own house, but there were quite a few other attractions to living in the little mountain town.

To the right was the entrance to the underground garage, to which Bianca had supplied the pass code. He'd memorized it, so in a matter of moments, the metal shutter was clanking upward, and then he drove quickly in. At this time in the evening, the parking places were filling up as people arrived home from work, and someone was right behind him, so he slotted the Ferrari into the first unmarked space he saw, even though it would mean walking right across the garage to reach the lifts. There was Protti's top-of-the-range German car, two along. They owned the apartment, so he'd be able to leave it garaged there during their time in the States. Convenient.

A Porsche had followed him in. Ignoring the glare from the other driver, he locked the car and headed for the lift, changing his mind at the last moment, when he remembered how long it could take to arrive. Instead, he entered the stairwell and pounded up to the fifth floor. He still managed a short run every morning, but with so much going on, he'd missed his regular workout sessions this week. Better make sure he was at the next one. Hardly breathing faster than normal, he arrived with two minutes to spare and rang the bell.

He waited. It was very quiet.

Surely, they hadn't left early. He'd already raised his hand to ring again when the door opened, and Adriano stood there, beaming at him.

"*Papà*," he shouted. "You've come."

Edmondo swept the boy up into his arms and walked in, holding him tightly, not wanting to bring their fierce hug to an end. He'd grown, all arms and legs now, and his warm, sweaty little body felt thinner than the last time he'd seen him.

"Where's your mum?"

Adriano, who still had his arms clamped around his father's neck, gazed up. "She had to go."

A shadow passed over the child's face. Edmondo tried to hold down the surge of fury that threatened to overcome him. He mustn't let Adriano see how badly this affected him, how angry it made him feel. Many things about Bianca annoyed him, but he'd promised himself a long time ago that he would never criticize her to their son. The boy deserved to have the best relationship possible with his mother, because it was going to be hard enough for him anyway. But it would have been good if she could have waited for his arrival today. It had all been arranged, leaving plenty of time to get to the airport.

Edmondo placed his son on the floor, but Adriano grabbed his arm.

"Swing me," he said. "Swing me around."

His father picked him up again and swung him round and round in a circle until they both collapsed in a heap on the rug. He took the boy's hand and led him over to the sofa, still thinking about his ex-wife.

Of course, she hadn't wanted to see him, Edmondo. That was why. She was drawing a very firm line under her life with him and appeared to be ruling out Adriano at the same time. She was an all or nothing person, and he suspected she wanted to give everything to her new relationship for the time being. She'd given everything to her relationship with him once, which had been a wonderful experience. Now, he barely remembered what he'd seen in her. They'd had a few good years together. He shrugged; she didn't do long-term, and when Basilio had come along with his exciting media job and all that entailed, she'd suddenly lost interest.

A door clicked open, and a woman in her late thirties walked in. Paola was a slightly less glamorous but equally beautiful version of her younger sister. She was a sensible woman with a doctor husband. Edmondo had always got on with her.

"Hello, Paola." He got up and gave her a hug.

"Thank you for holding the fort."

"No problem," she said, kissing him on the cheek. "You know this is my favorite nephew, don't you?" She nodded to Adriano, who was looking up at them. "I'm really going to miss him."

"You and the family are welcome any time. We have plenty of room, so just let me know when you're arriving."

"Thank you. So, how is *il conte* today?" she said, a little smile on her lips as she emphasized the words of the title.

"Very well. They love it in the town, having their tower occupied. As far as most of the townspeople are concerned, the right order of things has been restored." He grinned. "It took me a while to realize I'd automatically inherited the title when I bought the building, and even more, that people thought it was important, and I was supposed to live up to it. I've sort of got used to it, now. It does make you feel responsible for certain things, in a way."

"But there are no legal requirements? Just let me know if anything comes up. You know I can help."

Paola was a lawyer, although these days, she'd whittled her office time down to two days a week.

"No, it's fine. And I certainly don't want people honoring me for something I haven't worked for."

"I don't think you have much to worry about, Edmondo. You've probably worked harder than most to achieve what you've built in the last few years. Don't belittle it." She headed toward the hallway. "I'll leave you for a moment while I pack the rest of Adriano's things. Do you want a drink after your journey? Bianca asked me to close everything down before I leave, but I can still manage coffee."

He swallowed with difficulty at these words, surprised to be feeling more emotional about what was happening than he'd expected, with his ex-wife leaving the country and Adriano finally coming home to him as he'd always wanted. He wouldn't mind something a lot stronger than coffee—maybe a whisky would do the trick. But it would be irresponsible, given he had to drive back to Fortezza.

"Coffee would be great."

While they waited, Adriano and Edmondo sat down on the long sofa, the boy snuggling up to his father at first. Paola was back in a couple of minutes, bringing a juice for the child and a plate of *biscotti*. Adriano tucked in, chattering nonstop between bites. Edmondo watched his son as he ate. He wanted to gather him close, to eat him up like the boy was devouring the biscuits, but he mustn't crowd him. Theirs would be a long-term relationship and deserved being worked on carefully.

His love for the boy was swelling in his breast, a warm, wonderful feeling he'd held in check until now. Work couldn't be busier, but he would have to find the time for this new little person in his life, time to be a good father and provide the sort of home the child needed.

Now would begin a whole new chapter for them both.

Chapter 7

What was she going to do about her work? Isla sat at her computer table, her head in her hands. Instead of losing herself in her projects as she usually did, she kept having to remind herself that there were things to be done—and some of them had a time limit attached. She'd never in her life felt so reluctant to get on with her work, but she couldn't just sit there.

She'd always wondered how people could allow their feelings to dominate everything else. Surely, if there was something to be done, you got on and did it before attending to other things. And now here she was, in the ridiculous situation where her pulse rate seemed to double every time she thought about her client. And that would immediately send her thoughts in different directions, none of them related to the work she was trying to complete.

She opened the website and clicked through the pages of a furniture supplier, until she found one that showed the long, elegant sofas she recalled using on a project in London, which she thought would be the perfect fit for that tower-top room. Maybe not those with the steel legs—he'd said traditional but perhaps she could persuade him that the metal legs were the better option. She moved on a couple more pages and found the perfect combination. Hmm, purple, though. Isla grinned—he wouldn't like that. But the color chart showed a wide range. She'd introduce color mainly by means of artifacts, cushions, and so on but needed a grey for the furniture itself, and it had to be just the right shade, one that would go with the golden stone. She clicked back to the elegant, modern furniture displayed in the online catalogue against just such a stone wall and noted down the details. Two quite different designs, she had thought, and that's what she was going to do.

But even this fascinating research was interrupted by her thoughts diverting to her client. It was disconcerting—and it didn't just happen in office time when she was working on his project. It seemed to take up all of her free time as well. This was Monday, more than a week after she'd met him up at the tower, and she was filled with frustration at her lack of progress. She threw down her pen yet again, sprang up from her chair and paced about the studio, picking up objects and putting them down again, staring sightlessly out the windows. It was the fourth time she'd done this today. Eloisa raised her head from what she was working on, a concerned expression on her face.

"What's wrong, Isla? Can I do anything? If it's a work thing, maybe you'd like to talk it through."

"What? Oh, no. I'm just not getting it right yet. One of those things—it'll come together eventually."

There was no one else in the room, the others presumably out on site, while Tommaso sat hunched at his desk behind the glass wall, creating graphics and questions. He was very good at milking each successful project for publicity and had apparently taken to social media like someone a third of his age. Everyone knew he was preparing for an interview at a local television station and shouldn't be disturbed.

One or two of the team joked about his addiction to publicity, but Isla appreciated it. If any of them produced good work, he would go all out to ensure this was known in the right places. In the end, it was all about him and his business, but it would help her long-term plans. And they all appreciated the high-quality projects he landed. She had to use this unexpected chance she'd been given to build her portfolio, in order to persuade people to trust her with their projects when she set up for herself.

Yeah, right. She could definitely be trusted—just look at how she was behaving now. That was going to get her a long way.

Eloisa glanced at her phone and stood up. "Come on, let's go across the square and have a coffee. We've both worked through the last three hours. It's time we had a break."

It probably wouldn't do any good, but Eloisa was one of those people who was always willing to give support where it was needed, and she should not be pushed away just because Isla wasn't in the mood. They were close in age and had quite a lot in common. In fact, she was becoming a real friend, which was very good indeed, but maybe they hadn't yet reached a level of intimacy that meant she'd be happy discussing such personal matters.

What she couldn't ignore was that the obsession with the new client was interfering with the ability to give her full attention to the work. Something had to be done. Still reluctant, she followed Eloisa across the square.

"I thought you'd settled in really well," the girl

said minutes later as they contemplated the mound of cake, full of chocolate and nuts, that she'd insisted on getting for them, "but in the last few days, you've not been looking very happy. Is anything wrong?"

Isla looked up at her. Should she tell her, or should she not?

It could prove really embarrassing but, on the other hand, perhaps she could find out more about him from Eloisa. It would help her to work out if she was just going through a crazy period which would eventually pass, or if there was something much more serious going on. Frustrated by what was happening, she took an aggressive swipe at the cake with her fork, breaking it in two.

People said it was useful to talk when you had a problem. And one of those times had to be when you felt as confused about your feelings as she did at the moment. The girl knew him reasonably well because she'd assisted the architect who'd organized the dismantling and rebuilding of the tower. That was useful—and the opportunity to find out more was desperately tempting.

"It's my client," she said, before she had time to change her mind.

"But I don't understand. I can't imagine he's being difficult. He's lovely."

"Exactly."

"Oh—oh, I see."

Eloisa was quiet for a moment, stirring sugar into her coffee. How did she keep so slim? Then, she looked up, a little smile curling her lips.

"Isla! Don't tell me you've fallen for him." When Isla didn't answer, the grin widened. "You have, haven't you?"

A wave of heat moved up Isla's neck and into her cheeks, and she looked away quickly. This was so difficult, but she couldn't just remain silent now.

"Well, let's say he's had an effect on me." She paused, trying to find suitable words. "It's like I'm sixteen again, and everything's new and exciting and frightening. I don't really know how to handle it. And it's seriously affecting my ability to concentrate."

"I'm not sure how I can help you with that."

"No, I don't think you can. I have to learn to deal with it. Unless you can tell me that he's involved in the local mafiosi and is extracting their last pennies from his poverty-stricken tenants, there's not much you can do. I'm assuming he's got some tenants, seeing how rich he seems to be. That would be a serious deterrent."

"Has he shown any…is he…?"

"No, he's perfectly correct, very businesslike, you know. Just the way a client should be. And not the slightest bit interested in me." At least, she was more comfortable believing that. She added, "That ought to make it easier, but it doesn't."

"Well, I don't know anything to his detriment. On the contrary, I recall he contributed to the temporary housing during that big earthquake."

"Damn! That's no help at all."

She looked down and stuck her fork into the gooey mass on her plate, which looked heavenly. She didn't usually allow herself to indulge in such things, but she needed *something*—and there was no sense in it going to waste.

"Damn!" she said again and swallowed a large mouthful. "Eloisa, I can't deal with complications—not just now. I haven't recovered from my last relationship."

"Which was how long ago? Six, eight months? And *you* ended it, you said. That's long enough for anyone." She stopped, staring off into space, and then turned her gaze back on Isla. "And maybe you didn't love him, anyway."

"Of course I did," Isla said, affronted. "We lived together for two years."

Eloisa smiled. "It doesn't mean you loved him. From what you've said, I don't think you did. He sounded quite boring, and I can tell that's not you at all. Besides, it doesn't mean you can't be open to other possibilities, now that it's finished." She fixed her eyes on Isla's face, watching for a reaction. "I think he's divorced."

Isla tried not to show how interested she was in this fact. And failed. "Oh, really?"

Thank you, Eloisa. It would mean the field was indeed clear—and therefore that things were about to get a whole lot more complicated, because she wasn't sure she had the strength to resist.

"I know you're right, but I have things I want to do. I told you about my plan to open a design studio in the next couple of years. It'll all get out of control if I don't concentrate on that."

Yes, she needed to remind herself about the priorities—there was no way she could put all her plans at risk.

"I'd say that doesn't matter. It could even be a good thing. You can't cut out personal relationships. You just have to build the other things around them."

Ah, that was so difficult—and Eloisa was wrong.

Again and again, Isla had seen how couples had got together, and within a very short time, one of them had abandoned their career to run the home. And it was nearly always the woman—even now, in the 2020s. Especially when children came along.

****

When they got back to the office, she hadn't resolved a thing. But somehow, it had helped her to air the problem. She'd have a lot to think over later in the evening, but for now, she was back at work and relieved to find some self-discipline returning. She was caught up, pursuing exciting ideas which she knew would appeal. She tried out a few interesting variations, unwilling to settle on one approach until she could see where it might lead. When Eloisa left at six o'clock, Isla was deep in the scheme. She'd pushed all thoughts of her client out of her mind, after reminding herself that that's all he was—a client.

And that she was not a love-sick teenager but a woman of twenty-six who ought to know how to handle the different aspects of her life.

She pulled up the plan of the proposed stairs. Although she'd had a completely different idea for the stairs, they seemed to fit perfectly well as they were with the scheme that she had in mind. She'd discuss it tomorrow with Leonardo, the scheme architect, who had been away from the office. Tomorrow as well, she'd need to go on site to check a number of points off her list. *Il conte* wouldn't be there. It had sounded as if he wouldn't be around until the end of the month, so she didn't have to worry about a possible meeting. She telephoned Carlotta Forni, apologized for ringing so late, and arranged to visit at three o'clock the next day.

Aware she'd spent a disproportionate amount of her time on the tower project, she now put it to one side and worked on for another two hours, progressing work for her other clients.

Chapter 8

It was a lovely, cool day, perfect for getting some exercise. Somehow, with everything else occupying her, she hadn't been keeping up with that side of her life. She'd got into climbing at university and was keen, but she'd done very little physical activity recently, except for that walk with Eloisa on the Sunday of her first weekend in Fortezza—and that had hardly taxed her. The weeks were racing by. It was time to get out into the open and enjoy the fresh air, or she'd be going back to England without having benefitted from all the things the area could offer, and that had been part of the reason for coming. She swung the satchel over her shoulder and left the studio just after two o'clock.

Halfway up the slope, the road was very quiet, apart from the twittering of the birds and the scuffles of small animals along the wayside. Suddenly, that changed. A strange noise was beginning to impinge on her consciousness. What on earth was it? She looked ahead, but the road twisted and turned, snaking up through the trees, and she could see nothing. She'd swear that was someone singing, and there was a curious tapping, in time to the song. Coming around the next bend, she saw the source of the sounds: a little way ahead of her, a small boy was crooning quietly to himself. The gradient was growing steeper, but undeterred, he stomped along on his short legs, using a hefty stick to batter the vegetation on the edge of the road.

"*Buongiorno*," she said, smiling as she came abreast of him. "I'm Isla. What's your name?"

"Adriano. I live here."

She wondered if this was Carlotta's child, but when he turned to look at her, she changed her mind. He was *il conte*'s son, there was no doubt of it, the same deep-set dark eyes. He was six, maybe seven, years old. Surely, he was too young to be out on the road on his own? But perhaps things were different here. After all, this wasn't London. She thought of her cousin's little boy, who was much the same age. She adored the child and could not imagine ever allowing him out on the streets on his own, not so young.

"Do you want to walk up to the house with me?" she asked.

He stepped away. "No, I can walk on my own."

Well, at least he was wary of strangers.

"I'm going to see Signora Forni. What about you?"

"I'm going to my house," he said and ran off, disappearing through the gateposts.

There was no sign of him by the time she arrived on the forecourt, where Signora Forni was already heading toward her. The woman put her hand in her pocket and pulled out an oversized key as they approached the ancient door of the tower.

"With Adriano here, I've had to lock up," she explained.

"That must be the little boy I saw."

"Yes. He's gone missing several times, and he usually turns up in the tower if I leave it open. He's obsessed with it, but there are still no stairs and I'm terrified he'll fall through the floors."

"He was out on the road when I met him."

"Again! I cannot keep that boy in. *Il conte* says it's no problem, that this is his home, and we should let him wander because that's what small boys like to do."

"Maybe he's right. It does seem relatively safe up here. Anyway, I'll be here an hour or so, signora. If he wants to visit the tower, that's no problem. I'll keep an eye on him. You could tell him he can come in."

The woman laughed. "I won't have to tell him. Leave the door open a little, and he'll sneak in when you're not looking."

****

Rooms had now been partitioned off on the middle floor. Someone had thrown open the windows, but the air was filled with the smell of damp plaster. Isla ran her fingers lightly over a surface and decided the plasterers had probably only finished the day before, their work restricted to one wall in each of the bedrooms and to preparing a suitable surface for tiling in the individual bathrooms.

This new work presented her with many things that needed decisions, and she'd get down to it in a moment, but first she wanted to have another look at the top floor. She climbed up and stepped into the room. The wall to the left as she arrived at the top of the stairs was a long stretch of stone with nothing happening there.

They'd already talked about personalizing the decoration, and now she thought of the objects in the sitting room of the main house. If there were any more like that, she could make up a display which would be built onto the wall. It would be unique, and the fact that he'd collected the objects told her they were something that interested her client. The opposite wall, to the left of the loggia, cried out for a huge canvas, but that could be decided later.

A few moments later, she'd finished and dropped down a floor to begin the sketches and notes she would need for the bedrooms.

"What are you doing?"

She jumped, dragged out of her absorption in the color scheme she was planning. Adriano was climbing out of the hole in the floor, swinging himself nonchalantly off the top of the ladder. God, what if he fell! That drop had looked scary enough to her when she'd climbed up a little while earlier.

She was in the landing area that led off to the bedrooms that had now been created, down on one knee again, a favorite position for making a quick sketch. He ran over to where she was working.

"Can I see?"

"Here you are—have a look."

"That's not a proper picture."

"No, it isn't. It's a plan of the space. You see here—that line tells us there's a window in the wall, and this quadrant shows you where the first door is."

He looked at it for a few moments. "What's the writing?"

"I've written down my ideas about colors and things like that, so I don't forget. I have a really bad memory."

While she'd been talking, she'd taken another sheet of paper and had begun a rapid sketch of the room, in which she depicted a small figure wearing shorts and holding a stick, standing in the doorway.

"Is that me?"

"Yes. Here—you can keep it."

He stared down at the picture and then took it from her and darted off, clasping it to his chest as he somehow made his way one-handed down the ladders. She followed him down.

"Look what I have," he said, when they saw Carlotta as they were coming out of the building.

"That's very good. Say thank you to Miss Bruni," she told the boy.

"*Grazie,* Signorina Bruni," said the child, with a small bow. Then he skipped away, brandishing his picture.

"He has style," said Isla, laughing.

"Just like his father, but in Adriano's case, it goes along with a lot of naughtiness and cheek," the housekeeper replied. "So, don't be taken in by the charm. We used to get on really well, but since his mother's decided he should live here permanently, he's been quite difficult at times."

"Oh, doesn't his mother live here?" asked Isla, wanting confirmation of what Eloisa had said.

"No—Adriano stayed with her after the divorce, but suddenly, three years later, she's remarried and he's living here full time. It must be very different from being in the center of Rome. I think he's found it difficult to adapt."

So, it was true. She tucked the piece of information away—not that it was anything to do with her.

It wasn't hard to imagine what had happened to change the situation. Probably, the mother had met a new man—one who didn't want to be burdened with someone else's child. That would hurt, she thought, inevitably reminded of the way her father had gone off after her brother had died. She'd been ten years old, and she'd never seen him since. It certainly made you feel that you didn't matter when people behaved like that. She suddenly felt protective toward the child.

"Oh, I should have told you, *il conte* said to let you have a look in the glass corridor where he's put a few things that might interest you. He said you might be incorporating it into the design."

He wasn't all that traditional, thought Isla, or he wouldn't have agreed to that ultra-modern solution to joining the two buildings together. Hopefully, he'd like the idea of the feature wall using the archeological finds as well.

Carlotta Forni opened the door for her. Several cartons were lined up along one side. They seemed to contain a collection of pictures in various assorted frames, including two beautiful porcelain photographs of people in Edwardian dress, which would date from the early twentieth century, or even a little before. But what caught her eye was a superb pair of wooden skis. At a guess, they'd be at least a hundred years old. The beautiful old wood had been lovingly polished and was glowing in the afternoon light. She bent closer to read a card that was attached: "Could you use these? They belonged to my great-grandfather."

Now, she had something.

Chapter 9

Isla stared at the screen for a long moment, her hand hovering over her mouse. Then she clicked on *Salva*. It was an important moment. The scheme was finished—the two schemes, in the case of the upper room—and she'd organized them as best she could, to help the client understand the possibilities, especially for the middle floor of the tower, which they hadn't discussed in much depth. A few minutes later, she knocked on the boss's door.

"Do you have a moment, Tommaso? I want to run through this with you before I contact the client."

"Come in," he said, indicating the chair by the desk. "Sit down while I go through it."

Isla looked around her. It was the first time she'd been in here since that visit to the office on the Saturday after her arrival. Somehow, Tommaso had managed to make her feel much surer of herself than she'd been when working in London. Perhaps because there was no affection involved, as there had been with Susan. He just wanted good work, and he respected those who could produce it. She knew she was more than good enough, and that was all it took.

With Susan, there had been the feeling of owing something; and that had to be weighed in the balance when she made her decision about whether to accept the offer of a partnership or not.

She placed a selection of sample materials in front of him and told him how to access the work on his computer.

His eyebrows rose. "Two schemes?"

"The client is somewhat traditional in his tastes, but I can see so many possibilities for that upper room, so I thought I'd give him alternatives."

"These are not just alternatives. They are fully worked out schemes. Are we going to charge him for your time?"

Isla flushed. "I've stayed late most of this week, getting this together in my own time, so no, it won't be charged, and you haven't lost out."

He stared at her for a long moment and then returned his gaze to the computer and the materials she'd given him. She perched herself on the edge of the seat, and said, "Do you want me to explain?"

"No, I'll ask if there's anything I don't understand."

Isla was used to presenting to clients and had made it easy to follow, but she was anxious to know that it met with his approval. Everyone said he had very high standards, and this was the first important piece of work she'd done for him. He was flicking through screens and referring from time to time to the color and fabric boards she'd placed on the desk. Ten minutes later, he looked up at her.

"Well, I'm seriously impressed. The client hasn't seen this, you say?"

"No, not yet. I thought you ought to have a chance to comment first."

But her heart was singing. He liked it. It met his standards, and that's all that mattered.

They talked for a few minutes, and she scribbled down his suggestions, although the points were minor. Then, she went back to her desk, made a couple of changes, and composed an email to the client. He was always the client, never Edmondo or *il conte*. That way lay trouble. Impersonal was best. She gave two or three dates when they could meet, so they could discuss any issues which arose from the scheme and make a final choice. She would, of course, telephone the next day, but she wanted to give him a chance to look through things before they spoke. When she'd attached everything necessary and sent it, she looked around, wondering what to do next.

The empty feeling that she had now was familiar. It was always the same when she'd worked hard on a project and there was nothing to be done until she'd had the client's input. He'd seemed happy with her ideas when they toured the property, but now she'd worked them up, they'd arrived at what could often be a difficult stage: the point where clients would suddenly see how big a commitment they were making. Either they'd want to draw back a little or they were stimulated by what you gave them and wanted to add all sorts of other things—and the problem with that was what it did to the budget. Either of these approaches had to be dealt with before they went any further, especially if changes involved architectural services. She'd clocked up a good number of expensive hours, as it was.

She cleared things away and then called up the drawings of an extension to a nursery school. On this project, which was now in the later stages of building, she'd be working with Gianluca, who'd designed it. It was a lovely design with a small arena which would serve as a story and performance area. The retractable dome would make it usable at all times of the year.

Gianluca was very talented, and she felt privileged to work with him. While Leonardo devoted himself mainly to ancient buildings like the tower, the younger architect was involved in some very cutting-edge design which he brought to even the smallest of projects like this school. She frowned at the plans, fidgeting all the while. It was difficult to start work immediately on something so completely different. Besides, she wanted to talk it through with him, to ensure she understood all the requirements, but he was not in the studio today.

A short walk seemed like a good idea.

Downstairs, she looked out onto the square. The weather had changed during the morning, and now, it was several degrees hotter than when she'd arrived for work. She peeled off her jacket and dropped it on a chair in the reception area before leaving the building. A left turn brought her to the top of a sloping street, and she headed downhill out of the little town. But a quarter of an hour later, her navy cotton blouse was sticking to her skin, and she gave up on the walk, turning back toward the café to grab a cold drink. At least that side of the square was now in the shade.

When she'd ordered, she sat at a table under one of the two giant umbrellas, sharing the area with a couple of tourists who were enjoying the cool air. She spent two minutes considering what she would tackle next, while she waited for decisions from the handsome aristocrat.

That title—*il conte*—was a negative all on its own.

In fact, there were two points chalked up against him. She hated the business of inherited privilege. And if that sounds pompous, she thought, too bad! She was the child of a single mother, and she'd lived too close to real poverty not to think that the world was unfairly weighted against some people. Of course, it hadn't stopped her getting what she wanted—but wasn't that all due to the sacrifices her mother had made? And her own hard work?

She took a long sip of the cold liquid, the sharp ginger biting at the back of her throat.

And he was Italian. Of course, there wasn't a single rule that applied to everyone. Yes, she was inherently prejudiced against Italian men. No, she hadn't the faintest idea if he was unreliable and manipulative like her father. And yes, she ought to stop thinking like that. She gave a little, self-deprecating smile. Silly woman! It was completely ridiculous. But then, hadn't she had good reason to feel like that? She would hang onto her prejudices a little while longer.

Suddenly, she found herself tuning in to the couple at the other table who were speaking English. The woman was saying this was the best holiday she'd ever had, and she began a long list of the things she'd enjoyed about Italy. Isla listened.

"Maybe we could retire here."

"You're forgetting we're on holiday and it's the summer," the man said. "Things might look different if you were here all the year round."

But his wife was having none of it, and Isla was thinking, those were some of the reasons she'd wanted to come: the relaxed way in which people seemed to enjoy life, the wonderful architecture, the food she'd always loved—and so many other aspects of Italian life. Of course, it had been a combination of things, among them that Italy was a large part of her heritage and, increasingly, she'd wanted to know more.

And then, wasn't the country a mecca for people like her who were involved in design? If you looked at any aspect of design in the international field, you'd find seriously good Italian designers at the top of the list. When the opportunity had suddenly presented itself, she'd not hesitated.

Her mobile buzzed, and she pulled it out of her bag. Michele? She didn't know anyone called Michele. Oh, yes, she did. The guy she'd had dinner with all those weeks ago, the last night of the conference. She'd almost forgotten his existence, so involved had she been in thoughts of her client. Did she want to talk to him?

"Michele, I didn't expect to hear from you. How are you?"

"Very well. I am on business in Ascoli Piceno today. I have the idea that's not very far away from where you are."

"You're right—less than an hour, I believe."

"So, would you have dinner with me this evening? I'll finish by five, at the latest. I could pick you up."

Dinner. What a great idea. She could celebrate having got the tower project temporarily off her desk, leave for a while this tiny, claustrophobic town and the problems that were beginning to surface. And it would be nice to catch up. She'd spent far too much time obsessing about the impossible and trying to convince herself she didn't care anyway.

"I'd like that, Michele, provided you let me pay for

my own meal.'"

"Hmm…well it wasn't what I had in mind but, if you feel that's important, then I will."

"It is. And you don't have to pick me up. It'll be good for me to get away from here for a few hours, so I'll drive." She wanted to be able to leave when she felt like it and not be dependent on anyone else. "I'll enjoy the drive down to Ascoli. I can probably get there around six. Is that okay with you?"

Chapter 10

Isla took a huge breath, filled with a new sense of freedom. Closing the car door, she leaned back and rolled her shoulders to loosen the tight muscles. That's what far too many hours of computer work did for you. She started the engine and slowly headed the short distance up the mountain to meet the main road that circled around above the town. It would be exciting to drive fast—but very foolish on this narrow, winding road.

The evening was going to be great. She deserved this after working hard for weeks, not just on the tower but on several other, smaller jobs she was involved with, as well. Truly, she had scarcely allowed herself any time off.

Eloisa had been almost more excited than her when she'd mentioned she was going out for dinner in Ascoli. And with such a personable date.

"Sounds dreamy," she'd said, when Isla had told her a little about Michele. "Maybe he'll manage to take your mind off the unobtainable Edmondo."

Jealousy surfaced. It was all right for some. Unlike Eloisa, she didn't even have the right to call her client by his first name.

Going back down toward the sea for the first time since she'd arrived in Fortezza, and reminding herself not to overthink things, she relaxed into the drive. The warm air was gentle on her bare arms, but there was a hint of moisture in the air—and was that a flash of lightning? A thunderstorm would be quite something, up here in the mountains. Loving the drama of a big storm, she rather wanted that to happen, although Eloisa had said it wouldn't rain—or at least, not in Fortezza.

"There's a parking garage you can use, easy to get to and safe. It's very close to the Piazza del Popolo. Here, let me put the details into your phone for you."

It began to drizzle as she approached the outskirts of Ascoli, but she didn't really care. She'd put an umbrella in her bag, almost as an afterthought, and now it was looking as if it would be useful. Google told her in Italian to turn right and then take the first left. She was there.

A few minutes later, she changed into a pair of high-heeled sandals, locked the car, and headed into the town. There were so many interesting things to catch her attention. This place was different, sophisticated, a real contrast to the medieval simplicity of Fortezza. And she liked all that buzzy, low-key noise, which you always found in a place where many people lived close by one another—just like in the city.

She'd done some research before coming to Italy. Surely, she'd read that the population of Ascoli was less than fifty thousand people—hardly comparable with London's nine million. But after weeks in the tiny mountain town, it felt like a grand metropolis. Voices echoed off the walls of the narrow street as she hurried along, and the clinking of cutlery on plates floated out of upper-story windows as people began their evening. She stopped on a corner and waited, wanting to give herself time to absorb the atmosphere.

It was probably full of tourists, but that didn't spoil her pleasure in the lovely town at all. When she arrived at the piazza, a heavy rain began, the sky becoming almost black for a while. It swept across the square at a low angle, and despite the umbrella, her thin cotton frock was soon soaked. It clung to her legs, and when the streetlights came on, its vivid orange color was reflected in a dark glass door. Shops had rapidly illuminated their displays, and now golden reflections spilled out across the fine travertine marble flagstones, lending the square an air of magic.

She hurried across to a walkway that sheltered under jutting upper stories. Arches ran, cloister-like, along both sides of the piazza, and now almost everyone had retreated to the sides. Everyone except for the dancers, that is; in a restaurant enclosure, musicians played under a canopy, and people were dancing among the tables in the rain. It was an extraordinary contrast to a London evening, so relaxed and natural, although she knew that must only be on the surface; the Italians were a subtle, sophisticated people, and Heaven knows, certain aspects of their national character got bad press. Nevertheless, they did seem to have an ability to enjoy the simple pleasures. It was very beguiling.

Finding a spot under cover, Isla reached for her phone.

"Michele? *Buonasera...sì.* I've just arrived...yes, in the Piazza del Popolo, outside..." She looked around. "I'm outside a café—it's called Meletti, I think."

"Stay where you are. I'm five minutes away."

Entranced by the scene unfolding before her eyes, she jumped when he suddenly appeared at her side, surprised by how quickly he'd got there. They exchanged a quick embrace and began to walk arm in arm. The rain was stopping, and the early-evening sky grew a little lighter again.

****

There was a great deal on the menu Isla didn't recognize, but she settled for a simple main dish of *spaghetti carbonara,* and Michele chose *pesce al forno con salsa verde.* The waiter brought bread and olives at the beginning, and a big bowl of salad along with the main courses. Asked to recommend a wine to go with the main course, he came back a few moments later with a bottle of Santa Margherita Lugana. Isla knew little about wine, but when she took a sip, she liked its crisp dryness—and the bottle itself looked very attractive. But she kept this opinion to herself; she would sound so unsophisticated if she voiced it, a typical tourist remark. Remembering she was driving home later, she drank slowly, determined to restrict herself to one glass.

"This is a great place, and the food is excellent," she said, between forkfuls of spaghetti.

"Yes, it's a good thing we were early. I don't think we'd have got a table later on, with all these tourists around."

He was looking at her consideringly. She knew she looked good, having acquired a healthy-looking light tan, complemented by the glossy, dark hair which fell in a cloud around her face.

"You look well. I think life is suiting you in your mountain fortress."

She laughed. "Fortress, literally, I guess. Yes, I do like it, and I have made a good friend in my colleague, Eloisa. What about you?"

"Well, I'm back with my firm in Foggia, but we have this project up here in Ascoli. A contact of the boss, I think. Tell me about the work you've been doing. Are you enjoying it?"

"Very much. I've been working on a medieval tower."

"A tower! Tell me more."

She described it in general terms, and suddenly, he was quizzing her: where was it exactly? Was she working for a particular client or an anonymous company? But now she felt uneasy about going into such detail and gave some vague answers before switching to another project. It didn't feel like a good idea to talk about her clients in this way, and she wondered if she'd already said too much. Then, she remembered he was an architect. That explained why he was so interested. A lot of architects she'd met were like that, fascinated by any project that wasn't run-of-the-mill, which allowed them to indulge in what they called "real design."

She swallowed the last few strands of spaghetti and soaked up the remaining sauce with her bread. Her mother had probably anglicized the Italian recipes she made, because there was a noticeable difference between those and what she was eating now. Or maybe it was about locally sourced ingredients—or even the fact she was in very good restaurant with a charming man. Whatever the reason, the food was outstanding.

Isla relaxed, and they exchanged lots of information. She was in the process of making a new friend, someone she could enjoy meeting from time to time, in whose company she could spend a pleasant evening. Even so, he wasn't a potential lover. She did find him attractive—very much so—but her confused feelings about *il conte* made it difficult to appreciate anyone else. How could she even think about Edmondo when she was with this lovely man? But she could.

She looked at Michele, admiration for her so clear in his eyes and knew he wasn't considering things in the same way. Several times, she caught his look and saw she would have to decide about how this evening was going to end. She really liked him. If only her heart didn't race along in that absurd way, at double its normal rate, when the image of Edmondo Benedetti came into her mind, there wouldn't be a problem.

As it was, it complicated everything. She was being perverse, of course she was, passing up a wonderful opportunity to start a light-hearted relationship. Michele was every bit as good-looking as Edmondo, was attentive and charming as well. He even worked in the same sort of industry as she did, so as they'd talked, she'd discovered they had a lot in common. Whereas Edmondo—plastics. Ugh! She hated plastics.

But she didn't hate him.

She mustn't lead Michele into thinking her feelings for him were anything more than those of a friend because they weren't. It would be cruel to pretend otherwise.

They left the restaurant and sauntered down the length of the square, but her enjoyment of the evening had gone, in its place a nagging tension. The rain had long since stopped, and voices and music were carried on the warm night air. Her phone pinged. When she took it out of her bag, she was amazed to see it was nearly eleven o' clock. If she was going to be able to work in the morning, she needed to leave now.

"Let's head back to my car, Michele. I have a meeting first thing tomorrow."

He stopped where they were and pulled her into his arms. He began to kiss her, giving her no chance to pull away.

"I find you so sexy, Isla," he murmured against her hair. "I think I'm falling in love with you."

"I don't think—"

"Please, Isla, come back to my hotel with me. I already wanted you in Milan, but I could see you weren't the type just to pick someone up like that. But now—"

Why shouldn't she? It was eight months since Richard, and she hadn't slept with anyone during that time. It would just be sex, and with a very nice man. Wouldn't it? Truthfully, her personal life had been something of a desert since they'd broken up. She felt an answering surge of desire as he hardened against her.

But when she turned to respond, she picked up on the anxiety in his eyes, and she understood it was going to mean a lot for him, much more than for her.

"I can't, Michele. I like you a lot, but I'm not in love with you."

"We'll get to know each other better, then. This will just be the beginning, and things can change."

"No, I'm sorry. I'm not looking for that kind of relationship. But I did so want us to be friends." She paused a moment, knowing she had to make it clear. "I'm in love with someone else."

There, she'd said it, admitted her feelings for Edmondo were much more than just infatuation and sexual attraction. Although Heavens above, there was plenty of that! But she'd recognized it, and that changed everything.

"I can't do this to you, Michele. I like you too much for that. Please try to understand."

His eyes darkened. "I don't give up so easily," he said. "Who is it? Someone back home in England? Distance will separate you, you'll see."

She said nothing.

After a moment, he took her arm again. "Now, I'll take you back to your car."

Chapter 11

"Gianluca, do you have time to talk about the nursery school?"

Tommaso had asked her to take on a small but urgent project which she'd completed quickly, and only now was she able to turn her attention to this.

"*Sì,* what do you want to know?"

He brought the drawings up onto his screen, and they sat down, side by side, while he pointed out things he needed to draw to her attention and asked her how she intended to proceed. Working with an architect was quite different from responding directly to a client, and Isla enjoyed capturing his take on the building which of course had dictated the design. But a quarter of an hour into the conversation, Isla's phone rang. She glanced down and got to her feet.

"I'm sorry, Gianluca. I have to take this—it's my big project."

"No probs," said the young architect. "I'm going out on site now. Tomorrow, maybe?"

She'd try to meet him in the morning. Like her, he usually came in early.

"Isla Bruni," she said, as Edmondo's image flashed into her mind. She walked out of the door to the landing at the top of the stairs, her heart pounding.

"The designs look amazing. Thank you."

She hadn't realized how hungry she'd been for the

sound of his voice, how each inflection sent quivers of desire to tantalize her and undermine all her good resolutions. Now she longed to run her fingers over that tiny scar at the corner of his mouth, which lent him an oh-so-sexy look.

"I'm glad you like them," she said, her cool, professional voice hiding the riotous activity of her heart.

"I would like to discuss it with you, but I'm sorry—I can't make any of the dates you've suggested for meeting. The only time I have free this week is Friday afternoon, and that would have to be in Teramo, say around three o'clock, if you can make it. Would an hour be enough to go through things? I have another meeting at half past four."

"Just a moment. I need to check."

Isla was trembling, but she forced herself to walk sedately back to her desk and scrolled through her diary, unable to remember even what day it was. Okay, yes, it was Tuesday.

"I'm going to be in Teramo on Friday morning to visit a school we're doing a scheme for," she said, returning to the head of the stairs. "And I've nothing specific booked for the afternoon. I could probably stay on when that's finished."

"That would be good. I'd like to get going on this as soon as possible."

"Where shall we meet?"

"What about at my factory? If my earlier meeting runs on, which unfortunately it may do, you'll have somewhere to wait."

He gave her directions and rang off. She remembered his hands on the ladder at the top of the tower, the long fingers gripping as he hauled himself upward, and she imagined for a moment how they would feel on her skin. As the image took form, a surge of fierce desire swept through her and took her breath away. Why was it that, away from him, she was starved for the warmth of his gaze? Was it possible that she really was in love, as she'd said to Michele? No, she couldn't accept that, not with someone as unsuitable as this. This was more like lust, and these extraordinary feelings were nothing more than a sort of madness she had to get control of and quash.

Isla remained still for a moment, forcing herself to think over the arrangement they'd just made. She'd been going to share transport with Eloisa on Friday because her car had developed a fault and was sitting in a repair shop. But Eloisa had to be back in Fortezza by two, so that wasn't going to work anymore. The bus from Teramo came to Fortezza several times a day. She'd check the times of the later buses, though it would be better if she got her own car back before Friday.

She rang the garage, but the news wasn't good. They were waiting for a part to be delivered.

****

Isla waved good-bye as the electric-blue hatchback disappeared rapidly into the distance. The friends had managed to squeeze in an early lunch at a sandwich bar and had delayed Eloisa's departure until the last moment. Now, she risked arriving back late for her two o'clock appointment. Isla hadn't missed Eloisa's little smile when she'd understood that the meeting in the afternoon was with Edmondo. She wouldn't be able to wait to hear whether her friend had got together with her client for more than a business meeting. Of course, Isla intended to keep her thoughts to herself. As things moved on, she had less and less desire to talk about the situation. Eloisa could be very irritating on this subject, but fortunately, she seemed to know to stop teasing at the very last minute, before Isla rebuffed her.

Okay, she had time on her hands before she had to go to the factory. What should she do? Although not in the same class as Ascoli, this was also an attractive little town with plenty to look at, including a Roman amphitheater, and now, she walked slowly away from the cathedral and down through the Quartiere San Leonardo, in the hope of finding the confluence of the two rivers between which the town was built. *Il pranzo* was over, and a few people, mostly tourists, strolled along to help the digestive process.

Isla's mind was completely on the forthcoming meeting when she almost tripped over oranges, lemons, and tins of peas and beans that rolled down the sloping pavement toward her. Just ahead, an elderly woman was looking in distress at her groceries, now spread all around. Her bag had split. The woman slowly bent to pick things up.

"Wait, let me."

Isla delved into her shoulder bag, extracting a folding carrier that she almost never used.

"Look, you can have this." Quickly, she picked the items up and placed them in the bag and then hefted it up. "This is very heavy. Do you live nearby? I'll carry it for you."

The woman protested, but Isla insisted. After all, it was nothing to her—she had time to spare. They walked very slowly, and when they arrived at the door to a narrow little house, the woman was looking ill. She couldn't just leave her there.

"Can I get you a hot drink? Or ring someone for you?"

These suggestions were refused at first, but finally she accepted the offer of coffee. Half an hour later, there was color in her cheeks, and she was telling stories about the area she lived in. Now, Isla surreptitiously checked the time and was shocked to find she had only a few minutes to get to the factory.

"I must go now. Are you going to be all right? I could come back later."

"No, there's no need. It was just one of those funny turns," the woman said. "Thank you so much for helping me."

Soon, Isla was hurrying back, heading for a small industrial park on the outskirts, where her client's business was situated. The distance was greater than she'd expected, and it looked as if she was going to arrive late. She picked up speed, knowing she'd be hot and flustered when she arrived, which was not a great impression to make on a client. Especially not this client. But she couldn't have abandoned the woman any sooner. She'd just have to ring to apologize for her late arrival.

She was already taking out her phone, when suddenly, there was the signboard just ahead. She slipped it back into her pocket and slowed to walking pace. The building was an uncompromising, giant shed with neat, grey cladding, but a rather attractive brick and glass rotunda was attached to the front, and she admired it for a moment as she caught her breath. Nice—properly designed, not something off the shelf.

She needn't have worried about being late. When she walked in, the receptionist—fifties, frosted blonde hair, and comfortable figure—told her that the meeting was still in progress. Would she like some coffee? She would.

Isla sank gratefully onto the couch and used a magazine from the table to fan her glowing face. Finally, she'd cooled down enough to open her laptop and start transferring from her phone the notes she'd made on the nursery school she'd visited that morning. But when she'd finished her drink, the meeting still hadn't ended.

A dull noise, which she hadn't really noticed at first, throbbed in the background, and from time to time, a door swung open, emitting a blast of sound and a faint, sweetish waft of something chemical, as people hurried through into the vestibule and out through the main exit or into the toilets. Behind the door, she caught sight of a flapping, segmented curtain. Probably that kept sound and fumes away from the entrance. All this was interesting. She wanted to know about everything to do with her client. Maybe it would be possible to take a look? But at that moment, Edmondo came down the staircase with a man. They shook hands at the bottom, and he showed him to the door.

Oh, God, she hadn't got it under control after all. Her heart was beating fast as she rose to her feet, wondering why it was so difficult for her to admit that here was an attractive man she wanted to get to know better—because that was what she was feeling. He stirred something within her that she couldn't deny. She took a few deep, slow breaths, striving for calm.

When they'd locked eyes for that brief moment in

the bar in Milan, it had been an earth-shattering shock that left her dazed and numb. In the tower, she'd trembled at his unintended touch and the electricity between them—at least from her point of view—couldn't be missed. Why couldn't she just throw off all her nonsensical prejudices and respond to the moment?

Now he hurried over. "I'm so sorry to waste your time like this, but I could not end it any sooner."

"It's no problem," she said smiling and shaking his hand, completely professional. It was her heart that didn't know how to behave properly.

He ushered her up the stairs. It was quite a place, his office taking up the whole of the upper part of the rotunda. The walls were plain white, but that was perfect because the view was so good.

"You have a great place to work."

"Thank you. When I bought the land, there was just the shed. I added this building afterward. Gianluca from your office designed it." He smiled. "It's an extravagance, I know, but Maria and I enjoy working in it, so it was worth doing."

In the distance, she saw a green area, and he pointed out the Torrente Vezzola, a fast stream which rushed down the mountain and around the town. The elevated position gave him something much better to look at than the carpark.

For the next hour, they went through all aspects of Isla's designs.

"I told you I had confidence in your suggestions, and it turns out to be well founded. But you've done two designs—now what am I going to do?" He furrowed his brow, but there was a smile in his eyes. "I thought I could get this all signed off today."

"Hang onto them both over the next couple of days and then decide."

"You realize you've made me look at it in a completely different way?—*dannazione*, I actually like the more modern scheme. It looks amazing. I never expected that."

She smiled. This was exactly what she'd hoped for. "I'll let you into a secret, although I don't like to exert undue pressure on the client, of course: I prefer it, too."

"How soon can we get this done?"

"You really should take time to decide, at least a few days. You might not like it after you've given it some thought. You probably need to let the idea lodge in your head and see if it's consistent with how you see the tower."

"No, I can see it now, and that's what I'd like."

"Oka-ay," she said. "We'll need to go out to tender, in order to get quotations. It will take a while—unless you have people you already know you want to use, in which case, we can probably have them on site within four to five weeks. The work on the building won't take very long."

"Excellent. Isla, I'm grateful that you made the effort to come here today. It's been very helpful—and illuminating. I wonder—will you allow me to buy you dinner, to say thank you? My meeting will end by six."

Flushed and suddenly breathless, she was about to accept when she remembered the transport situation.

"I'd love to do that, but unfortunately, my car's out of service. I'll have to go back by bus this evening, and the last one's at half past seven, from the bus station. That doesn't leave much time."

"Ah, a pity." He thought for a moment. "Look, I'm

going home this evening myself. I thought it too late for a work meeting back in Fortezza—but I can give you a lift."

The phone buzzed, and he picked up. "Yes, we've just finished." He turned to her. "So, are we agreed?"

"Yes, that would be really good."

"About half past six? Will you meet me? Or would you like to stay here to work? I've already disrupted your day enough."

"Actually, staying here would be great if there's somewhere I can sit."

"Then I'll sort that out."

Chapter 12

Isla rang the office to let them know she couldn't get back for the end of the afternoon.

"I have work with me on the laptop after this morning's meeting, so I won't be wasting time," she told Chiara, the receptionist. "Could you pass that information on to Tommaso?"

Then she opened the nursery school file and got down to it, but a little while later, her mind began to wander. It probably hadn't been the wisest thing to do, to accept his invitation, had it? Of course, she'd invited clients to lunch before now, and sometimes been invited, cementing what would become a long-term business relationship.

A business relationship.

She had to be honest—this wasn't about business, was it? That wasn't why she'd done it. And it was dinner. Somehow, that was more significant than lunch. She'd been overwhelmed by her need to get alongside him on a personal level, and he'd offered the opportunity. It had hardly been a decision; she'd always been going to say yes. Damn, what was she getting into?

Taking more calming breaths, she dragged her mind back to the task at hand and went on the internet to consult a website that sold nursery school equipment. It was mostly plastic. Lovely bright colors, child-friendly surfaces. She'd like to look at alternative possibilities but using natural materials would increase the cost of the project, perhaps by an amount the client would not find acceptable. Nevertheless, she'd do the research. She worked on, but the brightly colored apparatus soon failed to hold her attention, so she went back to the notes and began making a list of things she must do before she started the job.

A while later, the telephone rang at the desk, and Maria picked up. Isla immediately found herself listening in but could make nothing of the conversation.

"*Sì, le chiederò si vuole.*"

The woman put down the phone and walked over to Isla to ask if she would like a tour around the factory. "I can get Pietro to do it before he leaves."

It would be a welcome diversion, given just how little work she'd managed to do. And she was curious. "That would be great, thank you."

She followed the receptionist into the work area and was immediately hit by a faint and not unpleasant, "new plastic" smell. The noise was insistent but low-level, which meant you could hear what people were saying without difficulty.

"This is our factory manager, Pietro," Maria said. He was the large, bald man, bulky like a rugby player, whom she'd seen walking through the vestibule several times during the afternoon.

Isla knew absolutely nothing about plastics except that she believed them to be fundamentally bad. Working mostly at the refined end of the design world, she was more familiar with natural materials and did try to inform herself about their sustainability before specifying. But plastic? She shuddered as her mind filled with visions of vast islands of plastic in the Pacific, and animals choking on the rubbish thrown down by heedless citizens. It was a pity it had to be a plastics factory—almost anything else would have been better. It had immediately colored her view of Edmondo, and not in a positive way. She was as repulsed by the idea he was involved in something less than commendable as she was attracted by him as a person.

"Why plastic?" she asked. "Aren't you just contributing to global warming?"

But Pietro soon set out to correct her assumptions about what he called "plastic crap." "What you say is true, I'm afraid, but it's a bit like internet hackers."

"I'm sorry, but I don't understand that."

"Someone says 'hacker,' and you think 'bad person.' In fact, some are good, and some are bad—but they're all hackers. It just depends on who they work for. There are factories churning out endless plastic objects that can't be recycled. But that's not what we do here."

"You don't?"

Her doubts must have been written large on her face because he came back with force: "No, we don't! We make things that are useful, necessary. You can't turn the clock back. Nobody wants to live like the medieval peasants did, so you have to find ways to work around the problems. And the boss is an engineer—a very good one."

He was leading her past gleaming machines that spewed out plastic pieces into vats of water.

"So, what does he do about it?" she asked.

This was okay—hearing about the boss would be

very interesting to her. Very.

"Well, for a start, he designed earthquake bearings for buildings after the 2016 earthquake here—and made them available at cost to anyone trying to rebuild their house, so that, next time there's a quake, it won't fall down."

This was news to her. Offering them at cost made it sound as if he had a social conscience, despite his apparent wealth.

"We've been producing those, among other things, for some time now. His designs were so innovative that he secured contracts right across the world. Of course, we sell those for a profit."

"You'd have to, in order to have a viable business. I understand that. Does Signor Benedetti—"

"Oh, and before you bring it up, we do recycle, although with the boss being such a good designer, there are very few off-cuts."

He continued at length on this theme, but she was rapidly losing the ability to take in the torrent of information.

"Do you think we could—"

"If you'd been here this morning, you'd have seen the recycling people arrive to cart it away."

The man was passionate about what they did, but she really didn't need to hear any more. How could she give up on the tour, without appearing too rude?

"Pietro, do you think I—"

"The real problem is single-use plastic like water bottles."

This was terrible. Isla tried again to concentrate on what he was saying, but she was beginning to tune out. It wasn't the fact he was giving her the information, but did he really have to ram it down her throat like that? She got the point. Why did he have to keep on about it?

Her mind wandered to the evening ahead, and she felt a frisson of excitement. How long was it going to be before Edmondo was finished with his client? She took a surreptitious glance at her phone as Pietro stalked ahead of her. Ten to six. Maybe the tour would end soon. Hadn't Maria said this man was about to go off duty?

"…and the fact that, despite all the publicity about the damage to marine life and other animals, people still discard them without a thought in so many parts of the world—and that's not just Africa."

"No, I know it's not."

Would Edmondo drive them somewhere for dinner or would they just walk into town? It didn't seem that far, so probably they'd go on foot. How would it feel to walk along beside him? Would he take her arm, like Michele had done?

"There are millions in Europe who couldn't care less what happens when they've finished their bloody 'rehydrating.' And *they* don't have the excuse of poor education."

Isla gave a sigh, totally losing track of where he'd got to with his explanation. How did his boss put up with him? Well, she'd had enough. Anyway, she did like the way he was talking about the company, as if he were completely involved in what happened there. That told her about how Edmondo ran things, that he was a good boss.

"I'm sorry, Pietro, but—"

"Look," he said, "you have to understand that plastic is a part of our lives. In fact, it can even be more sustainable than traditional materials."

What? This was rubbish. She wanted to get away from him. When was Edmondo's visitor leaving? But honestly, she had to respond to this ridiculous statement.

"That's simply not possible."

"It is if it's handled correctly—in the sense that some plastic objects will last far longer than the wood or metal equivalent."

She looked disbelievingly at him, and he suddenly stabbed an accusing finger at her white, sleeveless blouse.

"You wear linen. Don't you think there's an environmental cost in producing that?—at least as much as for modern, plastic-based clothing materials?"

"Well, of course, I don't know exactly—"

"And don't believe it when people say all the plastic could be biodegradable. In many cases, that would mean it wouldn't do the job it's meant to do. Sometimes, you don't want it to be biodegradable. People talk a lot of crap."

"Please stop, Pietro. I'm not responsible for other people's prejudices. I admit I have a few of my own—but you wouldn't blame me if you'd watched some of the TV programs."

A faint smile creased his face. He was human, after all.

"Well, I suppose there *is* a tendency to exaggerate, especially when people are so resistant to change. You have to get the message over somehow."

"I'm sorry, I can see you care a lot about this."

"Yes, we do. The boss is into doing it better. And he's actively looking at developing new types of plastic, better forms of the material that would not damage the environment."

Good, that was good. They should talk about the boss, about Edmondo. The factory was marginally interesting, but only in as far as he was involved. And she did want to know about what he did, of course she did—up to a point. She didn't need to know all the details of the industrial process.

With the dinner date fast approaching, what she really wanted right now was the opportunity to indulge in a little daydreaming. On the surface, Edmondo didn't tick any of the important boxes. But that was rapidly changing. She'd liked that bit about his helping during the earthquake. Her mood lifted, as this thought helped her see a relationship might even be possible. Could she get to know this complex and probably unsuitable man on a more intimate level? She sighed again. The more important question was whether she should.

A bell rang, and with escape in the offing, she heaved a huge sigh of relief. Technicians began shutting down the machines, the noise level quickly dropping, and soon they left the building.

"I have to go now. Feel free to wander around, but don't touch anything," he said, as if she were a small child. "And tell the boss to lock up! We had an attempted break-in last week."

He'd been tough to listen to, delivering the hard lecture with his humorless expression, insisting on making his point. But probably, she understood a little better now what they did. And he'd helped her to consider things in a different way, so maybe she'd take a serious look at using plastic in the nursery school—provided all that material could be recycled, of course—try to weigh up the advantages against the all-too-obvious disadvantages. The well-being of the children mattered as well, and expensive wooden equipment might mean they'd have to have less of it. Maybe. She would make sure her research went deep enough to uncover all the facts.

Pietro's footsteps on the concrete floor dwindled to nothing, and silence fell. Now she had the place to herself, she wandered around. It was basically just a massive space under a corrugated tin roof. Clear panels allowed in a little light, but she could see everything quite clearly, as he'd left the overhead lights on.

She walked down several aisles, and keeping well away from the guardrails, she again passed the machines, with the sacks of material in the pens, waiting to be fed into them. The whole of the far end of the building was filled with row upon row of metal shelving on which newly molded components were stacked in containers. Then came a packing bay and double doors. Right, she'd seen enough. Without watching people at work, it was very boring.

What was that noise? Isla stopped and listened carefully but could hear nothing at all. She took out her phone—six o'clock. Maybe she should get back to reception.

The aisles were broken at intervals by a cross-passage. As she emerged from one section, she caught a brief flurry of movement.

Chapter 13

The client frowned. "I don't see how we can rely on a small factory in the middle of Italy to guarantee a supply of bearings—or anything else, for that matter."

"*Dotoressa,* we can instantly convert our machines to deal with whatever we need. Remember how, in the pandemic, we were able to produce so many testing kits? And so quickly? I did email you that information."

"But your prices are the same as Lombardi's. You are smaller and should be able to cut the costs. Maybe we can discuss a discount?"

Ah—so that's what it was. No surprise.

"I'm afraid not. The costs of production are the same whether the firm is large or small. But I understand, signora, if you feel you must have someone more high-profile. That is your prerogative. Let me know your decision."

This was difficult. She didn't like the idea of paying the quoted price, and maybe she wanted the kudos of a big name. Or was she genuinely nervous of using a small firm? He wasn't quite sure what the problem was, couldn't see how it mattered. Anyway, it was time she went because she was keeping him from his dinner date. He stood up and held out his hand, managing to smile politely. Such meetings were par for the course and quite often led to nothing, but it was infuriating that she'd held him up. At last, he led her down the stairs to the entrance. As he passed through reception, he noticed that Maria Iannuce had already departed. A laptop lay on a coffee table by a pile of folders. They would be Isla's. But where was she?

She must have gone to the ladies'. He locked his office and then spent time turning out lights and tidying up. But five minutes later, she'd still not appeared. What was going on? Surely, she hadn't decided against waiting. But she wouldn't have left her laptop with all her work.

That was odd—the door that led into the factory wasn't properly closed. Pietro would never leave it like that at this hour—unless they were still in there. The slight anxiety he'd begun to feel left him. Of course, they must still be doing a tour. Poor girl! Pietro could be so serious when it came to his job. He'd be talking down to her, and she'd be too polite to protest. He'd better go and release her from whatever homily the man was delivering. He threaded his way through the flapping curtain.

All the lights were on, which was strange. Surely, they'd be shutting down by now.

"Pietro!"

No sound, except the quickly fading echoes of his own voice.

"Signorina Bruni! Isla!" he called. "Are you in here?"

Again, there was no reply, but now he heard a groan and a scuffle. He ran toward the noise and got to the loading bay in time to see Isla hauling herself upward by hanging onto the last of the metal shelving. His heart thumped. Was she hurt? What had happened? He hurried to her as heavy footsteps pounded to the door by which he'd just entered. When he swung around to look, there was no one to be seen, just the slight movement of the curtain.

He caught her in his arms before she began to slip down again. "Signorina Bruni—Isla—what's wrong?"

"Someone in here…hit me. Then I think…I must have fainted."

As he held her, his eyes raked the factory. If he hadn't been standing at exactly that point, he wouldn't have seen the red light flashing in a panel on the far wall. It signaled a malfunction at the very least, maybe something much worse. The machines were very safe— but not if you interfered with them. He was tempted to gather her up and race out of the building before something exploded, but he abandoned that idea when he realized he could probably stop anything happening by turning off the electricity circuit for the factory.

"Wait here, one minute."

Quickly, he lowered her to the floor, so she could lean against the shelf unit. He sprinted over, wrenching open the door to the cupboard that housed the electrics, where he pushed up a large lever. Instantly, all power was shut off and the shed went almost dark, the only light filtering through the roof panels.

He hurried back to Isla and helped her to her feet. "Can you stand? Let's get out of here."

"But someone—"

"Whoever it was is long gone. However, what they've done may still be a danger. Come on, we have to go."

She seemed to understand the urgency and forced herself to walk.

In the reception, which was still brightly lit, he sat

her down. Even if something exploded in the factory area, they were relatively safe here and could leave easily by the main door. He searched in the desk drawers for a first-aid box. There! Okay, he was going to do something about that gash on her head, but first, he needed to ring the police.

"We'll be here," he said, ending the conversation a couple of minutes later, and closing his phone.

But what about the flashing light? The only person who could deal with that was Pietro—if only to tell the police what had been done. He opened his phone again and scrolled his contacts list until he found the name. It seemed to ring for a long time. The man was probably driving. His fingers drummed on the desk, and he looked across at Isla. She was leaning back on the sofa, eyes closed, and her face was white. But she seemed to be holding up.

Ah, at last.

"Pietro, I need you back here…yes, there's been another break-in and something's wrong with one of the machines. Can you turn back?…Yes, okay. Police are on their way."

He shut down the phone and grabbed the medical supplies.

"Right, I'm going to clean that cut for you while we wait for them. I'd ring for an ambulance except I think the police will want to talk to you—if that's not too much for you."

"No, I'm fine, Edmondo," she said faintly. "Really, I'm fine—and I don't need an ambulance."

He liked that the formal manner had gone, and she'd called him Edmondo. It argued that she was prepared to trust him, in spite of the fact he'd placed her in danger. He went into the toilets and brought out a cup of warm water with some soap in it, flicking on the coffee machine as he passed. Then, he got down on his knees in front of her.

"Now, sit still and bend your head forward, so I can clean it up. It's going to sting."

As gently as he could, he parted the glossy hair to reveal a small, deep cut in her scalp. It had bled profusely down the back of her head and into the collar of her blouse, perhaps making it look more worrying than it was. So much blood! But scalp wounds were known to leak like anything, even when they weren't serious. He dabbed at it with cotton wool he'd soaked in the soapy water and decided it would probably heal quite quickly. Nevertheless, he cleaned the area carefully. Soon the blood stopped flowing, and he stripped two pieces of tape from a pack to close the edges of skin together, covering it with an antiseptic pad. Putting his fingers under her chin, he raised her head.

"There. All done."

"That was really painful."

His face was on a level with hers. Tears glistened on her lashes, and he handed her the cloth so she could wipe them away. She looked so fragile, he wanted to gather her to him and hold her close. He swallowed and fought the desire. He really couldn't afford to invite complications into his life—hadn't he enough on already? He could see she was trying hard to hold it together and that was good, so he smiled and turned away.

"Sorry about that, but it's better to make sure it doesn't get infected. It's probably going to hurt a lot more when you take that pad off your hair. What I'm worried about is concussion. I think you need to see a doctor."

"They're no better than anyone else at detecting it. They'll just insist I stay in overnight for observation. Look, I promise I'll stay awake. I really don't think the blow was that hard." She managed a smile. "See—I'm fine."

"Okay, we'll see how it goes." He got up and gathered things together. "Now, I'm going to make you a coffee with lots of sugar. It's good for shock, they say."

As he handed it over to her, flashing blue lights in the deepening dusk announced the arrival of the police, and a few moments later, Pietro's SUV swept into the carpark.

Chapter 14

It was half past nine before the police had finished. Pietro had checked each workstation carefully, explained to the officers what had been done, and made a temporary repair on one of the machines to make it safe.

"Someone's been altering the settings," he told them. "Could have been very serious. If the boss hadn't spotted that warning light, it would have wrecked that particular machine and cut production. It might even have caused a fire." He turned to Edmondo now. "I've shut everything down. I'll ring Franco and get him in early tomorrow to check everything out. Hopefully, we can start same time as usual. Franco will make sure it's safe."

He looked at Isla and said, "You really didn't see anyone here after I left? You didn't touch anything?"

It sounded like an accusation, almost as if he suspected her of conniving to let someone in. Or maybe, he thought she'd been responsible for the sabotage herself. She bristled. "No, I didn't! Why would I do something like that? What are you trying to imply?"

"Anti-plastic garbage. You might be from one of these groups. Lot of skewed thinking from people like that."

She broke into a peal of laughter but looked angry,

a dangerous spark in her eyes. "What? That's ridiculous! So, you reckon you didn't manage to convince me with your long, well-referenced arguments," she said, layering on the sarcasm. "And now, I'm a convenient scapegoat. If you felt like that, maybe you shouldn't have left me in here on my own! Maybe you're the one who's responsible."

Pietro's whole head flushed bright red, and his eyes bulged as if he were one of his own safety valves, about to blow.

"Hold on, hold on, Pietro. It's upsetting, but you can't blame the signorina for what's happened," said Edmondo. He was somewhat amused at the way the argument was developing. And it was reassuring that, in spite of her injury, Isla was clearly not about to collapse and, in fact, was giving every bit as good as she got. "For a start, she didn't ask for a tour—I suggested it. And she didn't hit herself on the head."

"Yeah—and how well do you know this woman? What if she's working with someone?"

"That's enough! I suggest you apologize now. You have nothing to base this argument on, and you insult Signorina Bruni. And me." He stared hard at the older man. "And that is not a good thing, my friend."

Isla raised her head at the tone of his voice, glimpsing the tough, successful businessman behind the suave exterior. You didn't create a highly lucrative business with clients around the world by letting others get the better of you.

Pietro finally dropped his gaze, and just as quickly as he'd flared up, he calmed down.

"*Scusa*," he grunted, finding it difficult to look at Isla. "But you have to admit there's something going on here. It's getting to me."

It wasn't much of an apology, but that was all she was going to get. Isla turned away from him holding her anger in check. She had to keep cool. He'd go away in a minute, and she'd be able to deal with the other things assailing her, like the throbbing ache on the top of her skull, which seemed to have worsened as a result of her angry self-defense.

"Of course, something's going on. We had a break-in last week—which, I might add, was unlikely to have been carried out by the signorina, who has never been here before."

These exchanges were listened to with avid interest by the two policemen, who didn't interrupt once, obviously feeling they might get an insight into the dynamics of the little group by remaining silent. Now they asked searching questions of their own, but neither Edmondo nor Pietro was able to give any reason why someone would wish to damage the business.

Finally, the senior officer radioed into his station and asked for a patrol car to drive by every hour to keep a check on things. But they made it clear they didn't have the resources to do that every night. Then, they left.

"I can't see what good that will do. Whoever it was won't be coming back tonight," said Pietro. "Right, I have to go. I'll be lucky if I get to see my kid tonight, and I promised. It's his birthday."

His annoyance was almost tangible, but with that, he stomped out. Edmondo and Isla watched him leave and, somewhat relieved, turned to look at one another. They both smiled.

"Let's lock up and go. To the hospital, okay?"

"Not okay. I'm fine. My head's a bit sore, but there's nothing else wrong. I'm not falling unconscious. Not sick. Not losing my memory. I just want to go now."

He looked at her for a long moment, taking in her general appearance, trying to get a read on how ill she might really be. "Well, one thing I know about concussion is that you're not supposed to be left on your own for at least forty-eight hours after the incident, so if you won't go to the hospital, I'll take you back to Fortezza and then I'll stay with you."

"Just take me home, Edmondo. I've had enough."

****

All through the journey, he tried to keep the conversation going. If she felt anything like he did after this endless day and all that had happened, she showed no sign of it. He was ready to turn around and head for the hospital at the slightest sign there was a problem, but she continued to talk and eventually convinced him there really was nothing he need worry about. Nevertheless, he wasn't going to leave her alone overnight.

He'd take her back to her flat and spend the night there in her sitting room. But why not back to his? He'd feel happier playing guard there. Adriano was staying a few days with his aunt in Rome, and Carlotta Forni had the weekend off. They'd agreed that weekends were hers, now that she'd added looking after the boy to her duties as housekeeper, and sometimes she took advantage to visit family. Which meant that no one would know Isla was there tonight, and in a small town, that was a consideration. He wouldn't want to embarrass her, particularly if their relationship never moved on from designer and client.

Of course, he wasn't prepared to believe that was how it would end. He knew now that it wouldn't—not if he could do anything about it. Then he sighed, aware again that he was heaping up problems for the future. How did he think he was going to cope if he started a new relationship just as his young son had come to live with him?—to say nothing of having to do something about the strange goings-on in the factory. And of course, the new contract he'd been negotiating.

Not that she'd shown any signs of wanting a relationship. What would it take to break through that cool, professional shell?—because it was a shell, tough and well-maintained. But, inside, he sensed a vulnerability.

From time to time, he glanced over, just wanting the pleasure of looking at her, but the road was narrow and dangerous in the dark, and he needed to keep his mind on the driving. When he finally drew to a halt on the forecourt of his house, she looked up at him.

"You don't know where I live?" she asked.

"I do, but I'm staying with you, at least for tonight, and this is more discreet."

"What about your little boy? I met him last time I came here. Surely—"

"There's no one here at all tonight."

He could see the protest coming, but suddenly she capitulated.

"All right. I'll stay."

He got out and came round to her, but she didn't wait for him to open the door. The car was low to the ground, and when she got out, she staggered slightly as she came upright. He took her arm to make sure she didn't fall, guessing she was more tired than she was prepared to admit. But hopefully, that was normal tiredness, not evidence of something more serious. He felt weary himself after the events of the evening.

****

The guest bedroom was on the ground floor. It was large and cool, with white walls, pale blue linen, and waxed, butter-colored boards on which was a sumptuous Chinese rug. She could hardly wait to get into that massive bed. He handed her a fluffy, white bathrobe and towels and opened the door to the bathroom, which looked almost as big as the bedroom.

A shower would be just wonderful—but maybe she wouldn't shower just now. She ought to, but she couldn't. She just had to sleep. "Good night," she said. "And thank you."

"*Buonanotte*, Isla."

He pulled her gently to him and kissed the top of her head, carefully avoiding the antiseptic pad and releasing her before she got the wrong idea about his intentions. On another evening, it wouldn't be the wrong idea at all. But that could wait.

"I'm out there, in the living room. Call me if you need me."

"There's no need. You go to bed. I have to sleep, that's all."

"There is a need. Remember—call me."

He left, closing the door behind him. Bewildered, she looked at where he'd been standing a moment before. Something had happened, something had changed, but she was too tired to work it out. For a moment, she imagined him stretched out on the sofa across the hall and felt comforted by the fact he would do exactly as he'd said.

She almost tottered over to the bed. Every part of her ached, from her calves, due to the walking she'd done in Teramo, to the stretched feeling of the skin on her scalp and the underlying throbbing pain. How could a blow on the head make you feel quite so dreadful? She dragged off her clothes and crawled into the bed. The cool cotton sheets enfolded her, and soon, she slept.

****

Edmondo went to his own room where he stripped off and had a long shower. It was only half past eleven, but it felt as if the night had been going on forever. The hot water pounded his muscles, and the tension began slowly to leave him.

His concern had all been for Isla. He'd dragged her unwittingly into a dangerous situation, when all he'd wanted to do was to spend some time getting to know her. He could only hope, when she woke up in the morning, that she'd forgive him. She had to. Because he wanted the chance to hold her in his arms, and not just to give comfort and support to someone who was too tired and ill to function normally. He wanted to hold that beautiful, fiery creature, with her layers of cool and red hot, trapped in his embrace. He wanted to taste her lips, to feel her body beneath his. Behind the sophisticated businesswoman, he'd glimpsed a flesh-and-blood female whose passions he was convinced he'd aroused—even if she hadn't recognized it yet herself.

But he couldn't just wade in and try to take what he wanted, that was for sure. She wouldn't react well to it—and there was a lot she was holding back. He gave a long sigh. Well, he had plenty of time to find out whatever was making her keep him at arms' length.

He stared unseeing across the bathroom, reflecting on what had happened. What the hell was he thinking? So much for keeping his life simple! Hadn't he just convinced himself there couldn't be any relationship between them? And if she was hiding something, it was part of her past and she didn't want people to know—good reasons why he should stay well away. Weren't there enough complications in his life already?

Edmondo turned off the shower and grabbed a towel. He dried himself vigorously, put on a bathrobe, and collected a pillow, sheet, and thin coverlet from his bed. His arms full of bed linen, he walked down the stairs into the lower hallway and listened for a moment at the door to the guestroom, but there was complete silence. He crossed to the sitting room and decided to leave the door wide open. If she called, he'd hear her immediately. When he'd made up a bed on the longer of the two couches, he got under the cover, before stretching over to turn off the lamp.

He'd been struggling to keep his eyes open, but now sleep was slow in coming. As soon as he lay down, he found himself dwelling again on the events of the evening. Who on earth wished him so ill that they were prepared to damage his business? Not a single person came to mind, but the fact it was happening was very worrying. He didn't really have competitors in the area—not people working at the same level. Who would want to do this?

He turned over, trying to push these thoughts from his mind.

Whatever happened, they had to find out what the

problem was, or his business was in peril. The police had treated it as a serious matter this time, unlike in the previous week when he'd called them out. That was a plus. Maybe the reason was that Isla had been assaulted, and it put the whole matter on a different plane.

It did for him too, he thought, shifting his focus to her. As he drifted on the borders of sleep, he imagined them both naked, arms and legs entwined, and he felt his desire grow. Now suddenly, he was fully awake, and he began to feel distinctly uncomfortable. Finally, abandoning the pretense of sleep, he got up and headed up to his bathroom—not that a cool shower was going to cure him of this malaise. He wondered if she'd felt the same way. But it was more likely she'd been too exhausted to think of him at all.

Chapter 15

Isla had been enjoying the delicious aroma of coffee for several minutes before she finally managed to open her eyes. When she did so, she found the room was filled with golden sunlight. Was this paradise? Maybe the blow to the head had been harder than she'd thought. Didn't matter. She should just lie here and enjoy it, listen to the birdsong that floated through the open window. That full-throated warble sounded like the thrush that used to occupy a tree outside her mother's kitchen, but she couldn't be sure.

She was rested. She stretched and inadvertently moved her head, and a sharp pain stabbed at her scalp, bringing tears to her eyes. When she moved again, more carefully this time, she concluded it wasn't so bad that she couldn't get out of bed—and with that tantalizing smell of coffee, she had no choice. It would be great to have a cup, or maybe even two. The hollow feeling in her stomach must be hunger—she'd eaten nothing since the panino at lunch time the previous day. Could it be that breakfast was on the menu?

Isla went into the bathroom, intent on a shower. As she picked up what she would need, the enormous bathtub caught her eye. In her flat, there was only a rather inadequate cubicle, tucked into a mean space off the bedroom, so an opportunity like this was not to be turned down. She spent a minute or two working out how the various knobs, buttons, and levers worked, eventually finding the one that covered over the plughole. Then she turned on the hot water and helped herself liberally from the array of bath preparations on the shelf. It was twenty minutes of heaven, and when she finally emerged from the steamy foam, she felt completely recovered. She'd even washed her hair, working carefully around the area where the cut was, in case it started bleeding again.

Back in the bedroom, she considered her clothes. Pity about the white linen top, which was completely ruined, but everything else was fine. Maybe...perhaps Edmondo's wife had left some of her clothes. She looked in the wardrobe and the drawers, but there was nothing in them. Never mind! She pulled on the blood-spattered garment, which appeared undamaged from the front but hideous behind.

She opened the bedroom door and looked out into the broad, central hallway, taking in the view into the sitting room, which was empty, all signs of Edmondo's night on the sofa having been removed. But there were sounds coming from a half-open door at the back of the hall which must lead to the kitchen.

Isla's heart began to pump faster, and she concluded wryly that she had to be more or less recovered, because she'd already forgotten about her various aches and pains and was, instead, reacting to the thought of seeing him again. There was almost an element of fear this time, as if this were to be a significant step in her life. As if whatever she did next would seal her fate for the foreseeable future. She smiled to herself; somehow, she'd turned into a drama queen overnight.

She pushed the door wide. The kitchen, on the same side of the house as the bedroom she'd occupied, basked in sunlight. Edmondo was sitting at a table reading, a cup of *caffè latte* in front of him, of which he'd drunk about half. And he was wearing dark-framed, serious-looking glasses. That was a surprise. It gave him a studious, uber-intellectual look.

"I didn't think we had newspapers anymore," she said, glancing at his reading matter. "*Buongiorno.*"

"*Buongiorno*, Isla."

She liked that he was using her first name. She should try doing the same but didn't feel she could, not yet anyway. Then suddenly, she had a memory of the evening before. She *had* done so. A tide of hot color washed her cheeks. He got to his feet, looking with interest at her expression.

He'd ditched the suit for black jeans and a soft grey shirt with long sleeves and a collar. Excellent taste. The shirt wasn't that fitted, but there was still a discernible ripple of muscle as he stood up. She noted that he wore a signet ring, and that was the only piece of jewelry. Too much personal ornament on a man was a real put-off, as far as she was concerned.

He came over to take her hands, looking critically at her.

"What?" she said, a little discomforted.

"Just checking to make sure you're all right." He switched to English. "You slept well? You are feeling better?"

"Much better—but I could die for a cup of coffee. And I'm starving."

"Hunger—this is a good sign. Sit down and I will make you breakfast." He pulled out a chair for her and then noticed the blood-stained collar of her shirt as she sat down. "Wait, you can't wear that. I have a few things here you could try on. I should have thought about it."

He left the kitchen and returned moments later with a couple of tops, still in their wrappings. "These belonged to my wife. When I moved here, I found them among my things. They are new. I hope that's okay."

"It's perfect. Thank you. I'll change."

"While I cook. Eggs?"

"Definitely."

She took the garments and went back to her room. There was a white cotton T-shirt, fitted, with long sleeves, and a pink cami top, both a little large for her, but the T-shirt was a closer fit and a lot better than the blood-stained rag she had on at the moment. It looked good with her dark linen trousers. Regretfully, the blood-stained blouse, a favorite, had to go into the bin. There was no way it could be reused. What a waste, she thought, reminded of Pietro's stabbing finger.

A quick glance in the mirror showed she looked somewhat healthier than she'd imagined. A little pale, perhaps. She tucked back a few strands of damp hair and opened the door.

Immediately, there was the smell of food, and her stomach responded with a low rumble. Returning to the table, where he'd placed a cup of coffee for her, she watched him in silence. How intimate this felt, as if they'd been together for a long time. Her heart started fluttering in that newly acquired, unruly manner it seemed to have just now. She sighed, trying to regain her equanimity.

He threw her a brief smile and then returned to his

cooking, while she slaked her thirst. Like most Italian coffee, it was delicious. She caught sight of a serious-looking machine on the worktop which must have cost as much as her car. Personally, she made do with a small stove-top jug—and that was still better than the coffee she was able to make back in England.

Although he had his back to her, she saw from his confident movements that this was a man at home in the kitchen. There was a sizzle as he poured beaten eggs into a pan and a few minutes later, he brought over an enormous omelet bursting with mushrooms, which he proceeded to divide in two.

"*Grazie.*"

She got on with the important task of eating and said nothing more until she'd finished and was wiping up the last of the egg and tomato sauce with a large piece of bread. Now, she sat back, replete.

"That's the biggest breakfast I've had in years, and I enjoyed every mouthful. You're clearly a very good cook."

"*Solo un cuoco per la colazione,*" he said. "A breakfast cook—but you can eat breakfast any time of day, of course. I had to learn how to feed myself when my wife left, but my culinary skills do not extend to anything else."

"And Signora Forni? Doesn't she cook?"

"Oh, yes, but for the first year, I was on my own, living in a flat in Teramo. It was before I had this house. And, frankly, it was enough for me. I was building my business then—long hours and no money. I spent nearly all my time at the factory. Sometimes, I'd get back after midnight and fall into bed, so the only meal I'd eat at home was breakfast. Dinner was always out in some local restaurant—if I even had the time. And then the earthquake happened, and we were working on the bearings. That left me even less time at home."

"Pietro really admires what you've done. He told me about it."

"Let's hope he remembers that. He's not just an employee—he's a friend, been with me since I started the factory. But enough is enough. I thought we were going to fall out seriously last night. And if he continues to treat you in the way he did, we will." He was quiet for a moment and then added, "The earthquake caused terrible devastation and loss of life, but for my business, it was a good thing—it put us on the map."

"So you felt you had to pay back? By helping people in the town?"

"Anyone would have done the same thing. I had the means to do it, and I was local."

"Not anyone. Some people never think to make a generous gesture like that."

"Well, I benefited from it in the end. The word spread, and I soon had new customers from far outside the area. I made a lot of money and continue to do so, so I didn't suffer at all. That's how I was able to buy the land here in Fortezza."

"But you didn't know at the time that would be the outcome," she said. "You did just do the right things. I'm impressed, Edmondo."

He looked at her, clearly considering her words. She smiled and hoped he'd understand that it mattered.

Chapter 16

Edmondo drove her down to the village after their lazy brunch. Several hours had passed as they talked, sipped coffee, and wandered around outside, enjoying the sun and the welcome breeze.

Now, he pulled up at the side of the road behind her car which had been delivered by the garage as promised. He leaned across and kissed her cheek. "I want to get to know you, Isla. I want to be with you."

The words were running through her mind: Yes, I feel the same. I've never before felt anything like this for anyone. But caution held her back. It was all happening very quickly. Was it true that you could fall in love like that, at first sight, as the songs promised? But maybe love didn't matter when she felt like this, the sight of him whipping her breath away when she least expected it. Then, suddenly, she was speaking the words aloud, saying how she'd never felt this way before. She laughed, a little embarrassed. "Did I really say that? I meant…"

"Yes, you did, so don't try to hide the truth." He smiled. "But we do have to work out what this means for us. Come down to the coast with me this evening for dinner. Do you like fish? I know a great fish restaurant."

"I love it."

He had work to complete but promised to ring as

soon as he was free. "It'll be after six."

****

In the flat, buoyed up by the words they had spoken and the thought of the evening to come, Isla put her phone on charge and caught up with a few chores. These mindless tasks were perfect, so she could concentrate on the important business of working out how she really felt about Edmondo and how she wanted her evening to develop. She'd have to make sure he knew there was no future in it, that she couldn't get tied down. But that was so difficult because it would suggest she was making assumptions about what he was thinking. The more she considered it, the more of a problem it seemed. But maybe he felt the same way. Weren't all relationships like this at the beginning? Then she relaxed. She'd just have to wait and see—and enjoy the process.

As she worked in the tiny kitchen, she could hear her phone bleeping and pinging with messages. She managed to shut the sounds out for a while, not wanting to abandon her happy thoughts, but there really had been quite a few, and she'd been uncontactable for at least twenty-four hours. What on earth was going on? Her phone had lost its charge the previous afternoon, and she'd not had access to the right kind of charger. Perhaps she'd better take a look.

She stared at it aghast. Eloisa had rung several times. Her mother's friend Penny had rung three times and left a voice message, and there were two other calls, one from Michele Verdino. This was a lot more than she would have expected, and the repeated calls were worrying. What had been happening while she'd been out of contact? First, she returned Eloisa's call, but there was no reply. She left a message: "Call me back. Phone working now." Something was definitely up. She rang Penny without listening to the voicemail.

The woman must have been waiting to hear from her because she answered on the second ring.

"Penny, it's Isla. What's going on? You've been trying to reach me?"

"Isla, thank goodness! It's your mother. She's had a car accident and is in hospital."

"Oh God! Is she—"

"She slips in and out of consciousness and has a broken leg, cracked ribs, and various abrasions. They'll keep her in until they've made sure there's no internal injury. But she's tough."

Isla's heart was beating right off the scale. Her mother in an accident, in hospital. Was she going to survive?

"She's been lucky—the car's a write-off."

"When did it happen?"

"Yesterday evening when she was driving home from her art class. A group of kids in a stolen vehicle came out of a side road and hit her car right in the middle, pushing it into oncoming traffic. She's in University College Hospital. I've just come away from seeing her. They're doing a brain scan, and they say she's as well as can be expected."

"But they *are* treating her? She *is* responding?"

"Definitely, yes, but I think it would do her good to see you, and I was sure you'd want to come over."

"I would. I'm going to get my things together, and I'll catch the first available flight."

"Don't be too shocked when you see her. The airbag engaged when she hit the other car, so she's covered in bruises and has a burn on the side of her face—that's from the airbag. There was no fire."

"Thank you, Penny. I'm on my way."

"I could meet you if you let me have the arrival time."

"No, I'll go to the hospital straight from the airport and come to you after, if that's okay. I'll give you a ring when I get into Heathrow."

Isla opened up her laptop to research the flights and soon realized there was some big event taking place in London and all flights were fully booked. So much for people flying less—it looked like the opposite was happening. The first available seat was at five in the morning. She booked quickly, aware that the only remaining place might be taken if she delayed. Then she texted Penny to say she wouldn't be arriving until the next day. She searched out a small travel bag.

Eloisa rang. "Have you had the message from your mother's friend? She rang the office when she couldn't reach you, and I happened to be there working. I was worried when you didn't pick up."

"I've spoken to her, Eloisa. Thanks for trying to get to me. My battery had no charge for some reason. I've booked a flight."

"I'm sorry, Isla. I hope your mother's going to be all right."

"Yes, me too. Her friend said they're doing various tests."

"I'll let Tommaso know you won't be in for a while."

"Thank you, Eloisa. You're a good friend."

"Michele rang the office. He said he'd already tried your number."

"I really don't want to speak to him just now. Could you ring back and apologize? Don't bother with too much detail, but say I'll call him later in the week."

She gave Eloisa the number and ended the call, thinking through all she should do. Then she remembered her date in the evening and rang Edmondo.

"Wait," he said. "I'm driving in heavy traffic. I'll ring you back in five minutes."

Isla packed carefully, trying to think about how she'd be spending the next few days but distracted all the time by thoughts of her mother. She might be a week or more in London. She checked through her things again—clothes, laptop, a couple of work files. Did she have everything she would need? And she mustn't forget the charger.

As soon as she'd spoken to Edmondo, she would leave for Rome. It would be hours early when she got there, but she'd rather be at the airport waiting, than hanging around in the flat. It would make her feel she was doing something.

Poor Mum. She'd been in good health when Isla had left London a couple of months earlier and had been excited about the art class she'd signed up for.

Her mobile rang.

"Isla, sorry about that. I was at a difficult junction, but now I'm out of it. What's the problem?"

"My mother's been in a car accident. She's in one of the big London hospitals, so I'm going over to be with her. I've booked a flight. That means I won't be able to see you this evening because I'll be driving to Rome. You do understand?"

"Of course. You must go. But I'll drive you."

"No, there's no need, Edmondo. There's plenty of

time. I can do it easily."

"Time, yes, but you're upset and stressed, and you still haven't recovered from what happened to you last night. No, I insist. I'll drive you. I would be going to Rome on Sunday morning to pick up Adriano from his aunt's house anyway. This will be just a little earlier, and I can stay with my father or with Paola. And I'm taking Adriano to the *Bioparco*—the, er, zoo—in Rome on Monday, so no problem."

He was right. She had sustained a vicious blow to the head and now, weighed down by the news and its dire potential, Isla no longer felt as good as she had in the morning. And it would be much better not to be on her own. "If you're sure, I'd appreciate that."

"Okay. What time is your flight?"

"Five a.m."

"Right, I'm almost home. I'll ring when I'm coming over to you. See you soon."

Chapter 17

Finally, the bell rang. Isla picked up her travel bag and checked again for her passport and other documents. And yes, she had put the charger into the bag. She took a swift look around the flat and then locked up. A few moments later, she opened the door that led into the courtyard, to find Edmondo waiting. He took the bag from her and deposited it on the step.

"*Tesoro mio,*" he said, pulling her to him. "*Come stai?*"

Her heart leapt as his arms enfolded her. She could have received an electric shock and it would not have had a greater effect on her. She drew in a sharp breath, angry with herself. How shallow she was. How could she even think of her own feelings when her mother, whom she loved dearly, lay in a hospital bed and was possibly dying?

"My mother," she began, pulling back a little.

"I know, Isla. This seems wrong to you, but these things have their own timetable. We can't deny our feelings even if they don't fit in with what we think ought to happen. I'm not trying to put pressure on you. I just want to offer you the comfort and strength you'll need to get through this."

"I know, I know. I'm sorry. I'm not myself."

"Then don't say anything else. Do you want me to let you go?"

"No!" she said, appalled at the idea. "No. I need you just now."

As tears spilled out of her eyes, his arms closed more tightly around her.

"What if there are internal injuries? What if she dies, Edmondo? I can't bear to think of that."

"But you said she's in one of the best hospitals. They will do everything possible."

"I should never have left her alone for so long."

"You had to. No parents really want their children to stay at home for ever—not good parents. You have your life to live."

"I'm finding it so difficult because it's been just the two of us for so long. Even when I was in my own flat, I would see her several times a week, go around to her if she needed anything, and she did the same. We've always been responsible for each other."

"Who rang you about this?"

"Her friend, Penny."

"So she is not alone. She has friends."

"She does have friends."

"That's good. Come on, let's go to the airport."

****

They entered a small bar on the outskirts of Rome, neither really wanting to eat, the projected dinner forgotten by both. It was not that sort of place, anyway, not if you wanted to enjoy a leisurely meal and start the process of discovery necessary at the beginning of a new relationship.

He wasn't even sure if she'd begun to think of him in any romantic way, even before the telephone call. Clearly, she'd shown some interest, but things had been complicated by the assault carried out in the factory, and this evening's emotional events only made it worse. He needed to sort himself out, try to understand if there was something here that they could take forward together—if that's what she wanted.

They were sitting in a booth, each nursing a cup of coffee.

She looked thin and washed out, a frail, tired version of the girl he'd been talking to earlier that day.

"Something to eat?"

"No—you fed me too well this morning. I'm really not hungry."

She attempted a smile, but it was obvious her heart wasn't in it. There were dark shadows under her eyes.

"So, when we've finished this, I'm going to get a hotel room where we can rest and wait for the flight."

"A hotel room? I couldn't possibly—"

"You don't trust me?"

Isla didn't have to consider this. Trust didn't enter into it. Her feelings for this man were so strong that if he so much as laid a finger on her arm, she'd follow him. Of course, she trusted him. The thing was, her body knew exactly what it wanted, but her mind still had to catch up with the program. What he said was just common sense. They had nearly six hours to wait. They ought to try to get some sleep.

"Of course, I do," she said.

But I'm not sure that I trust me.

There were several hotels near the airport. At each, buses ran in plenty of time for the flights—you just had to enquire at the desk. A little later, she stood listlessly behind him, all energy gone, allowing him to talk to the clerk and make the arrangements. How would she have coped if he hadn't insisted on coming? Probably she'd

135

have been slumped in a plastic chair in the departures lounge. He led her over to the lifts.

It was a perfectly good room with two double beds, although hot and airless. She opened the window and the stink of aviation fuel, and the roar of a plane entered—so that was why it had been fastened and the thick curtains drawn. In this busy airport, planes were arriving and departing several times an hour. As yet another sped past the building, she quickly shut the window again.

"I'll turn on the air-conditioning."

"That's a good idea."

She set her alarm on her phone to allow sufficient time to get to the departures lounge. Then she took off her jacket and draped it on the back of the chair before going into the bathroom. She came out a few minutes later wrapped in a bathrobe and laid her blue midi-dress on the chair to ensure it didn't get crumpled, before climbing under the thin sheet. Just as on the evening before, she fell asleep almost immediately.

****

Later, she awoke. She stretched across to the bedside table and looked at her phone. Only an hour had passed. She turned over, and then over again, but she was holding her muscles too tense to have any hope of falling asleep again. Gradually, she forced herself to relax, but it didn't change things, and she could not settle back down.

What would she do if her mother's injuries were really serious? How unfair life could be. *Please let her live, please.* Tears squeezed themselves out of her eyes.

Edmondo turned over in the other bed, and she could tell from his breathing that he was sleeping. She thought about him now, considering all the things she knew. He was quite different from so many of her ideas about men in general and Italians in particular. It was true that her frame of reference was quite small—her father, Richard, her ex-boyfriend…and Kyle, who had so cruelly affected her life all those years ago. Unlike them, Edmondo wasn't shallow or lazy or narcissistic; he wasn't cruel; he did care about others, and in fact, he had gone out his way to help when the situation demanded it; he was gorgeous and sexy, as well, and— and this seemed the most astonishing to her—it seemed he might even feel the same way about her.

But he knew nothing of her. How would he feel when she told him? Would he still want her then? She lay a long while thinking about this question, and then came to a decision. The longer she lay there, the less likely she was to sleep.

Carefully, she got out of bed and groped her way across the room. It was completely dark, and the air conditioning was turned up high. She shivered in the intense cold. Unable to see anything, she walked forward and slammed into Edmondo's bed. She bit back a cry of pain, not wanting to wake him. When the pain subsided, she raised the cover and got in beside him. He was awake now. She lay facing him.

"Hold me!" she said.

His arm slid around her, and he pulled her closer. Then, he unerringly traced the top of her cheekbones with the pad of his thumb.

"You've been crying."

He must have good night sight—or more likely, good insight into what she would have been doing, awake in the middle of this horrible night.

"It's nothing now. I was thinking of Mum and how little control we have over things. You offered me strength and comfort, so I've come to claim it."

"All I want is to make you feel good, to take away all this pain. Do you want to know why?"

"Yes."

"I'm afraid I'm falling in love with you, Isla."

"Afraid?"

"Yes, afraid, because it's changing everything for me. You've turned my life upside down. It happened on that day I saw you in Milan. There were two of you, two beauties. Some blonde girl—and you. Nothing has changed since then, unless it's that the feeling has grown stronger. I don't know where this is going, but I would do whatever I can to help you."

"Then, make love to me," she whispered, half afraid to say the words. "I need you."

"No, that's not what you need right now. You only think you do. I'd just be taking advantage of this situation." He was quiet for a moment, still holding her tightly. "Isla, I want you more than anything else, but I don't want us to make a mistake. This feels too precious to me to take the risk. We will make love when you are ready, when you've had time to think about things. We don't want there to be regrets."

"Edmondo, I—"

"No. What you need is to feel safe and cared for. That, I can do. Now, relax."

His arms were holding her close and slowly, his warmth stole over her, and she fell asleep.

Chapter 18

As Isla walked along the hospital corridor, she was trying to keep in mind what Penny had said about her mother's injuries: that things weren't as bad as she'd think at first. Not as bad. So she meant not to be too shocked. Poor Mum—she must look awful. At the nurses' station, they said her mother was in a small ward with three other beds, at the far end. That sounded hopeful—maybe it meant she really was recovering, since they'd placed her among other people—she had to hang onto that idea. But she would need to talk to the doctor; the first scan results should be available now, and they'd done various other tests. She swallowed, trying to calm her thudding heart, as she contemplated what the tests might reveal.

There it was, 5F. She felt sick.

From the doorway, only her mother's dark hair was visible on the pillow, but when she walked forward, her face came into view. Oh, God! It was one large purple and blue bruise, and the pink stripe across her left cheek would be the burn—but they'd left it to heal without a dressing so it must be relatively superficial. That had to be good—it just didn't look that way. The swelling was truly horrific, as if she'd been the victim of a brutal attack.

Isla snagged up a lime-green plastic chair and set it down by the bed, lowering herself onto it with care because it looked so flimsy. The next bed was unoccupied, and the patients in the other two appeared to be sleeping. She picked up her mother's hand, which lay on the sheet, and held it in both of her own, rubbing her fingers gently.

"Mum," she whispered. "It's Isla."

There was no response. She stayed where she was, holding onto her hand. This was terrible. She hadn't expected Mum to be unconscious. Frankly, she didn't know what she'd expected. But at least she was here, and whatever happened, she'd be able to help. It was such a shock to see her mother like this. She'd always been a strong person, and generally optimistic, and now she looked so…vulnerable. Tears started at the corners of her eyes, and a lump grew in her throat.

She mustn't cry, in case her mother saw her and was upset by it. Hopefully, she'd got it wrong, and Mum wasn't unconscious, just sleeping. She waited, and minutes ticked by. Then suddenly, the patient stirred and opened one eye, the other being swollen shut.

"Isla, you've come."

The voice was a croak. Her body was battered and torn, but she had no trouble in recognizing her daughter, and that was something to be grateful for. Isla squeezed her hand, tears of relief now finding their way down her cheeks.

"Oh, Mum, thank goodness! I was so frightened."

She leaned forward and got as close as she could to a hug, but there were too many tubes and tapes, and a drip, getting in the way. In the end, all she could do was hang onto her hand.

****

Several hours later, Isla left Penny's house, where they'd caught up over a cup of tea. She took a taxi to her mother's flat, having decided she would spend the next few days there alone. When Penny had tried to persuade her to stay overnight, she'd reminded her about the cat. The woman looked shocked, clearly having forgotten the animal.

Now, Isla would have to work out what to do about it. The poor creature was probably starving. Later on, maybe she could talk a neighbor into looking after it. Mum had lived in the same flat for a long time, and Isla had the idea there was a woman on the ground floor who'd looked after the animal when her mother had gone on the only holiday that she could ever remember her having.

The cab turned into the street, which was narrow and appeared dark and unwelcoming in the late afternoon, as the sun favored the back gardens at this time of day. Heavy clouds hung in the sky, and it was cold. Isla shivered and pulled her thin cardigan tightly around her. Tomorrow, she'd put on her leather jacket. She'd not been prepared for weather like this, and at the moment it was languishing at the bottom of her case. What a contrast it was to the balmy autumn weather in Italy. But this was England, changeable, and the morning might well turn out to be hot.

Isla used her own keys to enter the foyer and crossed over to her mother's flat, stopping for a moment to take in the familiar smell of lavender. They must have just done the monthly clean. When she unlocked the door and pushed it open, Tai-Lu shot out as if she'd been waiting in the hallway and wrapped herself with desperation around Isla's legs, meowing loudly. The beautiful Siamese was usually completely self-absorbed, so it was good to be welcomed, even though it only meant the animal was hungry. Stooping to smooth down the cat's ears, she murmured encouraging noises and promised to feed her.

Her mother was so proud of the flat, a roomy two-bed Isla had helped her buy from the council. It hadn't been difficult as she'd occupied it for so long, but owning her own place had given her mother a measure of self-respect. Isla dropped her bag on the hall floor as the door closed behind her, and she went into the kitchen.

Having put the kettle on, she opened the windows and searched the cupboards for cat food. The animal continued to wind around her ankles, purring loudly. But once Isla put the food down, she stayed just long enough to empty her dish, before exiting elegantly via the door flap into the garden.

Isla sank onto the window seat and leant her forehead against the cool glass, watching the animal scoot across the lawn. The sun was low on the horizon, and the tiny area was striped with long, black shadows interspersed with gold-green patches. In the distance now, Tai-Lu, with her bottom up in the air, bent to lap water from the pond. She'd have one of the goldfish straight out of there, if she got the slightest chance! But they'd probably learned to recognize her shadow for what it was and knew to keep out of the way. Forgetting the cat, Isla stayed where she was, thinking about her mother. It had been tough seeing her like that, but she was calmer now she knew she would survive.

Her unseeing eyes fixed on the dark patches as night slowly consumed the garden, she thought about where her own life was going and about Edmondo. She felt his arms tight around her and smelled again the musky tang of his cologne, felt the touch of his fingers as he discovered the tears she'd shed. She'd been distraught and he'd come to her rescue, and she'd taken what he offered without thought for him. What she did next would decide what happened to them. Maybe the path had already been traced, but if she followed it any further, there would be no turning back. What of her plans for the business she'd spent so long dreaming about? One step and she might lose it all. She knew how it went—life took over and sometimes you couldn't get it back on course. Not that she didn't want him—the opposite was the case, she thought, with a surge of longing—but she also wanted to realize her ambitions. Was it impossible to pair that desire with a relationship? Maybe. But for the time being, she just needed to talk to him.

"Edmondo's phone."

Who was this? Who could have access to his phone? The spike of jealousy took her by surprise. The woman's voice was pleasant, unchallenging. It must be…oh, yes, he'd be at his sister-in-law's place with his son.

"Hello, I'm Isla Bruni. I'm afraid we haven't met, but could I speak to Edmondo? I promised to ring."

"Ah, you must be his friend."

So, he had mentioned her. Of course, he had. What an idiot she was.

"I'm Paola," the woman continued. "Edmondo's here to pick up Adriano, but they've been out all day so he's taking a shower at the moment. I'll get him to ring you later, shall I?"

"Yes, please. When he's free."

She'd hardly given a thought to anything other than her mother since she'd got onto the plane. Of course, the two of them would have spent the day in the city. It seemed strange to her that they'd only parted that morning.

She made tea and almost immediately took a sip, but it was too hot to drink. So she waited, walking around the kitchen, stopping at the window to peer out, picking things up and putting them down again. She drank some more of the tea, but the minutes didn't pass any faster, and it was another half an hour before the phone rang.

"Sorry, Isla. I had to get Adriano settled, so that we can talk. The two of us are staying here tonight. How is your mother?"

His voice was like a balm, soothing her agitation, setting everything to rights.

"It's bad—but things are getting better. She's conscious. She's a very determined person, and she's already talking about when she comes out, even though she can hardly move at the moment. But I think I'll need to stay another four or five days, just to make sure everything's all right."

She pictured him at the other end of the phone, probably in a bedroom for privacy, maybe stretched out on the bed. She sat down again. "And you? How are you?"

"Missing you already. Please come back as soon as you can. Adriano wants you back as well."

"Adriano!" She laughed. "Are you sure he knows who I am? We've hardly even met."

"Ah, but you have impressed him mightily. He

talks all the time about the drawing you made of him, and Paola said she found it in the pocket of his shorts when she did the washing. It's obviously precious to him. He wants you to teach him how to draw."

"Okay. I'll show him when I get back."

"So what are you doing this evening?"

"Just now, I'm staying in my mother's flat. I'll get it ready for her return and organize someone to look after her cat, but I think Mum will stay with her friend, Penny, when she first comes out of hospital. You're right, she has friends and will be well cared for." She was silent for a moment and then added, "I miss you too, Edmondo. I feel…"

"What do you feel?"

Heat flooded her cheeks. "A little embarrassed about propositioning you. I'm sorry, I—"

"Don't be silly!"

"You were right. I wouldn't have wanted to…to use you like that. I was distraught. I hardly knew what to do to take away the worry and fear."

"But you turned to the right person to help."

"I did. Only now, I do realize we need to get to know each other, before we…first…we…"

"That's my intention. Let me know your flight, and I'll be there to pick you up."

"I will."

They talked for nearly three-quarters of an hour, about everything and nothing in particular.

He cared. Even if it went nowhere, he cared. Holding this thought tight to her chest, Isla fell into bed a little while later, exhausted, and slept dreamlessly until late the next morning.

Chapter 19

The marmalade was good. Her mother made a few jars every year, and Isla had found one open in the fridge. She ate two slices of toast on which she'd spread a generous layer and then sat down by the open windows with a cup of coffee, looking onto the tiny garden. Wednesday already—the days were passing quickly. At this time of the morning, only the extreme corner of the lawn was illuminated, and the rest lay in deep shadow. It would be several hours before the garden was in full sun, but the day was bright. A surge of optimism swept over her.

The charcoal scent of the bread mingling with the aroma of coffee filled the air and made her think of her childhood breakfasts, first with all her family in their other home and then here alone with her mother. In the early days, she'd be gobbling up cereal and milk from her special blue bowl while her mother ate exactly what she was eating now—toast with a cup of coffee.

Her father had usually been halfway out the door on his way to work by the time Isla came downstairs. And her brother, Jack, seven years her senior, already tall and masculine, would snatch a cup of coffee, ruffle her hair or pull a pigtail, and follow his father out. Father and son were devoted to one another and both crazy about cars. That was why her father couldn't wait to buy the smart, fast car for his son's seventeenth birthday.

The door would close behind the men and then, it would just be the two of them, and she'd loved having all her mother's attention.

And later, after the accident, it was always just the two of them, her mother and her.

Today, the smells and the flavors were the same, but there'd been a different quality to that long-distant time. She had changed a little, but more changes were due; now it was up to her to create the fabric of her adult life.

Inevitably, she began to think about Edmondo. Were he and Adriano sharing breakfast right at this moment? Whenever he spoke of his son, she could see how much he loved him. It must have been so difficult that his ex-wife had insisted on having custody. And especially sharing him with the new husband, in a place that wasn't really suited to a child.

What must that be like, to have to give up your child? Although some men, like her own father, seemed to manage it. Bitterness, usually buried deep at the back of her mind, surged up, its intensity taking her by surprise. She swallowed, trying to remove the sour taste in her mouth. Were people forever marked by the things that happened in childhood? Could she never forget? Never escape?

But for most parents, it must be very painful. And Edmondo was sensitive.

Sipping the cooling coffee from time to time, she checked emails. She needed to talk to the contractor they'd decided they would probably use on the tower, so she could send him the plans and he could arrange a site visit. Hopefully, work could start within the month, depending on how much he had on just now. A short email to the man brought that up to date. Having visited the nursery school and reread the notes she'd made on Friday, she emailed her suggestions for the project. And that new client out at the farmhouse who'd contacted the practice—she must remember to arrange a meeting with her for the end of the following week. She sent an email suggesting she would make contact later in the day. Isla had learned a long time ago that making sure people knew what was going on was one of the basics of running a business. There was apparently nothing else that needed her immediate attention, so she shut down the laptop and put it on charge.

Visiting hours at the hospital were not until after lunch, and it wasn't yet eight o'clock. Should she use the time to visit Design 501? This had been at the back of her mind for a little while, and it would be lovely to see her colleagues. But meeting up with Susan, her boss and friend, was going to be awkward, because she'd be delivering unwelcome news.

Before she'd left for the exchange, they'd talked about a future partnership. She'd wondered if Susan had suggested she do the exchange to put off the moment when the decision would have to be made—and, of course, anything she learned could only be good for the studio. And meanwhile, she was investigating ways to make it easy for Isla to buy her way into her business. It was lovely to have her talents so much appreciated, but now she was certain it wasn't what she wanted—which she'd told her boss months earlier.

"Isla, just think of the advantages of coming in with me. How on earth will you live while you build up your client list?'

Convinced she was unlikely to change her mind, Isla had nevertheless promised to think it through. It was incredibly generous of Susan, but she was sure it wouldn't work for her. She sighed, not wanting to confront the issue but knowing she must.

And now, there was an added complication: Edmondo.

But whatever the future of their relationship, she wouldn't be accepting the opportunity in London.

"I'm going to stay in Italy," she said suddenly.

She'd changed. Everything had changed. The country had got to her, touched some part of her that had hitherto lain dormant.

Finally, it was time to face things. She sighed and detached her phone from its charger—still only eight fifteen, so there was plenty of time for a walk. She would set off in the general direction of the office, although she hadn't decided quite yet if she'd go in. After feeding Tai-Lu, she locked up. Thank goodness the Williamses down the hall had said that when Isla left, they'd look after the cat. It was one less thing to worry about.

It was a lovely morning, cool and sunny, as she left the short Putney Street in which her mother's flat was situated. It was great being back in London, seeing all the places that had once been so big a part of her life. She missed it, and yet she didn't. As she walked along, her eyes were fixed on the Thames, where small craft crisscrossed from one bank to the other; it sparkled to her left, and central London gradually opened up ahead.

But suddenly, she was thinking about the walk up to the tower in Fortezza. She heard the buzzing of late bees, and it was the drowsy warmth of the Italian sun on her skin that she felt, not the brisk morning breeze blowing off that great artery of the capital. And there was Adriano skipping along in front of her, thrashing at the bushes and clumps of greenery that grew by the side of the road, releasing the heady scents of sage and rosemary. And Edmondo smiling thoughtfully from the ladder when she'd met him in the tower. She had to get back. These things had become so important to her that her soul felt starved by their absence, and she was diminished.

By the time she'd got to Waterloo Bridge, she'd worked up a thirst. She must be near the Strand, a good hunting ground for coffee shops, so she turned away from the river, wincing at the ache in her calf muscles. As she entered the ancient thoroughfare at Somerset House, she found a place with a couple of tables outside and ordered a latte, settling down to watch the passers-by.

Surely, she shouldn't be this tired, with pains in her legs and a tightness around her neck. But some of it was probably due to her recent experiences. Maybe she should try bathing in the Roman bath that was rumored to be somewhere along this road—if it was a Roman bath. She settled back and sipped at a half decent coffee, though it wasn't as good as the Albertos' brew.

The last few days had been stressful, so now she lowered her tense shoulders, telling herself to relax. It was true that being in a big city kept you fit, and she'd got out of the habit of walking, which went some way to explain the aching muscles. A few things would have to change on her return to Fortezza, that was certain. Fitness, yes, but one of the things was not to allow any procrastination. And perhaps she should start with this now. She took out her mobile and called Design 501.

Half an hour later, she stood outside the old Victorian industrial building that housed the design studio. The entrance was an imposing doorway with a terra-cotta arch, between a barber's and what she considered to be one of the finest bakeries in London. On reflection, that hadn't been great for remaining fit and keeping her figure when she'd been working here. That was why she rarely ate cakes—the ones from this shop were just too good, and the only way to manage things was to keep away completely. But she was strong this morning, so she went in and bought a loaf, aware that there was almost nothing in the larder back at the flat. Then, ignoring the lift, she climbed the metal stairway that rose in three flights, angled around the central space, and deposited the visitor at loft level. How strange it was to be here. A little scared to plunge back in, she pushed open the door.

Everything felt different, although she would have found it difficult to say exactly what had changed. There were about twenty people in the large room, among them Christiano, who looked up and waved. Smiling at everyone and saying hello, she went over to shake hands and exchange a few words with him, because they'd never in fact met. Then, she kissed her friend, Magali, who introduced her to a tall youth with a full, black beard, the most recent intern from the art college. They always had someone on placement, but the face hair was quite a surprise, because the last few interns, both male and female, had sported earrings and tattoos—and virtually no hair at all. For a while, she socialized with her colleagues. Then, taking a deep breath, she backed away toward the inner office, knocked on Susan's door, and walked in.

They embraced.

"Come and have some tea," Susan said, drawing Isla over to the deep leather chairs at the window that gave a view over the station. Susan only ever drank green tea, and Isla elected to have the same, to make things simple. She watched the street below as Susan busied herself with the drinks. A cloud crept over the sun, and people scurried along with hunched shoulders, looking as if they expected rain. So different from the golden days she'd left behind.

Having asked why Isla was in London and passed on good wishes for her mother, the woman came straight to the point: "Have you given any more thought to my suggestion?"

"I have, Susan, but I'm afraid my answer is still no."

Her look of disappointment said a lot, and Isla felt guilty, although she'd always made it clear that she wanted to go her own way.

"Well, I can't say I'm surprised. I've rarely met anyone so determined to do her own thing, but I don't think you'll get a better offer from anyone."

"I'm sure that's true, and I'm sorry. But there are things I have to do. I'll email my notice to you as soon as I get back to Fortezza. But I will come back for a while at the beginning of the year to work out the month if you need me. Unless you manage to find someone by then."

"Thank you. I'll let you know, but I expect we can sort something out—though I doubt we'll get anyone at the same level. You know I'll always support you, Isla. Have you made any plans yet?"

"Not really, nothing definite. That's what I'll need to do in the next couple of months."

"I suppose there's a man involved in all of this?" said Susan with the scorn of a woman who did not find the opposite sex remotely attractive and generally made sure they knew it. "I can't believe you've been there all this time and not found someone."

Isla blushed, although she shouldn't have been taken by surprise. Her boss knew how to read people. It was part of what made her successful.

"There is, but things haven't progressed that far." She paused, considering. "And my decision isn't to do with him." It was good to realize that this was true.

"We enjoyed the Zoom session. Thanks for doing that. I was sorry to miss such a stimulating conference."

"It was great. I picked up all sorts of new ideas, got a lot out of attending, as you could probably tell."

They discussed it further and, for a short while, talked about her mother, before Isla said good-bye.

It was hard to get out of the main office. Everyone wanted to know what she'd been doing and asked about her mother's accident. They were keen to know about the office in Fortezza as well.

When she finally left, visiting hours at the hospital were about to begin. If she wanted the full allocation of time, she needed to get moving. A 205 bus was just drawing up outside when she exited the building, and she hopped on board.

Chapter 20

Mum was sitting up, which was a plus. And the tubes and the drip had gone. Nevertheless, it would be a while before her face looked any better. A yellow edge to the purple and red abstract design that she appeared to be wearing was gradually becoming visible. Poor Mum—that must be very painful.

"I'm so much better, Isla. You really don't have to stay any longer."

"I can't just leave you like this. What if you have a relapse?"

"Yes, you can. And I won't have a relapse—they've already told me they're letting me out tomorrow morning, after the doctor's done his round. They're just waiting for the final test results—but he said today that I'm recovering much faster than they expected, and that I'll be better off at home, as long as I have someone with me."

"Exactly. You need someone at home with you."

"It's taken care of, Isla. Penny's coming to get me as soon as I ring, and I'm staying with her for the next couple of weeks. She'll look after me."

"Doesn't Penny have to work?"

"No, she's quite a bit older than me, you know. She's retired now."

"Mum, are you sure this is going to be all right for you?"

"Yes. You have your own life to live, and it's time you got back to it. I can tell you're wanting to get on with things."

They talked for a while, and Isla began to relax. A new personality was emerging, much more decisive than before. Here, in her hospital bed, her mother had no doubt found plenty of time to think about what had happened to her, and where her life was going. Isla decided it was being faced with the idea of her own mortality that had given her this new zest and determination.

"If you're really sure you'll manage, I could ring the airport and confirm my flight for Friday morning."

"Do that. I'll tell you what—when I'm well again, I'll come and visit. Maybe I can persuade Penny to come with me."

"That's a really good idea, Mum. I'd love you to do that, love to see both of you. Only, don't forget, the exchange finishes at Christmas, so don't leave it too long before you come."

"But you're staying on?"

That was very acute of her. She was obviously getting better fast.

"Well, you're right that I'm thinking of it, Mum. I really love it there, and I...I've met someone. But no decisions yet."

Her mother tried a grin but winced. "So, this is the girl who told me just a couple of months ago that all Italians are too smooth and unreliable? Am I right in thinking he is Italian?"

"Yes, but of course, he's not like that!"

"I'm only teasing. You don't need to tell me anything if you don't want to."

"I…well, there's not much to tell, but it looks promising. I'll let you know what I decide."

It was promising. At least she now knew how she felt about Edmondo, though whether this was love or not, she couldn't tell. Despite her preoccupation with her mother, the yawning gap in her life that had suddenly opened up when she'd left him behind in Rome had helped her understand her feelings at a deeper level. It wasn't just the physical attraction, which she had to admit was huge. She felt a connection with him unlike with any man she'd met before. But did he feel the same way? It seemed possible. And he was so sensitive to her needs. She'd never met a man who cared that much, who didn't think about himself first. One thing she did know was that this was certainly going to interfere with her carefully laid plans. What was she going to do?

"I'm glad you've finally found someone after Richard," said her mother, looking very pleased. "And I have to say, I never—"

"I know." Isla laughed. "You never really cared for him. He wasn't a bad person, you know, just not the right man for me—and I should have recognized it a lot earlier. But maybe mothers know these things."

"Probably. Anyway, you've left me with no choice—I'll just have to visit you, now. I'm desperate to meet him."

They both laughed at this enthusiasm, and then her mother broke into a fit of coughing that brought tears to her eyes.

"My ribs—so painful. I have two that are cracked."

Isla said, "You must be careful," and then, she added, "Mum, I think you'll like him."

"What's his name?"

"Edmondo. And that's all I'm telling you for the moment."

She passed on the news about the cat and stood up. "I'm going now. Give me a ring after the doctor's visit to let me know if he's allowing you to leave the hospital. Is your phone charged?"

"Yes. Don't fuss—and do confirm that flight, Isla. Whether I leave tomorrow or the next day, I'll be fine. I'll call you, okay?"

"So, either way, I'll see you tomorrow afternoon, because I'll be leaving early on Friday morning. I do know you're going to be in good hands with Penny."

With the vague feeling their mother and daughter roles had been reversed, she bent to kiss her mother and waved as she left the ward in a much happier frame of mind. What a relief that Mum really was getting better so quickly. Penny was a decent woman. She could trust her to do everything necessary to keep her mother safe, but she would have to insist on being told immediately, if there were signs of things going wrong.

It had been so good to see how much had changed in just a few days. A burden had been lifted, and she could allow herself to think of the future. At the beginning of the week, she'd been so worried about the extent of the injuries, that she'd wondered if she ought to be cutting short her stay in Fortezza, in order to take care of her mother. It was a huge relief to know that it wasn't necessary.

****

Back in the flat, with Tai-Lu doing her usual, sinuous dance around her ankles and giving her insistent, low-pitched meow, Isla telephoned Penny.

"Of course, she's staying with me, what are you thinking, Isla? How long have your mother and I been friends? It must be more than thirty years, well before you were born when we met. I'm glad to have the chance to do something for her. She helped me so much when Phil died, you know. She didn't intrude because that's not her way, but she just wouldn't let me mope around at home all the time, the way I wanted. I've always been grateful for that."

That had been five years earlier, when Isla was in her last year as a student. Wrapped up in her own life and the exciting prospects that were opening in front of her, she'd hardly been aware of what was going on at the time.

"Thank you, Penny. So you think it'll be all right if I leave on Friday morning? I'll need to confirm my flight this afternoon."

"You go right ahead. I'll look after her."

Isla ended the conversation and rang the airline. Then she keyed in Edmondo's number.

Chapter 21

Edmondo closed his phone at the end of a long conversation and tucked it into his pocket, his mind buzzing with the news that Isla would fly back on Friday morning. Two days. His heart had leapt at the knowledge that he would see her again so soon. She'd sounded reassured that her mother was doing well. That was great, of course, but for him, the good news was that they would be together again. It had been difficult, her having to go off to London like that, just as things were beginning to develop between them. He could hardly wait for her return.

It would need some organization on his part because his son was a major priority, but he was used to having to solve problems with his work, and surely this situation would not prove too much for him. The little boy was probably missing his mother, although he hadn't once mentioned her. Was this a bad thing? Wouldn't it be more natural if he talked about her? Perhaps he was bottling things up only for them to have problems later. It was worrying.

He'd arrange another chat session for him. He'd bought a tablet, which meant it could be done relatively easily, but the difference in time across the Atlantic often seemed to get in the way, and they'd only managed to hook up a couple of times so far. But whatever the case, he needed to spend as much time as he could with the boy, to help him settle in.

He rang the number Bianca had given him and was relieved when she answered after a couple of rings. He could hear loud chatter and dishes and cutlery clattering in the background.

"Everything going well, Edmondo?"

"Yes, I wanted to set up a session with you for Adriano. Can you manage it today?"

"We're having breakfast with a couple of film people at Pitchoun. Remember, we went there years ago—that French place on Olive."

He smiled, noting the fact she was speaking English, and with an American accent. That was weird.

"But it should be all right later on—say in a couple of hours."

"Okay, speak to you later."

That's what their communications were like these days—brief and to the point, but it was good that she seemed happy. He shrugged. It was Adriano who was important.

They'd had very little money when he was a child, but his parents had been loving and encouraging, and that was the good start in life he'd like to give to his son. He only had to look at his cousin, Giacomo, to see how badly wrong things could go if those qualities were missing in a family. So making sure that Adriano knew how much he was loved was very important. And he mustn't forget the boy would soon be going to a new school, with all the challenges that could present. There might be quite a few difficulties ahead, but hopefully, Isla would understand this and not expect his undivided attention.

Still, he wanted to devote this weekend to her,

would have to if he wanted their relationship to go anywhere, and it wasn't appropriate to take her back home with him while his son was there. Not quite yet. He rang Paola, knowing that he'd already relied far too heavily on her with regard to Adriano.

"You don't mind, do you, Paola? This is really important to me."

"Of course, I don't. And Adriano loves being here. Look, I would be the first to admit that my sister was—still is—a difficult woman. I think the way things turned out was really hard on you." She sighed. "And you've been on your own for nearly four years, Edmondo. It's time things changed. I'm really pleased if you've found someone you care for at last."

"Blame on both sides, I expect. I didn't pay her enough attention. I was too taken up with the business, long hours, late nights. I can see that now."

"And she's a person who needs constant attention. I think that's what she's getting now, and she does appear to be happy, so let's concentrate on you and Adriano. I am looking forward to meeting Isla."

The result of this conversation was that his son would benefit from more time with his aunt and younger cousins. He told Adriano they'd be leaving for Rome early on Friday morning, instead of late in the afternoon. The boy was quick to pick up on things, and the first thing he said was, "Is Signorina Bruni coming back? Can I come to the airport with you? Please, *Papà*."

It wasn't a bad idea. It would help his sister-in-law if he dropped the boy off late morning, give her a chance to get her own children organized.

"Just a moment so I can check," he said, and

quickly texted to Isla—*Adriano will be with me when you arrive, okay? We'll take him to Paola's afterward.*—

She texted straight back. —*Sì, bene.*—

He smiled. It was that simple, with none of the histrionics he was used to from Bianca, whenever he wanted to do something that she hadn't counted on or set up herself. He sent Isla a smiley face of approval, wryly noting that this was the first time he'd ever used such a thing. She was only twenty-six, seven years younger than him, and probably used emojis with her friends as a matter of course. But he'd never really got into the habit—while everyone else had been playing around on social media, he'd been building for the future. But the business was fine now, and it was time he changed a few things.

****

When they walked into the arrivals hall, Adriano was super-happy about the visit.

"Can we look over an airplane, *Papà*? Can I talk to a pilot?"

It was great he was so curious but disappointing to have to tell him they wouldn't be able to do that.

"Why not, *Papà*?"

"Because we don't have tickets. They won't let us get near an airplane. But if you really are interested, maybe we can arrange a proper visit on another day."

Edmondo wasn't sure if a commercial company would allow such a thing, but he had a friend with a small plane. It should be possible to set something up.

"Yesss!" Adriano was jumping up and down in his excitement. When he'd calmed down, he asked, "Are we going to see Signorina Bruni right now?"

162

"Yes, she's going to drive with us to Aunt Paola's."

"Will Signorina Bruni show me how to draw today?"

"Probably not today. She's going to be tired after her journey—and we have to get back to Fortezza for a…a meeting."

Well, that was true. It was definitely going to be a meeting. Except it would just be her and him.

"Oh!" The sound carried a huge weight of disappointment.

"You know, you could ask her if you can call her Isla. When you say Signorina Bruni like that, it sounds as if you don't know her."

"Well, I don't really." He looked as if he was considering something. "Do you like her, *Papà*?"

"Very much. Do you?"

He furrowed his brows, giving it serious thought. "Think so," he said after a few moments. "She's a good person. And she can draw."

Unwittingly, Isla had found a way to make friends with him.

She saw them immediately she came through the gate, the tall man and the small boy, and waved. The latter had spotted her and was now darting around the clusters of people greeting each other.

"Signorina Bruni, you've come! We've been waiting so-o long."

"Yes, so-o long," said Edmondo, arriving close behind and dragging out the word as his son had done. "At least ten whole minutes—or, in my case, six whole days."

He leaned forward and kissed her cheek, noting her

blush. This time, things felt different. She'd come back, and the sight of her had him fizzing as if he'd just imbibed a glass of champagne. The force of his desire surprised him. He couldn't remember such an intensity of feeling for any other woman. Did she care about him in the same way? He tried to analyze what the feeling was, and the only thing he could come up with was happiness.

Which created a major problem: now, he had to have her in his life because, if he didn't, he'd be incomplete, unable to function properly. How had she done that to him so quickly?

"Let me take your bag. And I'm sure Adriano will carry one of those for you. You seem to have so many more bags than when you left."

When he took it from her, his hand trembled as it brushed against hers and he felt her reaction. She looked quickly away, down at the boy, and handed him a Selfridges carrier bag.

"Take care of that for me, Adriano, please. It's biscuits and chocolates for everyone in the office, since they've covered for me while I've been away."

"Did they have to do your work?"

"Well, some of it, so I need to say thank you. It's so good to be here," she added, smiling at them both.

****

Paola was a lovely woman, that was her first thought. She welcomed them and insisted they stay to lunch, and neither Edmondo nor Isla could do other than accept. There was real affection between her and Edmondo, which meant she would want the best for him, and that included having Adriano to stay. And to her, offering lunch was no more than a basic courtesy.

It couldn't be easy to cope with a lively six-year-old when you had a baby and a preschooler of your own, but she seemed to be one of those serene women who take everything in their stride. Even her children were calm, and Adriano immediately toned down his behavior here, apparently without any effort.

"I've brought you some things from London," Isla said, placing on the table a bag of interesting packages from the Selfridges Food Hall.

Paola looked inside. "Ah, thank you. That's very good—I know this shop." She kissed Isla. "It was kind of you to think of it."

"And I have a present for Adriano."

The little boy, who'd been doing his utmost to see into his aunt's bag, now looked up, his eyes round. "For me?"

"I could have bought you chocolates or sweets, of course." His face fell. Clearly that's what she should have done. "But instead, I got this." She pushed an oblong package wrapped in shiny green paper across the table.

The boy snatched it up and began to tear at the wrapping, but Edmondo and Paola said in unison, "Adriano!"

"*Grazie,* Signorina Bruni." And without taking a breath, he added, "Can I look now?"

Everyone laughed.

"*Prego.* You're welcome. You can open it now."

Quickly, he ripped the paper, fretting at the tape that bound it. Finally, it fell away to reveal a small sketchbook and a blue tin box of pencils with a sketch of a lion on the front. Not children's colors. These were the real thing, drawing pencils that ranged from hard to very soft.

"This," he said, suddenly subdued, "is better than sweets."

"That's good. I'm glad I chose the right thing. But, just in case it wasn't, I did get some chocolate bars as well."

And his face broke into a wide smile.

****

In spite of the lovely welcome, Isla wanted to leave. Lunch, of which she'd eaten a minuscule amount, was over, and she was sitting politely next to Edmondo while they drank coffee, scarcely listening to the conversation. Instead, her thoughts, prompted by her body's reaction to his nearness, filled her mind to the exclusion of all else, and it astonished her that no one else knew what she was thinking. Twice, Paola asked her a question, and she had no idea what the conversation was about.

"Sorry," she said. "I'm just a little tired."

She hadn't realized how she'd stored up her feelings, pushed it all away while she visited her mother, supported her while she talked to the police when they'd come to ask questions, dealt with the car insurance company, and a hundred other matters. Even making arrangements for the cat had occupied her mind. Then, there was keeping in touch with the office and trying to work remotely, although that had not been difficult under the circumstances. It had given her the time to write most of the specifications for the next stage of Christiano's long-term project, in order to get a contractor on board. There were just a few things to check on, back in the office, before she sent it out.

And, at night, she'd fallen into bed exhausted,

sleeping heavily, and sometimes waking later than usual. Afterward, once she'd felt that her mother was getting better, she had allowed herself the luxury of thinking about the man she hoped would soon be her lover. Would he ever be anything more? It felt so good to be with him, and she knew he was the right person for her—even if he didn't.

Her mother was happily ensconced in Penny's house in Barnet, a short distance from Elstree Studios, and was being treated as an honored guest. She was so resilient. Truly, the difference between Mum on Sunday morning and when she'd said good-bye to her yesterday afternoon was wonderful. Now it seemed likely she would make a full recovery. Now Isla could pay attention to her own needs.

Chapter 22

They left Rome after lunch. The great city was built on hills, but they looked fairly low to Isla, and it wasn't until they approached Tivoli that the land began to rise. As they drove along, Edmondo pointed out the picturesque ruins, clearly visible from the road.

"One day, we'll come here. You must see the Villa Adriana. It's so big, it's like a town in itself."

Did this mean that he saw a future together? She'd already decided it was what she wanted, but now, she was scared. It felt as if every word, every gesture bound her more tightly. Living with him in her life could offer so much. She couldn't let that go by, but she must not lose sight of herself and her goals. But all she said was, "Is that the same emperor who built the wall in the north of England?"

"It is."

"He certainly had grandiose ideas."

They drove through the warm afternoon sun of early September, along the A24 and over the backbone of Italy, the chain of mountains that divided Rome from the Adriatic. Patches of aromatic herbs grew close to the roadside. Woody rosemary bushes had forced their way between the stones on the lower slopes, their pale purple flowers looking washed out in the glare of the sun. Here and there in the hollows, velvety sage reared its head. She sniffed, reveling in the scents they released as these were carried toward them on the breeze. At another time, she would have liked to get out and gather some, maybe to add flavor to a meal, but just now, she was anxious to keep going. Slowly, slowly, the air began to cool, and the light became less intense.

He was such a good driver; in Britain, Ferrari seemed to be synonymous with speed and arrogance, but Edmondo handled his beautiful car with the sort of tenderness you reserved for something you loved, not going particularly fast, nursing it around the bends and negotiating a series of spooky tunnels, blasted out of granite and limestone, which Isla hadn't even noticed on her frantic journey to Rome the previous week.

They didn't talk much, each lost in their own thoughts, but now, as they rose higher, he started telling her about the mountains of the Abruzzi, about compression and extension. A picture grew in her mind of those rocks thrusting up and folding toward the Adriatic.

"And there's a lot of history. Did you know this area was occupied by the Celts in the fourth century BC?—that's where the name comes from."

"What name do you mean?"

"Apennines—from *pen* or *ben*, I think. You have this in England—the Pennines. And Ben Nevis in Scotland."

Well, she sort of knew about this, but she was a Londoner, and she was certain she'd never visited those places. "I'm very ignorant about these things, even what's in my own country."

His enthusiasm and love for the region and its history was wonderful. She'd have to find out more, in order to share in what he found so fascinating.

"Does your family come from the area? From Fortezza?"

"Originally, yes. My grandfather moved to Rome when his older brother inherited the house and the land."

"And now you've inherited it."

"No, my grandfather's brother left it to his eldest son, but he had no children, and in the sixties, he was penniless after a business venture went bad, so he was forced to sell it. But the new owner never got to grips with what had to be done, and it fell into ruins. I bought it back from the estate."

"That was lucky, that it came back on the market."

"Yes, and at a very low price—because it was unlivable and there's almost no potential for growing things on the land—it's all rock. Also, there'd just been an earthquake—people weren't rushing to buy property in the area. It's been a lot of work to restore the tower."

"And in the meantime, you renovated the house." She was quiet for a while, and then she said, "So, I noticed they call you *il conte* in the town. Did you inherit that or is it just a courtesy title for someone who's been a benefactor in the area?"

"Neither. The title is attached to the land, so I am genuinely *il conte*. It's an anomaly. My father, who is still alive, does not have a title." He flashed her a wide grin. "But I'm no aristocrat, so don't run away with that idea. My dad worked all his life in a factory in Rome. But he *was* an inventor, a great engineer. Our house was full of his prototypes. Still is, I guess."

"Like father, like son, as they say," she said.

This was perfect. It explained why he was so relaxed. He worked hard and had no expectation that other people owed him something.

What was going to happen next? Needing the physical contact, she put out her hand and touched his arm. He turned to give her a smile, but then his eyes went quickly back to the road.

It was time she worked out what this relationship would mean. All she'd done in London, when the thought of him had floated into her mind, was to feast on the sensations that coursed through her body as she remembered the way she felt each time they met, how every touch set her alight. It got in the way of clear thinking. She folded her arms over her chest and sat up straight. It was time to sort things out.

"You're looking very determined. What is it?"

"Nothing important. Just thinking."

But it was important. Of course, they could just have sex, and that was something she'd missed over the past year, but it wasn't as simple as that because it wouldn't be casual. If they went ahead, she would change, and her goals would be compromised. Somehow, she had to bring the two things together— life with Edmondo and her career.

They'd begun the descent into Teramo now, and a few minutes later, they turned into the narrow road which led to Fortezza. Soon, once again, they were climbing.

What if he didn't feel the same way as her, if this was just a pleasant diversion and later, they'd part, no hard feelings on either side? Could she do that? Could she not do it? She'd breathed in his essence and now everything was topsy-turvy, her emotions and desires whirling in space, and there was nothing she could do to bring them back to order.

Maybe a simple liaison was all it could ever be, since his son must be the most important thing to him. She'd seen that he loved Adriano. Perhaps he'd feel it wouldn't be suitable to introduce someone else into the boy's life.

"Shall I take you to your flat?" said Edmondo.

He hadn't wanted to ask the question, because he thought he might not like the answer, but he knew that's what he should do. He had to allow her to make a choice.

"No, Edmondo. Let's go to your house."

Only a short distance now. My God, he wanted her so much. When they got back, he'd carry her out of the car and straight up to his bed. Maybe he'd tear off her clothes, if she'd let him. He'd pictured this moment several times over during the very long week he'd just had, imagined what he might do to please her. He remembered her body against his in the hotel bed, how difficult it had been to turn down her request. He was hardening even at the memory.

It was late afternoon by the time they arrived, and the shadows were lengthening. With Signora Forni gone for the weekend, the place was deserted. He stopped the car, and they got out. She looked uncertain standing there by the wall, gazing over the sweeping terrain, the features of which were beginning to meld into a low mist. It wasn't surprising if she was nervous—so was he. But she was smiling, and that boded well.

"Come on!" he said.

She held out her hand, and he drew her toward him. He started kissing her, tentatively at first, inviting her to contribute.

Isla kissed him back, thinking it was the first time they'd done this, really kissed, that was—and yet he'd filled her mind so much, if the house door had been open, she would have skipped the kissing, rushed upstairs, and thrown herself onto his bed, and waited for him to plunder her. Plunder—she liked that word. All of her was there for his taking. She blushed, embarrassed by the scene she'd conjured up. And then thinking how much she wanted to hold him, she laid her head on his breast. He stroked her cheek.

"Pink as a summer rose. What was going through your mind?"

God, could he see her blush, even in this light?

"Oh, the usual. You know."

"You do this a lot, do you?"

He was looking deep into her eyes. Her throat was suddenly dry, and when the words came out, they sounded like a croak to her ears. "No, not so I've noticed. And it's never felt like this."

Her heartbeat had edged up a notch. Somehow, it was getting difficult to catch her breath. And the kissing was good after all, getting better all the time.

His hands slid up her arms, and he caressed her neck. Of their own volition, her fingers worked their way through his floppy, Italian curls. She loved them, wanted to twist them around her fingers. Where had she got the idea that she didn't like Italian men? She must have been mad.

They came together in another kiss. This was what had to happen, as if they'd known each other in the distant past, and it was a matter of finding each other again, simply a continuation of what they'd had then.

They were still kissing as they burst into the house.

In the semi-darkness, he pushed the door closed behind him with his foot, his eyes on hers, and then he pulled her toward the stairs. A red light was winking somewhere on the wall by the sitting room door.

"Alarm," she said, suddenly realizing what was going to happen.

Hanging onto her, he stretched across her shoulders and punched in the numbers, and the light went out.

"You see what you do to me," he whispered, "how much power you have over me? I never forget the alarm—my mind must have been occupied with something else."

They climbed the stairs. It was a slow climb, their steps punctuated by kisses and quickly indrawn breaths. She hadn't been up here before, but she didn't find herself paying any attention to her surroundings. In the room, she moved toward him. It was coming to her now, how important this was going to be, how it mattered that he felt the same way, that she had an active role to play.

She stretched out her hand and began to unbutton his shirt. Her fingers were trembling, and the buttons were too small, so she couldn't do it one-handed. Freeing her other hand, which he'd clasped behind her back, she concentrated and got the job done. Fine black hairs covered his chest, and she laid her head there a moment, as she'd imagined doing earlier, drinking in his scent, musky and lemony at the same time.

Edmondo gently caressed the nape of her neck, making her shiver. When she pulled away, the same long, blue dress she'd worn in the hotel in Rome dropped to the floor and lay puddled around her feet.

He couldn't help a gasp, overwhelmed by the sight

of her after all his imaginings. She seemed to be wearing nothing more than a few wispy pieces of black lace with some vivid blue, satiny material gleaming through. He brought his hands around her back and unhooked her bra clasp, releasing her breasts. Small and rounded, fitting exactly into his hands, the nipples already standing proud. So beautiful, with her slim waist.

He trembled, trying to hold back a little, knowing it would be better to take it slowly. But she wasn't passive; already, her hands had found his belt, though her fingers slipped on the buckle, before she succeeded in opening it. He said, "Let's lie down."

They lay naked on the wide bed. Rays of late sunlight striped across them through the shutters, creating mysterious dips and hollows in their skin. He moved across and began to trace patterns on her arms, dropping feathery kisses onto her shoulders and throat.

"So soft," he whispered.

A moan escaped her lips.

He moved farther down, trailing those wonderful fingers across her breasts and down, down. The lighter his touch, the more sensitive she became, and suddenly, she erupted in a great shudder.

"Now," she said, "now, please, if you have any…mercy."

"*No, non ne ho.*"

His grin was devilish as he took her mouth, teasing with his tongue.

Then his hand slid lower still, down between her legs, and there he found her cleft.

****

Later, they lay side by side once more and gazed

into each other's eyes, drinking in every nuance. How had he made her feel like this? She hadn't been able to respond that way before, with so much abandon, the sheer wantonness that had overtaken her. She hadn't known it was possible to derive so much pleasure from the simple, carnal act. And she'd been right: everything had changed.

As the tides of passion began to recede, she was re-experiencing the ways he'd brought her to climax. How had he known where to go, what to do to make this happen? She tried to read his eyes, hoping she hadn't disappointed him. He leaned forward and kissed her, lingering a little at the corner of her mouth. Helpless, she moved toward him, and his hand began once again to caress her face, her neck, her breasts. She turned on her side, and when suddenly he ran his fingers lightly down her spine, she was fired up again.

It would take time to discover all the things that would please him, things that would be particular to them, but for the moment, this was all she needed.

Chapter 23

It was still relatively early in the morning on Sunday when Isla climbed out of the car outside her house and waved good-bye to Edmondo, as he turned in the direction of Rome to pick up Adriano. It was such a pity she couldn't go with him, but there was work to be done and she had to learn to fit him in around the other things in her life. What she really wanted was to spend all her time with him. She smiled, acknowledging the situation was getting ridiculous—and that pleasures deferred were always keener. She had to pace herself.

The church bell clanged another dozen times and abruptly stopped. Now the partially shaded square was a silent place, although the sound still rang in her ears. Across the way, chairs were stacked outside the little bar-restaurant, and tables were upended against the wall. Suddenly, crockery clattered in the kitchen at the back of the building, and the espresso machine hissed fiercely. In a few minutes, Signor Alberto the Younger would be opening, and his first clients of the day would appear.

Isla turned away and entered her courtyard. It was going to be a long day, as she got ready to return to the studio. But Italy was teaching her a different rhythm of living, how to be civilized, to enjoy the moment and not always be onto the next thing. It was a serious—and entirely pleasant—lesson, and one she intended to heed.

The flat was a little musty after being shut up over the week. She put down her bags and went to open all the windows. Sweet fresh air and the scent of thyme from the box she'd planted outside the sitting room window wafted in, making a big difference to the atmosphere. She would do a few chores, but first she put on coffee, and while waiting for it to brew, she unpacked and watered a couple of drooping plants. When the liquid began bubbling in the pot on the stove, she put everything on a tray and took it out onto the tiny balcony with her laptop.

She checked the state of play with the various projects in which she was involved and responded to a couple of emails. There was one from Christiano, saying what a pleasure it had been to meet her finally, and she wrote back, saying likewise, and that she was glad there'd been time to drop in. Then, she began to plan the week's work. It was necessary to ring Eloisa, but given it was Sunday, it would probably be better to wait until at least mid-morning.

The coffee was good, helping her get back into work mode. But once she'd dealt with the more pressing items, her attention began to wander, and it didn't take long before she found herself thinking over the weekend. God, they'd spent most of Saturday in bed. She'd never done anything like that before. She flushed; it was so *abandoned*. Even now, she trembled when she remembered the things they'd done, and just how wonderful it had been. He was such a thoughtful and sensitive lover.

No, this was no good. She must get down to work. Tomorrow would come all too soon. Anyway, she wouldn't see Edmondo until Wednesday.

How would Adriano feel about seeing her around more, especially with his father? This question was beginning to occupy her mind. He might react badly if he got the idea his mother was being supplanted in his father's affections.

She drained her cup and took the tray back inside. As she washed up, she pictured the little boy's enthusiasm over her gift. She'd established a connection with him, there was no doubt about that, but becoming a substitute mother was altogether different. It was selfish, of course, but not unreasonable to want to pursue her ambitions—and caring for a child of that age could definitely stand in the way.

Of course, the question hadn't arisen yet, but the circumstances of her own childhood meant she was sensitive about this. What might her reaction have been if another man had come into her mother's life? Probably, she would've been jealous—jealous and difficult. Although this was quite different, she was going to have to go carefully because she'd grown fond of the little boy and cared about what he felt.

Her mind still on Adriano, she filled the washing machine and set it going.

She was excited that he was so keen on drawing, with an understanding way beyond what you'd expect for a child of his age. How old was he? Not quite seven, she thought. It was astonishing. He was already producing pictures that looked—well, they looked like real pictures, with an extraordinary level of detail, such as a much older child or an adult might make. Was it possible he had a photographic memory?

At eleven, she rang her colleague.

"How's your mother, Isla? You must have been so

worried."

"She's much better. Thank you, Eloisa, for being such a good friend this week."

"No problem. Anyone would do the same."

"I *was* worried about her...and when I saw her, you know, I couldn't quite believe how bad it looked. But at least, her injuries weren't life-threatening. I'm discovering that she's tough, so I think it's going to be all right. She's left the hospital and is being looked after by her friend. Now, tell me what's going on in the office."

They talked for another twenty minutes, while Isla caught up with the various happenings. Somehow, she managed to avoid saying that she'd arrived back on Friday, but she was sure someone would have seen her and Edmondo together, despite her conviction that she'd scarcely left his bed. And they'd be quite happy to spread the news—it was that kind of town. Used to the anonymity of London, she did find it somewhat claustrophobic but was gradually coming to understand that people's interest could be motivated by kindness, and even that curiosity was no more than that. Not much went on in the little town, so anything out of the ordinary drew people's attention. Discretion was a good idea.

Tommaso was courteous and affable when she spoke to him. Did she feel able to come back this week? She did, she assured him, and brought him up to date on the work she'd already completed, insisting she'd be in the following morning.

Duty done, Isla had no inclination for anything further to do with the office. Instead, she'd give the kitchen and bathroom a thorough clean. She spent a good hour working off her surplus energy, and soon, the flat gleamed and smelled wonderful.

It was still not quite noon, but suddenly aware that she'd eaten scarcely anything over the weekend, she investigated what remained in the fridge. There wasn't much choice beyond hard cheese and week-old tomatoes, which somehow seemed to have survived. It would have to do. In the tiny ice compartment, she discovered some frozen slices of bread, which she defrosted by toasting them before making sandwiches.

When she'd filled a thermos with coffee, she carried it all down into the courtyard, along with a book she'd been meaning to read for a while. The place was deserted. She'd never seen any of the people in the neighboring flats use this garden to sit in, although there was an elderly woman who trimmed and cleared it regularly.

The book was one of a Nicci French series that a friend had given her on her last birthday nearly a year before, with strong assurances that she would love it. She'd brought it with her, somehow imagining she'd have more time for things like reading in Italy. When she read fiction, she liked to settle for several hours, even finishing a whole book in a day, and this seemed like the ideal opportunity to indulge.

Fascinated by the character of Frieda Klein, she was still perched on the iron bench several hours later when the sun disappeared from the courtyard, and she'd grown too cool to be comfortable.

She gathered her things together and went back inside. It was only fiction, of course, but she was touched by the story of the abduction of a small boy and still found herself immersed in it as she climbed the stairs. There was a darkness in Frieda's background. Things happened to her that shouldn't. And that reminded her of the incident in the factory. She must ask Edmondo what he'd done about it.

Chapter 24

Two days later, toward the end of the morning, Isla's mobile rang. It would be a call from the nursery school, probably to confirm they were comfortable with the start date for their job. It wasn't. Instead, there was Edmondo's name on the screen. Her pulse stepping up at the sight, she walked out into the stairwell to take it. But Adriano's bell-like voice rang out, inviting her to dinner.

"Well, that's very kind of you, Adriano,' she said, recovering quickly. "But I—"

"I asked *Papà*, and he said it was a good idea."

"Did he now? In that case, I would like to accept. What time shall I come?"

"*Papà* said half past seven, but if you come earlier, you can teach me how to draw."

"I can teach you some special ways of doing things, but you already know how to draw, Adriano. Nobody needs to teach you. But I *would* like to see what you've been drawing. Would you show me? Shall I come half an hour earlier?"

"Yes, please. Oh—here's *Papà*. I think he wants to talk to you. Good-bye, Signorina Bruni."

There was a clatter as the boy put down the phone, and a moment later, Edmondo was on the line.

"Hello, Isla. Has he persuaded you to come to dinner?"

"That's a very accomplished young man you have there, so I found myself agreeing straight away—but I assure you, I didn't need to be persuaded." She laughed. "I promised I'd be there about seven so we can look over his drawings. Is that okay?"

"I'll see you then, *tesoro mio.*"

She closed her phone and stood there at the top of the stairs, looking out through the glass wall. He'd called her his darling. It was the second time he'd used the endearment. From someone else, the words would denote nothing more than affection, but coming from him, they conveyed an exquisite sweetness that set her heart beating fast. Once again, a stab of desire played havoc with her. God, she was at work, here. Was she really incapable of behaving in a professional manner? She took a couple of deep breaths to calm herself but was sure the ready color would not yet have left her cheeks.

Slowly, she made her way back to her computer station. Eloisa was gazing quizzically across at her, and Isla knew she was dying to ask questions. Well, she'd have to keep them to herself for the time being. She ignored her friend and forced herself to get back to work. There was no time to indulge in any thoughts of Edmondo. Her phone rang again—the firm supplying the wood for a raised dining area she'd designed for a private house in Teramo.

"Impossible to get hold of any, I'm sorry."

Damn, if they didn't have the right wood, it would mean a number of changes to the scheme, which had been based around the dining area. This was a bit of a disaster.

"Surely you can just try another source?"

"Since the pandemic, it's been more and more difficult to get hold of this particular wood—all wood is difficult at the moment. I have a wide range of suppliers as it is, but they all have the same problems and prices are sky-high."

"Okay. Look, I'll come back to you and place a new order when I've had a chance to discuss it with my client."

She called up the client's number, hoping it would be him and not his wife who answered. Carlo was easy-going and open to her suggestions, while Alessandra had very defined ideas about what she wanted. It might prove difficult.

****

"All right," said Eloisa as three o'clock approached. "I'm desperate for a cup of coffee. Coming?"

"Well, I guess I can allow myself half an hour off."

In fact, after the frosty telephone call with Alessandra that morning, she was feeling distinctly wrung out. She'd had to promise to go out to their house early the following day to sort out the problem of the wood and had rearranged two other appointments to fit the visit in. And it didn't sound as if the client was going to make things easy for her.

"Of course, you can," said Eloisa, who was now waiting by her desk. "Everyone else went out to lunch, and you didn't move. And I did notice you hadn't brought in anything to eat. You're not going to keep that figure on glasses of water, you know. A girl has to eat."

"I haven't yet had a chance to go grocery shopping. And I have a lot of work to catch up on."

She must do something about the empty fridge, though. Last night, she'd eaten baked beans on the remaining two slices of the defrosted bread. Eloisa was right, so she shut down her computer and picked up her bag. Down in the square, they chose a table that was out of the direct sun.

"Right, sit down. I'm supplying the coffee, and you're supplying the information."

Isla smiled weakly at her. There was to be no getting out of this.

A pimply boy, in a starched white apron that brushed his ankles and accentuated his skinny frame, came over to take their order. It looked as if the Albertos had taken on a new member of staff in the week she'd been in London.

"Add a cheese panino to that," said Eloisa. And scarcely allowing him time to move away, she said to Isla, "So I'm guessing that was gorgeous, sexy Edmondo phoning you this morning, and that it wasn't work related."

"It was actually his son, Adriano."

"His son! Oh dear, I am reading things wrongly."

Isla sighed. How could she have ever imagined she could keep things to herself? Of course, she couldn't. When she looked at Eloisa, she tried to frown but couldn't help grinning at the same time.

"Ah-ha! Well?"

"Well—you're not so far off. It *was* Edmondo I was speaking to at the end."

"So!" She sat back with satisfaction. "How are things between you? Have you got together with him?"

Isla still felt reluctant about sharing with anyone else, but her friend was waiting for an answer. When none was immediately forthcoming, Eloisa said, "Come on, Isla. You can't pretend there's nothing happening."

The girl's expression was so hopeful Isla burst out laughing. She couldn't believe Eloisa was so invested in someone else's future. How little she seemed to understand about other people.

The coffee and sandwich arrived, giving her a few moments to think about what she was going to say. She was starving and bit straight into the panino. Then taking pity on Eloisa, she said, "Okay, you're right, we have got together."

"And?"

"So that Friday, he invited me to dinner to thank me for—"

"Oh yes—for doing your job! I'm sure."

"Yes, and I was really looking forward to it," said Isla in a hurt tone, "when everything went terribly wrong."

She gave an edited account, pretty much everything about the incident in the factory, but somewhat lacking in detail about the weekend of her return. And she said nothing at all about the time in the airport hotel. She'd been worried, upset, and full of confused desire. That was private.

"That's great, Isla. I think you're just perfect for each other. And how are you getting along with that suave six-year-old? I had to go up to do an inspection on the tower for Leonardo, you know, while you were away, and he followed me around the whole time, prizing information out of me. Did I work with Signorina Bruni? Did I know she was in London? Had Signorina Bruni told me her mother was in hospital? Was Signorina Bruni coming back soon? Was she going to be doing an inspection as well? And quite a bit more along those lines. I can tell you, I began to feel quite jealous."

"Don't be upset—it's all about the drawing. The child's a bit of a whizz. He soaks up information and wants to learn everything. And he thinks I've got something to teach him."

"And Edmondo? No doubt, he thinks you've got something to teach *him*, as well."

"… is very pleased we get on so well." She smiled at Eloisa. "Just so you don't spend the whole of the next twenty-four hours wondering about it, that call was an invitation to dinner tomorrow evening from Adriano. Oh, and yes, his father will be there."

Eloisa sat back, a wide grin spreading across her face, while Isla swallowed the last of the crumbs. Feeling much better, she stood up, stacking their cups on the tray, ready to take them back inside. It would save Signor Alberto the Elder a journey. Then, she remembered the pimply boy and put the tray back down on the table. He could do with the experience.

"Now, I'm going back to the studio, so that Tommaso looks favorably on me next time I have to take time off—which will definitely happen if things don't go smoothly for Mum."

Chapter 25

Supper was a massive plate of salad with ham and boiled eggs, and tiny, salty little anchovies. It looked as if Signora Forni had been baking that day as well, and the fresh bread was delicious. They finished eating but remained at the table, talking a while longer. Three whole days ago on Sunday morning, Edmondo's car had disappeared down the road toward Rome, and Isla hadn't seen him since. She longed to be close to him.

So far this evening, Adriano had kept her firmly anchored in the present as he chattered about anything and everything, but he'd gone very quiet now. He was probably hoping no one would notice him still sitting there, up way beyond his bedtime. He was beginning to get that droopy look, along with an absolute determination to keep his eyes open. It was a battle he was going to lose.

"Time for you to go to bed," Edmondo said, getting to his feet a minute later.

"No, *Papà*. I want to do some more drawing."

"Adriano!"

They'd already covered several sheets of paper with triangles as she sought to demonstrate, by moving the focal point, how perspective worked on the drawing of a house. It was enough for today. The boy really did need to go to bed and besides, it would be great to have his father to herself for a while.

"We can do more drawing another day," she said. "I'm sure I'll be able to come back some time to do that. People don't do their best work when they're tired."

"That's a good idea, Adriano. Come on, okay?"

"Oka-ay!"

Reluctantly, the boy took his father's hand, and when good nights had been said, they left the room. Edmondo popped his head back around the door.

"Don't go anywhere. I'll be back in a few minutes."

Isla had enjoyed the child's company, but now she looked forward to his father turning his full attention on her.

She got up from the table and stacked the plates. Then, she wandered around the room, admiring a charcoal drawing of the original tower. She bent toward it, trying to see the signature, and realized it had been done by Edmondo. So that's where the boy's talent came from. Beside it hung a small, framed photograph of the same scene.

She continued around the room. Adriano's new sketchbook lay on a side table by the window, and now she turned the pages carefully. Some of the drawings were quite childish but had strong, confident lines, and one or two really captured the spirit of a scene. How clever he was, so observant.

The door opened softly behind her and clicked shut. She continued looking at the book as if she had not heard. She wanted to leave the next move to him, and she waited in delicious anticipation. Edmondo came across, placing his hands on her shoulders. A shudder ran through her whole body. Then he turned her around to face him and gazed into her eyes.

"I've been waiting for this moment all evening."

He bent his head and began a gentle kiss. It was sweet and warm and innocent, the light pressure of his lips drawing her in. But the way he was stroking the hyper-sensitive area at the back of her neck was knowing. Little tingles coursed through her, and soon tension built and the beginning of a desperate hunger for him. He'd learned so quickly how to get a reaction from her. Now, he dropped his hands to her waist and increased the intensity of the kiss, pulling her in close, until he seemed to possess her entirely. Then, he moved away, taking her hand, and he led her over to the sofa.

"Shall we have a drink? I'm going to have a Campari. What about you?"

"For me, too."

With Adriano seated at the table, they'd drunk only water during dinner. A moment later, Edmondo lowered himself onto the couch beside her and handed her a glass.

"*Salute!*"

"*Salute*, Edmondo. Your good health!"

She took a sip, but the drink was strong, and she pulled a face.

"Would you like some soda with that?"

"I think so. I don't drink anything much other than wine—and sometimes gin. I'm not used to it."

"You see, I don't know even a simple thing like that about you. We have a lot of ground to cover."

She gave him the glass, and he stood up. As if on cue, his phone rang. He took it out of his pocket, looking mildly annoyed, but then, his expression changed, and he put down the glass.

"Sorry, it's the surveillance company. I'll have to take it."

He was already on his way out of the room and his voice came to her from the kitchen, but she couldn't make out what he was saying. Then he was back, his face wearing an unaccustomed frown.

"You set up surveillance?" she asked. "On the factory?"

"Yes. The attack on you was not the first incident. A few weeks ago, we had two deliveries together and had to store some of the materials outside in the small portacabin."

"Someone stole them?"

"No, but they broke in and the whole place was turned upside down. It was deliberate vandalism, and quite a lot of it was unusable after. Then there was the graffiti. The board at the entrance was daubed with red paint last week and I had to replace it. And two days later, someone broke into the main factory."

"That's terrible, Edmondo. I can see why you had to get help."

"The attack on you was definitely an escalation. I couldn't ignore it any longer. A person who's prepared to knock you on the head and tamper with the machines, and possibly endanger lives, isn't some small-time thief—as the police have been at pains to point out. So we've put in cameras and alarms with a link to the security guys."

"What's happened?"

"Someone's just tripped an alarm. Two guards went out to the factory straight away, but there was no sign of anyone."

"Have they got video?"

"Yes, they're emailing it. I told them to send it straight to me and not waste time viewing it themselves, because I'm much more likely to recognize anyone carrying out such a concentrated campaign against me. Do you want to see? I am sorry, *cara,* it's spoiling our evening."

"Yes, but it's important to you. Let's have a look."

He crossed over to a door on the left of the fireplace and led her into a room at the back of the house. The windows were uncurtained, and as the light went on, they became black mirrors, stark in the white walls.

A computer occupied a workstation that looked like the set-up they had in the studio. Presumably this was where he did his designing. On the wall facing the windows were bookshelves with a huge assortment of books. She spotted *Per Una Storia della Geofisica Italiana*, and another volume on earthquakes, titled *Prevedere l'imprevedibile*—the loose translation must be something like foreseeing the unforeseeable; maybe how to predict a forthcoming earthquake? Mmm, living here would create an interest in such things, that was true. A book lying closed on the desk was named *Ingegnera degli Acquiferi.*

"Give me a moment or two to set this up." Edmondo sat at a desk, opened a laptop, and fired it up.

She looked at the other shelves and lusted after an entire row of books on Roman and pre-Roman history in Italy. She'd tried reading up before she came to the country, just a little information in preparation for her six months' exchange, nothing of this standard. Her heart gave a tug as she remembered that it would soon be October and nearly three months had passed already.

"Here we are."

Pulling up a chair, she sat down beside him, and he put his arm along her shoulders, pulling her close. "I'm sorry."

"This is important, Edmondo. I understand."

The section of video had been wound back to twenty minutes before the triggering of the alarm.

"I'm going to watch this in real time. Maybe I'll be able to identify who it is."

The first ten minutes passed slowly, grainy black and white images showing the whole of the forecourt and carpark. Apart from the odd branch waving in the breeze or an animal setting off a security light as it scuttled by, there was nothing of interest.

"It's all from this one angle?"

"No, he's sent video from all the cameras."

It looked as if it was going to be a long, slow evening, and not much fun. But then, always observant, Isla said, "Stop it a moment. Wind that backward a little."

Edmondo did as she said, staring at the screen. "What have you seen?"

"Now, go slowly forward." Something had caught her eye on the far right. "Okay, play the last five seconds again." Knowing what to expect, she easily saw the movement this time. "There! Someone's standing right at the corner, but then he moves away and disappears. I don't know how this works. Are you able to look at the footage from the camera on that side of the building and start it from around the same time? It says 21.20 on this. It might save some time?"

There appeared to be security lights around the whole building, but the next camera showed a much dimmer area than the carpark. They watched as the film unfolded, straining their eyes, and starting to think what they'd seen was an anomaly. Then, suddenly, two men appeared on the screen, back view only. Isla grabbed Edmondo's arm, caught up in the drama of the moment. One of the men crouched down to work at the lock on a small side door. It took two minutes before the lockpicker stood up and the two men entered the building.

"As easy as that," said Edmondo. "So much for security."

They looked at each other, wondering what was going to happen next. Seconds later, the door was flung back and both men came running out, oblivious to whether they could be seen by the cameras. In two seconds, they had vanished.

"*Dio mio!*"

"You know who it is?"

"I do." He was looking troubled. "Not the one who opened the lock, the other one. I guess the interior alarm went off, and that's why they came out so quickly."

"Who is it, Edmondo?"

"It's my cousin. Second cousin, I should say."

"Your cousin! But why would he break into your factory?"

"Why wouldn't he? He's good for nothing, a waster. And he's obviously teamed up with another just like him."

"Is he jealous of you or something?"

"Maybe, but the real reason will be that he believes that by living up here in Fortezza, I've done him out of his inheritance. I don't even know how he found out."

"But you bought the place—from someone else altogether."

"Yes, but Giacco doesn't recognize that. His grandfather was the third brother—how do you say it?—*la pecora nera*?"

"The black sheep?"

"Black sheep, yes. He vanished when my granddad went to Rome. But by the time I was at school, they were in Rome as well, living in the same area as us, and Giacco and I were in the same class at school."

"Ah! And now, he's back and he's claiming his rights. Is that it?"

There was plenty of potential for trouble in that scenario.

"Yes—except that he doesn't actually have any rights. He's quite mad. Even when we were kids, he did crazy things, always in trouble at school, and nearly got himself killed a couple of times."

"So what does he base this claim on?"

"He thinks that when the house was sold, the money was shared with my father, that there was some sort of deal, and his father was excluded because of his behavior. And basically, it's not fair. And conveniently forgetting that several generations have passed, he believes I have the money and have used it to buy back the land. His heritage."

"Not true?"

"Definitely not true. He's completely delusional. When he settled his debts, my great-uncle, Simon, hardly had enough to live on, and he died a poor man. My dad even arranged and paid for his funeral at the end, so if anyone's owed money, it's my father. Simon certainly didn't give us any."

How strange families were. This went way back and seemed to be based on a lot of pride, resentment, and greed. It threw her own family problems into perspective. Not that it made her feel any more warmly toward her father, wherever he was.

"So what are you going to do, Edmondo? Report him to the police?"

"I don't know. He's family. I need to think."

"He may be family—but he can't be allowed to damage your business and hit people over the head. What if he came here?"

Edmondo looked up, startled.

"I'm just asking the question, since he seems to believe he has the right. And he sounds as if he could be dangerous. Think about Adriano."

"I know."

He was silent for a long moment. They were sitting close together in front of the computer. He pulled her toward him and caressed her cheek with his lips. "Darling, I'm going to have to cut short our evening. I'm so sorry."

"It's very disappointing, very." It was, but she smiled to let him know she was just teasing and kissed him. Of course, it was disappointing, but it couldn't be helped. "It's not a problem. You have to sort this out. What are you going to do?"

"I need to tell Signora Forni that I won't be here tonight and she's in charge of Adriano. Then, I'll take you home and drive on into Teramo. But first, I have to ring the security guys. They should patrol there until I arrive." Edmondo was looking really upset.

Isla slid her arms around him and held him close. "Get onto them now—and try not to worry. We'll work something out."

Chapter 26

Falesia Bianca. White cliff or maybe white crag—
it sounded so romantic. And apparently, it had some of
the best climbing in the region. Below the famous
rocks, and about five kilometers away from Fortezza,
was a small town.

It was Friday afternoon, and people at the studio
were making plans for the weekend. Isla was only half
listening, intent on finishing an email, but then
Leonardo said, "We're going climbing, Isla. Would you
like to come with us? Eloisa said you've done some
mountaineering in Wales. I hadn't realized."

"Yes, I have—nothing very difficult, though. I
don't seem to have found much time for climbing since
I came here, but I do enjoy it."

Which was bizarre, really, when she was living in
this wonderful mountainous region. Why shouldn't she
go with them? Edmondo was down in Teramo until late
today, probably until the early hours of the morning,
and again most of the day tomorrow, so she wouldn't
be seeing him for a while. Besides handling a rushed
order at the factory, he'd started trying to track down
his cousin, Giacomo, and was determined to talk to him
and bring him to his senses. He'd said he might be able
to sort something out. Something that would keep him
out of their lives for good. This had sounded vague, but
Edmondo was never vague. He probably just didn't

want her worrying about things. So she'd asked him how he was going to manage that.

"I'm thinking of hiring an investigator and working with him."

"What—a sort of private eye?"

"Yes, these people know how to go about it. He's coming in to see me next Friday afternoon, and we're going to work out a strategy."

"Take care, Edmondo. Your cousin sounds quite wild—dangerous even."

He'd just kissed her and said, "Don't worry about me. I'll be careful. And you know, I could even help him buy a place, if that's what he wants."

"Let's hope that'll do it, then," she said, but as she learned more about Giacomo, she was less sure he would be placated by such an offer, obsessed as he was with the tower. Was it possible there was even a streak of insanity there?

They'd talked a little longer. She was still worried about his proposed search for his cousin, but she couldn't do anything to change things. They'd kissed a little more then, and by the time he'd dropped her off, she was in a heightened state of arousal, damning the crazy cousin to hell for disrupting their lives.

"I promise you we'll go for our dinner down on the coast on Sunday."

That was something to look forward to, but there was nothing she had planned for Saturday. And she really would enjoy a day in the mountains.

"I'd like that, Leonardo. I have no equipment with me, though."

"No problem. We can easily help out—as long as you have your boots with you."

"Yes, I brought them, but that's all."

She'd made a point of searching out high-quality boots before leaving England, hoping to get some decent climbing, but had only used them a couple of times, walking with Eloisa and Giorgio. Eloisa had made it clear she was no climber, so they hadn't really been tested.

"Great! So we meet in the square here at half nine tomorrow. Make sure you bring lunch and plenty of bottled water."

Later, when Edmondo rang her, she told him what she intended to do the next day.

"That's great, Isla. They'll work you hard. Tommaso told me how keen they are. Have fun, and I'll see you on Sunday, my sweet. Take care!"

"How's Adriano settling in?"

The boy was just completing his first week at his new school.

"So far, it's sounding good. He's made a friend who lives in the town near where you'll be climbing. Carlotta says he's invited for the whole day tomorrow, so she's volunteered to take him up there during the morning, and I'll pick him up later on."

"You really are lucky to have her. Isn't that into her free time?"

"Yes, but she took time off today, shopping in Teramo. She told me she won't be going home this weekend. And yes, I do appreciate it."

After a few minutes, Isla closed her phone. That sounded positive for Adriano. Enjoying his new school would depend a lot on making friends.

Chapter 27

Isla was early again—she couldn't seem to help herself. But she'd locked up, and there was no point in going back into the flat. Anyway, it was pleasant enough to hang about in the square. She wandered across to the bakery and looked into the window, where there was an interesting display. Signor Pirovano had just taken over the business, and not only had he introduced new lines, but he was now selling a selection of sweets. There, in the center on a stand, was a box in the form of a racing car, containing a variety of candies and chocolates. She decided to get it for Adriano.

She glanced around, but there was no sign of her colleagues. She could always hear cars coming up the road from the Teramo direction, as they had to change gear at the corner, and just now, the little town was very quiet; she had enough time to buy the racing-car pack. Five minutes later, having managed to escape the enthusiastic baker's conversation only by announcing the arrival of her lift, she hurried out, pushing her purchase into a side pocket of her rucksack. Later, she'd bury it at the bottom of the bag in case the chocolate melted.

A car appeared at the far end of the square, one of those with about seven seats. It pulled up in front of her, Leonardo opened the back door, and she slid in beside him. He introduced her to the driver, Davide, and Jessica, the woman sitting next to him, neither of whom she recognized.

"We're meeting the others up there at the carpark," Davide said. "They're coming from the north."

****

Edmondo was right about working hard. These people were very fit and serious about their sport. Leonardo said he climbed most weekends, and if he'd known she was interested, he'd have invited her before.

"To be honest, I've had a lot to do, so don't worry about that."

She enjoyed the challenges of abseiling down a sheer cliff and crawling under an overhang, which almost proved too much for her. Of course, she was roped up, so it wasn't particularly dangerous, but she'd done this before and knew from the experience that there was nothing pleasant about losing grip and dangling from the end of a rope with a huge drop below. It hurt, and she had no desire to look stupid. Thank goodness she didn't make a fool of herself.

It seemed like hours later that someone shouted, "*Pranzo!*" It was going to be a bit of a late lunch as it was already after three. They scrambled up the last stretch to a bluff which overlooked the town, talking about a much more demanding spot farther along, where they could finish the day's climbing. Davide had tried it out a couple of weeks earlier.

It had grown hot for the time of year, she thought, remembering the distinctly chilly temperature back in England—but Leonardo said it was about normal. She walked around, allowing the air to cool her, and felt some movement in the ground—or was the heat making her dizzy? No one else seemed to have noticed, a lively conversation going on, now that everyone had settled to eat.

So she sat down and chewed on the corner of a cheese sandwich, not really hungry.

"You know," she said to Jessica, who sat next to her, "I could swear that building down there, the nearest one with the tower, actually moved."

"Might be heat haze."

It wasn't that hot, surely.

Then there was a shudder, and a few small rocks came tumbling down either side of where they sat. They all looked at each other, reserving judgment, but when it happened again a minute later, this time with much more force, they sprang to their feet.

"Quick, we have to get off the mountain."

Leonardo was already stuffing his possessions into a rucksack.

"Get your things together." He threw a coil of rope to Isla. "Here, you take this. We're going down. It's an earthquake."

She slung it over her shoulder and followed him. It took twenty minutes for them to arrive on the outskirts of the little town, and by the time they'd done so, there'd been several, much more severe tremors, and rubble blocked their end of the main road.

"We need to get to the cars and leave."

Now, Isla could hear her phone ringing. Where had she put it? She found it in the top pocket of her sack. Edmondo.

"Where are you?"

"Falesia Bianca, on the edge of the town."

"But you're all right?"

"Yes. We just got off the mountain."

"How bad is it?"

"Bad, I think. I can see a collapsed building just ahead."

"That's where Adriano is."

Oh God, of course. She'd forgotten.

"Are you in a safe place?" His anxiety came through in the way his voice was rising.

Perhaps she could help. "Edmondo, what's the address? Maybe I can get him, and we can wait somewhere for you."

"No, you need to get out while you can. Go with the others. You have no experience of earthquakes."

"But maybe I can help, get him out of the town long before you can get here."

"I want you safe, Isla. The family will take care of him. Stay away."

"Edmondo, I'm not going to do that. I'll find him. Give me that address."

"Okay, okay. But keep away from buildings. I mean that—stay out of the way." He gave her the address and cut the connection.

Chapter 28

No tremors had been felt in Teramo. Edmondo had heard nothing about the earthquake until a machine operator working overtime on an urgent order in the factory caught it on the radio.

"Have you heard the news, *signore*? Another earthquake—in Falesia this time. Isn't that up near where you live, *signore*?"

Edmondo's heart slammed against his chest wall. Adriano! He had to get him out. And then he remembered that's exactly where Isla was climbing. In seconds, his world was turned upside down. Scarcely stopping to think, he swept everything off his desk, locking the sensitive information in the safe and then securing his office. How could this have happened? It was the first time he'd let the boy out without Carlotta or himself, and there he was, right in the middle of all the chaos.

First, he had to check what was happening. But the family's landline wasn't answering, and he didn't have a mobile number. He rang twice more, and now he was getting an out-of-order tone. Either that was all it was, or the house had been impacted and the line was damaged.

The address where Carlotta had dropped off Adriano that morning was in the middle of a long row of town houses. Which should make it relatively risk-free in an earthquake because the buildings were close-packed and should support one another. Or that's what he'd tell himself. He took a few deep breaths then. It was no use panicking.

Finally, he spoke to Isla. At least she was safe, and he'd told her not to go anywhere near buildings. Most injuries and fatalities during an earthquake were caused by falling masonry, not by the earthquake itself. If people stayed out in the open, they'd feel nothing more than the tremors, unless they were very unlucky. He just hoped she'd take the warning seriously. If he lost her now...if he lost either of them...no, he mustn't think like that. He hurried back into the factory area.

"I have to leave straight away," he told the techie. "My son is up there in Falesia. Lock up when you're done."

And he ran out to his car. He'd change it for the truck he kept up at the house in Fortezza. Two minutes later, he was on the road.

It was a leisurely Saturday afternoon for most people, and he was able to drive fast to the outskirts of Teramo, but then, the narrow mountain road with its sharp corners and switchbacks forced him to slow down. Desperate for news, he turned on the radio. A report was coming through about people being evacuated and then about the collapse of the front wall of the church. It was a building that had stood for more than six hundred years, the announcer said, as if the earthquake was likely to respect that. He tried to go a little faster.

Swapping to the truck in Fortezza took just a few minutes. He always had safety equipment on board. Most people living up here took the same approach, knowing how easily emergencies could arise in the mountains.

He rang the number again, and then Isla's phone. No response. Why was the family not ringing him to let him know that Adriano was safe? Was Isla okay? The questions were whirling around in his head. He was halfway there when he tried again, but he'd lost the signal. Of course. It would only pick up again just outside the town. He vowed he'd get a satellite phone. Why hadn't he done it before?

Suddenly, there were blue lights flashing behind him. He pulled in as close as he could to the side of the road, and an ambulance and a fire truck roared past. If anything was likely to increase his fear, this was it. Things were serious.

Fifteen minutes later, he arrived at the edge of the town and was met by chaos. He steered around rocks that had bounced down the mountain onto the road. Oh God, what had happened to Adriano? Where was Isla? He skirted another obstruction but immediately saw a pile of rubble farther on, and the road was blocked by a barrier. It was manned by a policeman who told him to go back to where he'd come from.

"My son…I have to find him. He's only six."

"We'll find him, *signore*. Leave it to us. Leave it to the professionals."

The policeman's job was to keep the spectators out, but Edmondo knew in circumstances like this, everyone who was able to had to pitch in and do their best. He certainly wasn't going to leave it to others.

He'd noticed a layby a short distance back, and now, he began to reverse. There was enough space for three vehicles and just enough for him to turn around, which he did, before tucking himself in at the front. If rocks came down the mountain and crashed onto the vehicle, there was nothing he could do about it, but it was of no importance under the circumstances.

His heart was beating uncomfortably hard as, in a fever of impatience, he turned off the engine and picked up his emergency backpack. Where were his old trousers and walking boots? Trying to tamp down his panic, he searched around in the back of the truck, finding them exactly where he'd left them, rolled neatly and stashed in a corner in a container. Ripping off his suit and shoes, he changed. Finally, he grabbed a fleece and gloves and stuffed them into the pack. He wouldn't be coming back to the vehicle until he knew the score.

Then, taking a coil of rope, he slung it over his shoulder and set off.

The policeman would stop him, and they'd waste time arguing, when he should be searching for his son and for Isla. He looked up the mountain and finally spotted the goat track he'd known must exist. There! A faint line ran parallel to the road, way above him, only just visible in the gathering dusk. In moments, he hauled himself up and then loped along, anxious to get into the center as quickly as possible. As the track swung around above the town, there were further tremors, and he heard the rumble of toppling masonry. And screams. *Merda!* What was happening? Please God, let them be all right. Why wasn't Isla in touch? His spirits plummeted. The people he cared for most in the world were in this town, as its buildings split apart and crashed down.

He'd already lived through one earthquake in that region and knew from experience how fragile the human body was, how little defense it had against blocks of stone. But last time, the people he loved hadn't been involved.

A long way below, he could now see the barrier with the policeman on duty. Almost immediately after this sighting, he found a branching path on the right that led down to the town. It obviously wasn't only goats that used this track.

He began his descent. The route was hazardous, and the coming darkness was accelerating, forcing him to slow down. There was no point in risking a fall. As he made it into one of the back streets, a flurry of rain hit him, the drops freezing on his face. He turned quickly toward the center.

Chapter 29

A short while earlier, Isla had passed by the same spot. Her climbing companions had piled into the two cars in the carpark and headed straight over the mountain. They intended to make a circuit around to Aquila to avoid the blockage they rightly assumed would have occurred in Falesia. No one would be likely to get through the town for many hours, if at all that day. Only Leonardo had elected to stay with her.

"I'm a good climber. Maybe together, we can help someone," he said. "Everyone's needed in a situation like this, especially people who know what they're doing."

It was good that he cared enough to take the risk, and Isla was grateful for the company, having little idea of what to expect. She told him the address where she hoped to find Adriano.

"Okay, I have a good idea of where that is. Let's go there first and get the little fellow, and you could wait with him in an open space, far from any buildings."

"Thanks, Leonardo. It's good of you to help."

"*Prego.*"

He led her farther in by small side streets, avoiding police and other officials. A lot of the houses were shut up, and people were hurrying away from the center as they went toward it. That felt scary, but she could not imagine doing anything else but looking for the boy and getting him out. Even as they walked, there were further tremors.

They emerged onto the main street. The buildings here were undamaged, and no vehicles passed them. Occasionally, they saw a police car and ducked out of sight.

"We keep to the middle of the road. If you see any movement, run," said Leonardo. They passed a tall house, the front wall of which literally began to craze before their eyes. They sped up and, a few seconds later, heard the building crash down to the ground behind them. Nowhere was being spared.

"Here we are," he said. "It should be around here."

They were looking up a narrow street. An official orange-and-white-striped barrier had been placed across it because a crater had opened up halfway along. Balanced right on the edge was a car, and a police officer was trying to restrain a man. He was probably the owner of the vehicle and wanted to be allowed to move it. The situation had descended into a physical struggle and the vehicle owner, who was twice the size of the policeman, appeared to be winning.

They turned away from the strange tableau. People did crazy things in circumstances like these. Why would you risk your life for the sake of a battered old car? What about helping people who'd got trapped?

Leonardo looked around.

"There's a stretch of wall all the way around this side of the town because it's built on the very edge of the mountain. We can't be far from it here. I think these houses may even back onto it."

"You think we could get to the house from behind?"

"Well, it's possible. Why don't you check that? I'll go behind the houses on the opposite side of the street and work my way around the crater. Maybe I can get to it from the far end."

They parted quickly, and Isla took the first street on the left, an ancient thoroughfare so narrow, she could hold out her arms and touch the walls at either side. This certainly wasn't the sort of place Edmondo had suggested she wait in, but it meandered between ancient houses that leaned comfortably against one another, so there was a good chance they wouldn't fall, even if shaken by the tremors.

A minute later, the street ended at a T-junction, facing the town wall, a structure that was double her height. She turned right and now jogged along the narrow, curving, paved lane at the back of the buildings. It was growing dark, but ahead, a knot of people became visible in the gloom. What was going on? They were staring up at the row of houses, and there was a lot of shouting and gesticulating. So something had happened. She hurried toward them as a greasy drizzle began to fall.

Isla sucked in a breath, shocked by the extent of the devastation. This was beyond appalling. The whole back wall of several houses had disappeared, and then, the rest of those buildings had lurched out toward the town wall. You could see straight in, as if they were dolls' houses, all the rooms and items of furniture revealed. The floor of a bedroom in the central one had slid down toward the distraught group, but a wide gap yawned between the slanting floor and the remains of the back wall of the house—which was now reduced to just below head height. How on earth had that happened? Several very elderly men, a heavily pregnant woman, and a scattering of children were gathered in the narrow lane.

Isla had a sinking feeling as she hurried up to the group, knowing exactly what she was going to see. Two small boys were at the far side of the bedroom, high above, and they looked terrified. Fear smote her in the chest when she recognized Adriano. With one hand, he held onto the handle of a door in the far wall, and with the other, he was clutching the wrist of the second child, who was lying on the floor, about to slide down toward the abyss. Tears gathered in her eyes. They were six years old, and they looked so small and vulnerable. They had the courage, but did they have the strength to hang on and keep each other safe?

The woman said Enzo had gone off for help, and now he could be seen returning with a plank which he placed to bridge the gap. As Isla studied the scene, he began to encourage the children to slide down and cross it to safety, but she could see straightaway that they were never going to be able to do that. If Adriano let go of his friend's hand, the way the floor was tilted meant the boy would not head naturally toward the group but toward the gaping space. Something had to be done. She worked it out. It was going to be up to her.

"No, I can't," said Adriano, not letting go. "He'll fall."

"Hang on," Isla said. "I'll try to bring you down."

Everyone turned to look at her. Who was this newcomer who thought she could solve the problem? But they were desperate, and any help was welcome. The group parted to let her through.

She was still carrying the rope she'd brought down

the mountain with her. She knotted one end securely around her waist and handed the other to Enzo, who seemed to have more of a clue than the others.

"Get this tied around something—that lamp post over there looks strong enough—so that, if I fall, I can get back out again."

She was trying not to think about the other possibility—that she might not be able to get out. She was a reasonably good climber, but this wasn't rock. The vinyl-covered floor was smooth and now slippery with rain and would give her no purchase.

A bed in the corner of the room began a slow journey diagonally down the slope, its legs ripping at the floor covering, and the group gave a collective gasp. It came to rest partially over the gap.

"Is this your son, with Adriano?" Isla asked the woman.

"Yes, Marco. They were just playing…" She broke into tears and began to wail.

"Please, signora, calm yourself. We don't want to frighten the boys. We have to be strong because they need to feel this is going to work."

The woman fell silent, but tears continued to course down her cheeks. Her hand went to her bump and rested there, reassuring the unborn child, or maybe just herself. The ground shuddered.

Choosing the simplest language she knew, Isla explained to the men what she wanted them to do. She hoped she'd made sense. Then she climbed up onto the broken house wall. She didn't look down and she didn't hesitate, or she wouldn't have found the courage to do it. She jumped the gap, rather than using the wonky plank, and landed lightly, immediately running up the slope. Thank God for the new boots; they really did have a good grip. She positioned herself on an exposed wooden floorboard which looked relatively dry, all the time talking to the boys, reassuring them, telling them what she was going to do.

She'd deal with the smaller boy first. He was in a more precarious position, and it didn't look as if Adriano could hang onto him much longer. Right as she had that thought, the child slipped from his friend's grasp and grabbed wildly at a cot which had now begun its own slow move downward. Isla flung herself to one side and managed to get hold of his arm. She dragged him to his feet, and a moment later, they heard the furniture crashing down into the hole. Isla ignored it. She pulled a few loops of rope up toward her so that she could pay it out gradually, and then she wound the rope several times around him and snapped a carabiner into place to hold the cradle she'd formed. The loop should give him something firm to grip, so he wouldn't slip.

"Hold on to that and don't let go, whatever happens. Understand?"

His eyes big and luminous in the murk, the child nodded solemnly.

"Even if you fall, we'll pull you up. *Ma non mollare la corda, capisci?* That's your job, to hang on. Don't let go. Have you got that?" Again, he nodded. "Now, start walking backward, fast as you can, down toward the road."

Her commands were calm and firm, and the boy didn't question anything. There was no time for more. She had to get Adriano off as well.

The old house was creaking, as if to remind her how dangerous it was, and how little time was left.

She looked up and said with a smile, "Hang on, Adriano."

Then she turned once more to the other child. "Is that your granddad down there?"

"*Sì, mio nonno.*"

"Well, don't worry. He'll catch you when you reach the bottom of the slope. Just hold on tightly and walk backward. You can do that, can't you?"

"*Sì,* signora."

She trusted to the grip of her boots, braced herself, and paid out the rope. He was a slight child, no weight at all, but it seemed to take forever before he got to the plank. All the time, he was looking up, seeking reassurance.

"That's right. Don't stop. Granddad's right there behind you."

A moment later, eager hands grasped the child and pulled him to safety.

As soon as the weight was gone from the rope, Isla continued up the slope to where Adriano clung to a doorknob, snapping off her helmet.

"Hello, Signorina Bruni," he said.

"You're a very brave boy, Adriano," she said, a lump in her throat. "Now, you saw what Marco did, didn't you? I want you to do exactly the same."

Even as she spoke, she could feel a tiny tremor beginning. She clipped the helmet on his head. There was no time left. Repeating the whole process with the rope, she pulled him around, just as she'd done with the other boy, forcing herself to take the time to do it properly, aware of the increasing movement of the building. Adriano was a bigger child, so now, she formed a loop to anchor herself to a sturdy-looking bracket fixed in the wall, so that she could take his weight while he made his way backward down the slope. She'd only use it if she began to slip, because she couldn't be sure it would hold her.

"Hold on tight!"

Everything was wet now, and the rain was increasing. Adriano was determined, but the slippery surface was making things difficult. Then, halfway down, the house gave a further shudder and lurched sideways. Her heart thudded hard, and she almost leapt toward him as he lost his footing, but she restrained herself because there was nothing to be gained by doing it, and she had faith in him. Things settled down again. He was on his knees but still clinging to the rope. Her heart was beating so hard, it almost choked her.

"Well done! Well done! That's right, try to stand again if you can."

Finally, the crowd grabbed the child and hauled him across the gap. She heaved a sigh of relief, and ready to follow him, she unhooked the loop from the wall.

Then, the house lurched again and threw Isla across the floor. She rolled away from the group, tumbled over the broken edge, and fell into blackness.

Chapter 30

Isla stopped screaming when the rope bit into her skin and knocked the breath out of her. As she'd gone over the edge, she'd thrown up her hands and grabbed the rope, taking her weight on her arms, but still it slipped through her fingers and tightened around her waist. She let go with one hand and tried pushing her fingers inside the rope loop to loosen it, but she couldn't. It was so painful. She'd been frightened about the abseiling—and how stupid that was. That was just playing, but there was nothing remotely fun about this. How long was she going to be able to hang here?

Lumps of masonry were still falling, objects hitting and scratching her. And she didn't have her helmet. At first, it seemed totally dark, but light entered through tiny cracks high above her, though not enough to gain any idea of what was around her. Screams from outside faded into the distance and then stopped altogether, leaving a thundering silence. Did that mean if she shouted again, they'd not be able to hear her?

But the pain around her waist was growing, and she had to do something about it. She hauled herself up a little farther and tried wrapping the rope around her arms like she'd seen in circus acts, which allowed her to breathe more easily, though the rough surface of the cord added another layer of pain. Then, she struck out with her feet, searching for something on which she could stand, and the movement set her swinging from side to side. This was terrifying. If the people on the surface didn't gradually pay out some more of the rope to allow her to land somewhere, she would die.

The minutes went by, and she shouted periodically. There was no way she could just hang there with the rope gradually crushing her waist. Her arm muscles were already cracking with the strain, and the pain was sheer torture. The more she wriggled around, the worse it got. If she'd been a more experienced climber, she might have fixed the rope in a better way in the first place. But there hadn't been time to think, and she'd gone with instinct—to tether herself and then get the boys to safety.

Forcing herself to calm down and maintaining her grip on the rope, she reached out carefully with her left foot, and something clunked against her toe, some hard object, an edge that was about on a level with her knees. And it wasn't moving.

She began to swing gently, pendulum-wise. If only she could work out how to get on top of it. She was nearly there, so close, and twice she managed it—but twice, trying to get upright, she slid off again. Finally, she swung aggressively at it and clanged into an enormous frying pan suspended from a hook on the wall. She grabbed it, teetering for a moment, and then she righted herself. All right, that was an improvement.

The surface on which she now stood was shallow and uneven, and she guessed it to be a kitchen worktop. Allowing her feet to take her weight took the pressure off and brought indescribable relief. She succeeded in loosening the rope around her waist by a tiny amount.

"Help! Help! I'm in a kitchen," she shouted, but

the words bounced around her and no one answered. Who knew if they could hear her out there? "*In una cucina. Sono qui.*"

The space muffled her words, and then came silence again. Okay, that wasn't going to work. More masonry must have fallen, blocking the sound. She'd try to deal with that in a minute, but she'd had a much more worrying thought: what if something fell on her directly? She touched a sore spot on her arm, and her fingers came away wet.

Reaching the point of desperation, she felt the rope suddenly slacken. The people outside must finally have realized they needed to let it go slack. And then they'd tie it back to the lamppost—at least, she hoped they would. Guided by the rope, they would have a fair idea of where she was. Anyway, somebody was thinking about the situation, imagining what might be happening below the rubble. *Grazie, Enzo.* People knew she was here, and she had to be grateful for that.

She forced herself to take deep, slow breaths as she crouched on the top of the kitchen worktop and thought out her next move.

If she sat, she might be able to slide down to the floor and find a spot where she'd be sheltered—if any of the floor remained. Gingerly, she lowered herself. Okay, her feet were now on the floor. There was a list to it, as if she were on a gentle slope, but it held her weight. It was time to explore.

Of course, they'd do their best to get her out, she knew that. Of course they would, but it could take a long time, and the house might disintegrate further. If something hit her head, it could cause serious damage. This was a horrible thought, and she wanted to be sick.

It was far too easy to imagine it as a possibility. But it was no use panicking. Instead, she had to work out how to get through this.

Another tremor and her foot slipped. She was hanging in space again and had fallen at least half her own height. Once again, the rope cinched tight, and she cried out in pain. She couldn't keep on letting this happen. Now that miserable little piece of worktop was looking like an oasis in the desert—and she had to get back to it. She hauled herself rapidly up the rope and again managed to wind it around one of her arms, knowing she had to move quickly. Swinging now by one arm, she repeated her earlier technique with the frying pan and finally managed to scramble back up onto the counter.

Isla was bruised and battered and terrified half to death. She was shaking by the time she'd completed her maneuver and wanted to cry, could even feel the sob rising in her throat. But there was no point in being miserable. She fished a tissue out of her pocket and wiped some of the grit and dust from her face. That was better. Right, think of solutions instead of dwelling on how hopeless things were. She had to find a place of safety. Yes, that was a good idea: she should search the room for some large object or a piece of furniture that might protect her. Only this time, she'd avoid that bit of floor over to her right.

Things had gone quiet, and the tremors had stopped. No more falling masonry. Even the trickle of rubble had ceased, so now was the moment to have a look around. But this time she'd use her head. With more slack in the rope now, she set about retying it around her legs and waist to form a proper harness, just in case she found herself suspended again. This made her feel much more in control, and she climbed down.

The safest place was going to be close to the walls, but very slowly, she ventured away, worried about another hole in the floor, or that maybe she'd hit her head and knock herself out. Yeah, okay, it could happen—but she couldn't just sit there, waiting for the next lump of concrete to land on her.

Ah, there *was* something. She ran her hand along a hard edge. It was a chunky old wooden table, perfect for what she had in mind. But she had the sense of a gaping void lying just beyond it. There was no evidence for this, just the feeling, and it terrified her to such an extent that, for a while, she couldn't bring herself to move forward. No, don't go there. Use your common sense.

She stretched out a hand, and very gently, she pulled at the table. It stuck for a moment and then moved slowly toward her, upward across the rucked-up tiles of the floor. If she dragged it right up to the wall, maybe she could wedge it in place between the cupboard and the corner and it would give her a small amount of protection.

The last tiny slivers of light had disappeared by the time she got it in place. That must mean it was night outside, but her other senses were working harder, and she knew she would succeed. She just knew it—she just had to keep on going. And they *would* come for her. Of course they would. She was sure of that as well.

Mission accomplished. She was breathing hard, more from tension than physical effort. Now she needed to calm down again. It was fantastic she'd managed to do what she wanted and could crawl into the space under the little table. It was only just big enough to cover her but would do the job of protecting her head, and even the rest of her if she organized herself properly.

Still tethered to her rope, she placed her back against the cupboard and bent her knees, with her feet up against the leaning wall of the corner. If the wall fell on her, there'd be no chance, equally if the floor suddenly caved in, but she didn't want to think of that. She eased her legs into a more comfortable position. The space was cramped, but as long as nothing dislodged her little niche, she'd be reasonably safe.

Minutes later, there was another collapse as if the rest of the house had come down. Chunks of masonry and furniture descended into the space where she sat, rumbling, banging, and crashing all around her, and other things were tumbling farther down, into that void. Screaming wasn't going to help her, but she couldn't stop herself. She was going to die.

Slowly, slowly, things stopped moving, until there was nothing but a fierce hiss. Silence. Then, suddenly, a massive metallic clatter blasted in her ears—pans, maybe, or cutlery, scaring her almost more than anything before.

Okay, okay, she was in control again. She forced herself to sit quietly. Her throat was raw, and her breath was coming in great whoops, but it slowed, and finally she was breathing evenly. Ugh! What *was* that? It was disgusting, a rich stink of excrement gradually spreading through the air. A sewer pipe must have fractured. That was all she needed. She was definitely going to be sick.

After a quiet moment, the wood above her head

gave a sharp crack as a large object hit the top of the table and bounced away. But her shelter remained intact, and she was unhurt. Petrified but unhurt.

She waited for silence, and then she shouted again, determined to let them know she was still alive, but she couldn't hear voices from outside, nor the sounds of rubble being moved. Surely, they weren't going to abandon her. They couldn't do that.

No, that was ridiculous. She'd seen on TV news how in earthquakes, they'd still be out days later with diggers and cranes. And what about those miners in Chile? They'd been underground more than two weeks and not just a few feet below either, but nearly half a mile. They didn't stop until they'd accounted for everyone. But she didn't like those words "accounted for"—that meant alive or dead.

Actually, she wasn't in such a bad situation, was she? Why wasn't she thinking about all the positive things? She'd be unconscious now if she hadn't found the table—big plus. This was a well-protected corner here—another good point—and hopefully, her bit of the floor would stay put. There was plenty to hope for. Plenty.

Isla thought of Edmondo. She loved him. That was clear now, and all her silly hesitation and inability to show her real feelings just seemed stupid. What on earth had she been doing, wasting precious time, when maybe there was no time left? Would she ever see him again? But of course she would because Edmondo had been on his way to the town, and Adriano would tell him where she was. And all those people knew she was there. Edmondo would get her out. Oh, if only he would come. A big sob filled her throat, but once again, she choked it down and then, as a thought occurred, she gave a little laugh mixed with hiccoughs.

These were the moments when the hero should be riding in on his white charger, to the rescue of the damsel in distress. Actually, a red Ferrari would be good. She spent a few minutes indulging in the fantasy of being rescued, inventing various ways in which it might be achieved. But it was a fantasy; there was no way Edmondo could do more than anyone else. And very likely, emergency services would soon be on the scene. They would be the rescuers.

Squeezing up tighter into her improvised shelter, she allowed herself a few quiet tears—but only a few. *Come on, girl! Do you want them to find you crying?* No, she didn't. But for a while, she couldn't stop the flow. Just when she'd found Edmondo, when she'd experienced a few moments of happiness with him, was she going to lose all that? Finally, she wiped her eyes and stared blankly into the dark, a dull ache at the back of her head.

It took a while for the idea to penetrate. She moved around trying to find a more comfortable position, but something was sticking into her back, and it turned out to be her climbing sack. How had she not realized she was still wearing it? She hadn't had time to remove it before the rescue, and she'd tucked herself in against the cupboard, without being aware it was there. She shrugged it carefully off her shoulders and found that gave her an extra couple of inches of room.

Suddenly, her mood shot up from dire and miserable into overdrive and she laughed—of course, there were *things* inside the sack, as well. She must have got knocked on the head after all, since it'd taken so long for her to think of that! Feverishly, she opened the buckles and pulled at the string. There was the sandwich she'd nibbled at and nearly half a bottle of water; there was another, unopened bottle; and there, nestled at the bottom, was a beautiful racing-car box full of sweets and chocolate. At first, she just wanted to devour it all, feeling very hungry and thirsty, and she glugged down the water from the opened bottle. It removed the dust from her mouth.

The desperation was probably the result of the adrenaline rush—it wasn't as if she'd lacked food or water recently. But she'd better ration it out, especially the water. What if she were to be down here for many hours, days even? With this appalling thought in mind, she ate a very small amount of the bread and cheese and took a couple more sips of water. After she'd fueled up, she felt more in control, and everything looked better. She broke off the wheel of the chocolate racing car and placed it in her mouth. Allowing it to melt slowly on her tongue, she gave herself up to the bliss. She'd have to get another box for Adriano.

Chapter 31

A huge crater filled the street, the roofs had gone, and the front walls of the three houses in the middle of the row were cracked. A door swung on one hinge. The sight hit Edmondo like a punch to the solar plexus. People were saying it was that hole that had undermined the houses, because the rest of the dwellings to either side of the three were virtually undamaged. It must have been there forever, a big underground cavern, and no one'd had the slightest idea it existed.

Edmondo's desperation had no effect on the officials in charge. They wouldn't let him pass, and there was no way of finding out what had happened. He tried ringing Isla again, but there was no answer. From the distance, he couldn't even tell if they were the right houses. Turning away, he decided the back street was the only possible way in. He ran down a side alley and along by the town wall, and soon he saw a group of people ahead.

His heart thudding with terror, he arrived just in time to see Adriano being handed down to the ground, a cloud of dust rising into the air behind him. He rushed forward and clasped the little boy to his chest, almost crushing him in his relief. The earth shook again, and behind him, a large section of wall fell into the hole, pulling with it the undamaged rear of the house next door. The screams suddenly stopped.

"*Grazie Dio! Grazie Dio!*" he cried. And when he'd managed to calm his emotions, he turned to one of the men and said, "You saved my boy. *Grazie del profondo di mio cuore.* The other boy, too? Is he well?"

"*Sì, signore.* But the young woman who saved them has fallen in. The house moved, you understand, and she had no chance. *Lei è così coraggiosa.* So brave."

As if to underline this, there was a further tremor and the crash of falling stone just a few feet away from where they stood.

"Young woman?" Edmondo began to feel sick.

"*Sì, sì,* it was she who rescued the boys. Now, we must rescue her. Aldo has gone to bring help."

He didn't need Adriano's reference to Signorina Bruni to confirm his fear. She was down there, under a pile of stone and more was falling on top of her. She was almost certainly wounded and might even be dead. And she had saved his son.

Marco's mother, recognizing him, tapped him on the arm. Tears streaked through the thick layer of dust on her cheeks.

"You want to help with the rescue, *signore?* I will look after Adriano. Please help, *signore.* I have my son back because of her, and so have you."

"Where will I find you?" he asked.

"If the road is clear, we will drive down to my cousin in Fortezza to make sure the children are safe. We will keep Adriano for you."

"*No, Papà.* I am staying here to get Signorina Bruni back. I am not going."

It took all Edmondo's powers of persuasion before

he agreed to go. The boy had to leave, so that he could focus on what he must do next and not worry about the child's safety.

He kissed his son again, holding him in a tight embrace.

"Adriano, it will help me more than anything if you are out of danger, so I can concentrate on getting Signorina Bruni out of there. Do you understand?"

The boy had tears in his eyes, but he nodded and brushed them away with the back of his hand. "*Sì, Papà.*"

The child walked off hand in hand with his little friend. Edmondo desperately wanted to comfort him, but getting Isla out was even more important at this moment.

A couple of minutes later, a red-haired man, made unrecognizable by a thick layer of dust, appeared from the other direction. Surely, he'd seen him before.

"Leonardo Guzzi," he said. "Your architect at the studio."

Of course. The men shook hands, and Edmondo explained the situation.

"We split up," said Leonardo. "I never imagined this."

"Help me," said Edmondo. "Please help me. I have to get her out."

He choked back a sob as he was speaking and blinked rapidly, trying to shut out a vision of her body mangled beneath the pile of rock. They'd just found each other. Was it only to lose one another so soon? No, he wasn't going to allow that to happen. He bent down and heaved a lump of masonry to one side.

So began the laborious task of removing blocks of

stone. It was back-breaking, careful work if they were to do it without causing possible further damage to the girl trapped beneath.

This was going to be a long night.

Chapter 32

Below ground, it was dark and mostly quiet. At times, wood creaked, and stone settled, or a rush of rubble and plaster was suddenly released as the buildings moved, which they continued to do throughout the night. Things dropped into that void she'd imagined, just a few feet away. It wasn't the broken edge of floor where she'd fallen. This was something vast, and there was a coolness in the air that seemed to come from deep underground. She could feel it. It had grown in her mind as an entity waiting to swallow her up, an abyss. This word, charged with emotional overtones and suggestions of evil, only served to wind her up even more. Each time the thought occurred to her, she pushed it away. The present was bad enough without working up her fears with a fantastical possibility. No, she didn't want to find out if it was a reality.

But she knew it was.

She'd got her feelings under control now as long as she made herself think about quite specific things, practical things, like how she could secure herself better with the rope, or how long she could make the rations last. She had to be practical so she could deal with whatever happened.

But suddenly, out of nowhere came the thought of her mother almost dying. Mum was now recovering—

but would she ever see her again? In spite of her determination, tears squeezed themselves out of her eyes and tracked down through the dust and grit on her cheeks. Mum had already lost her son and husband. How would she cope if Isla died? Wasn't this exactly what her mother had feared when she'd said it was an earthquake zone?

When she allowed herself to think of Edmondo, a racking, throbbing pain opened deep within her. Could it really be that they might never meet again? No amount of being practical could wipe away that possibility. Tons of rubble were piled up above her. It wasn't even reasonable to imagine she could escape from that. More tears flowed without her even being aware of them.

But, at some point, she fell asleep, exhausted. She was watching a film, a black-and-white film, but even in her dream, she knew it had to be a dream. The shadowy scene was dramatic, with clumps of gnarly, old trees, moonlight filtering through the upper branches. She tried to make out what was going on, but at first it was difficult. Then it became apparent she was in a churchyard as the vague outline of the church suddenly solidified. Now, she lay down carefully on the grave—*the* grave. She arranged her clothes neatly and joined her hands in a position of prayer, like the medieval stone effigies of long-departed knights and their ladies located inside the building.

And then, Kyle was back. The fear snatched her breath away, suffocating her, taking everything. He leant over her still figure on the grave and brandished a long, Italian stiletto in her face. Only the recumbent figure wasn't Isla after all; she was the one looking on, and it was her mother who sprang up from the now open grave and tried to grab the handle of the dagger. Instead, she caught the blade and blood began to drip, quickly forming a dark, viscous pool. Isla screamed and came awake.

Sweat coated her skin. Terror had taken a hold of her, and she couldn't move. Gradually, the memory of her surroundings came back. She wasn't being stabbed in a churchyard. There was no Kyle. Her bunched muscles slowly relaxed, but she was still shaking, as if she had been attacked with that long, cruel knife. She would go mad if this continued.

Still thinking of her mother's care for her, she extracted the filthy tissue from her pocket and once again wiped her face. Then, she scrabbled about in the bottom of the rucksack and located a couple more pieces of chocolate. Slowly, she savored the taste, and after a while, she grew calmer. It was just a dream after all, a horrendous dream, but it wasn't reality.

But reality was horrible as well. Still, there was no need to panic because everybody would be doing their utmost to rescue her. Now, many hours after being buried below ground, this fact hardly had the power to make her feel any better.

At least the boys were safe. Adriano was safe. That wasn't something she'd imagined, was it? She recalled their terrified little faces. How brave they'd been. How well they'd followed her instructions, in order to keep themselves from falling. At least, she'd succeeded with that. It was a comforting thought to hold in her mind as she endured the long night. They'd managed to contain their terror. The least she could do would be to emulate their courage.

She moved a little, wincing at the dreadful pain where the rope had bitten into her waist, the dull ache in her arm muscles, and the growing soreness in her legs. Cautiously, she turned in place and allowed herself to straighten them, which brought a little relief, but she soon had to swing herself back in again because the slope had increased, and she feared sliding off.

It must be the early hours of the morning. She checked her phone for the umpteenth time, but there was nothing to be got out of it at all. Smoothing her finger across the screen, she searched for a crack. Though everything seemed normal; it simply wasn't working, and she couldn't tell him she was still alive and uninjured. What was he thinking right now? He must be terrified, imagining all the same dreadful things that had been going through her mind. Would they let him get near enough to help?

She tried to send him a message of love with the power of her mind, a reassurance that she was all right. Working hard at that occupied several minutes. But suddenly, she stopped. It was hopeless. She sighed, trying to regain control. Maybe it wouldn't help, but she'd hang onto the idea of him. She'd imagine what he was doing out there, where exactly he was working, picture him picking up blocks of stone and throwing them to one side. This occupied a little more time, before reality came rushing back in.

Maybe it'd be better to check that she really didn't have any injuries. A lot of debris had scraped and hit her while she'd hung from the rope, as she sought to orient herself, and she must have a bruise where that heavy object—a chair or a box, maybe—had banged into her hip. Taking great care, she stretched again, first one leg and then the other. God, she was so stiff! She knew about the cut on her arm, but what was this sticky stuff on her right leg? Blood, certainly, drying now. Otherwise, there were just a few small cuts and grazes. The fetid air was making her feel nauseous again, and a moment later, she was throwing up.

Ugh, that was disgusting. It was better she didn't think too hard about where the smells were coming from.

A little while later, sleep claimed her once more.

****

Outside, as dawn came, the crane driver forced Edmondo and Leonardo to step back. With the growing light, he was able to position his crane safely and now, he could begin moving some of the larger pieces of stone and concrete. The work was delicate. Moving the big blocks might dislodge others and even a single, small one could prove fatal to anyone down below. They couldn't be certain of where she was, or if she was still alive.

The two men watched in agonized silence. Both had worked all night, stopping only minutes to glug down coffee and, once, to eat something—what, they didn't know. They'd only accepted food because someone had shoved it toward them, and they knew they needed fuel. During that time, they'd cleared a large area and exposed the bigger problem—huge blocks such as these could only be moved by using the crane. Finally, the grabber clamped onto a massive stone lintel and was poised to swing it away.

"I think that's where she'll be, from what I've been told, so as soon as I've moved it, I need one of you to go down on a cable to get her out," said the driver. "But don't get your hopes up—we don't know she's there. She could have...You need to be ready—the whole lot could collapse once we move this."

"That'll be you," said Leonardo, grinning. "Anna will kill me if I do anything like that."

As if he hadn't already risked his life several times over, during this horrible night.

But Edmondo had no intention of letting anyone else do it and was already being fitted with the harness they used for the job. Someone handed him a small, sharp knife—"You'll need this to cut the rope if she's still attached to it."

****

Inside the collapsed houses, beneath the rocks and fallen masonry, everything was still black, but Isla could now hear something was happening—a scraping and banging. Then a clinking sound. Could that be shovels? Only it sounded bigger, and a powerful engine was turning over nearby. It was getting lighter. The engine came closer, the sound filling her head as it reverberated against the stone. Some machine. She must let them know where she was, close to the wall. She began to shout, "Here I am! *Sono qui! Qui, vicina al muro.*"

Then a huge chunk of concrete swung away, and light flooded in. She blinked. It was difficult to make out what was happening, the sudden light too much after the total darkness.

Edmondo. He was high above her, hanging from a cable. They were lowering him into the chasm, so that he could get her out. Of course, it would be too dangerous for people to climb down. Relief nearly overcame her, and she struggled to breathe, thinking she was dreaming again. Then her eyes focused better, and that great, gaping hole swung into view, exactly as she'd imagined it, only a few feet from where she sat in her precarious shelter. The remaining piece of floor looked set to break away from the wall at any moment.

A tense silence emanated from the watchers. Everyone knew that, even at this stage, something could go terribly wrong. Her mind filled with an overwhelming joy that Edmondo had come for her, and she began to shake at the sight of him there, almost within reach. He could do nothing to help her yet. But Isla's wits had come back, and she was already working out how they were going to do this; common sense told her she was the one who had to move.

There was another tremor, and something poked into her back. Her niche was no longer safe. She couldn't just throw off the rope and get ready for him to reach in and pluck her from her eyrie, because if the wall gave away, she would need that rope. The pace at which events were unfolding was agonizingly slow, every moment elongated. She eased her legs out from under the table while they lowered him farther, and farther again, until he was exactly opposite the place where she sat and coming closer. Close enough to touch. Very carefully, she turned her body around to face him. Then the wall behind her split open, and she launched herself into his arms.

"Edmondo?" Her voice came out a croak; trying to speak hurt the back of her throat.

"Oh God, I've found you. I've found you. Oh, thank God," he said.

Stones cascaded down into the void, and the rope slid down behind her. It had broken away from whatever they'd tied it to, and there wouldn't have been anything to hold her in place.

"Put your arms more tightly around my neck," Edmondo said, desperately hanging onto her. "Now, quickly."

His heart was hammering against her breast, and he held her so tightly, she could scarcely breathe.

They moved away from the collapsed building at last, and she took deep breaths of clean, fresh air and didn't care who could see the tears streaming down her face. The driver winched them up together, and they rose into the air, dangling for a moment over that dreadful void. There was a sudden crack behind her. First, the split widened, and the whole wall where she had been sitting slowly disintegrated. Then chunks of masonry, the table, and the cupboards toppled down and disappeared.

For a brief moment, Edmondo and Isla hung there, watching as everything vanished. And then, there was nothing left. The sinkhole stretched from the opposite side of the street, right under where the house had been, and up to the place where she'd been sitting. Then the jib swung around and deposited them on a safe patch of ground. He kissed her, ignoring everything else, and there was applause from the people who had been working nearby.

"You're the fourth person to be pulled out," said Edmondo, kissing her again.

It was fantastic to know others had been saved, but she was sure she was the first to emerge in the arms of her lover, kissed in front of an audience of twenty observers and a crane driver. As far as announcing a relationship went, you couldn't get much better than that.

****

They insisted she go to the ambulance to be checked. She didn't think it necessary until she tried walking.

"I'm fine," she said, standing up straight, but her legs felt numb, pins and needles beginning to prickle as she hobbled over to the vehicle in the early dawn light, leaning heavily on Edmondo's arm. She quickly sat down on the step, unable to climb in as they urged. Her legs were wobbly and painful because of the cramped position she'd been in all night. A paramedic came to dress the wound. It was Eloisa's partner, Giorgio.

"She said you'd gone climbing at Falesia," he said, "but I didn't expect we'd be pulling you out of that hole. You okay now?"

"I'm okay," she croaked. "Just glad to be out of there."

Someone handed her a bottle of water, and she guzzled it down, reserving the last few drops to splash over her face, to wash away the dust.

All the while, Edmondo stood close to her, his hand on her shoulder, as if he feared she might disappear if he let go.

"You're the one who rescued the two little boys, aren't you?" the female paramedic said.

"Are they okay?" whispered Isla. Speaking still hurt. "It must have been so frightening for them."

"Physically, they're fine, but you're right, they may be a bit traumatized. We shouldn't worry too much, though—they're very young and it had a good outcome for them. Children are resilient."

Then they pronounced Isla fit to go.

"I think you're a bit of a heroine here," said Edmondo, holding her close again. "And you're definitely my heroine—*every* bit of you."

His shirt was torn, he had cuts and grazes, broken fingernails, and a large, reddish-purple bruise on his right cheek. He was in a worse state than she was, covered in a thick, grey dust. But battered and grey-haired, he still had the means to turn over her heart—even more than before.

She smiled up at him. Was this how he'd look in twenty years? Very sexy, very distinguished.

"What are you looking at?"

"Just counting your injuries. I think you win over me by quite a distance."

"Well, it's not surprising. That hole in the ground got in the way, but Leonardo and I worked most of the night and we moved a lot of stone in the dark. There was no way they could fit any machinery around the back, so in the end, we had to wait until the front was cleared. But we kept hoping we'd find you before that by working from the back street. We weren't going to sit there doing nothing, were we?"

"Where is Leonardo?"

"Let's go over and say hello."

"Yes, I want to thank him."

Leonardo was equally cloaked in a grey dust and had the same sort of injuries as Edmondo. He limped across and enveloped her in a hug. "Great to see you, Isla. Eloisa would never forgive us if we hadn't got you out."

They talked for a short while, and then she said, "We can give you a lift. Come back with us."

"No, thanks. I need to get back to my wife. She's

seriously worried about me although I have been in touch during the night, but I'm not sure she believed me when I said I wasn't doing anything dangerous. I've got a lift lined up. It'll get me all the way home."

Isla felt better, but suddenly, she wanted to be away from there, far from the rubble and dust, the gaping crater, and the heart-rending destruction. How many people had died? There'd been no warning this time, no smaller tremors in the days preceding the earthquake. It was possible some people had not got out alive.

"Can you walk as far as the car? It's down the road, not too far from here."

"Yes, it'll be good for me." She tried a stretch and grunted. "I'm so stiff. I need to warm up these muscles. What's happened with Adriano?"

"He's with his friend, Marco, staying at the house of a cousin of theirs in Fortezza. We'll pick him up him on the way past, shall we?"

"I'd like that. Where's that poor family going to live?"

"I suppose they'll stay with the cousin while they sort things out. I know them—they've got quite a large house."

They'd been walking as they talked, and now, the truck came into sight, and she laughed.

"I was expecting the car! When I was sitting in that black hole, I imagined you sweeping into the village in the Ferrari and coming to get me."

"I'm sorry I don't match up to hero status, but this is more practical up here."

She hugged him and whispered in his ear, "Oh, you definitely match up—and here I am to prove it."

They got in, and he said, "Let's go home."

The mention of home warmed her heart. And into her mind flashed the picture of the house by the tower.

****

Adriano was sitting very still in the seat behind them. He'd said hello in a quiet voice when they'd gone to fetch him from the cousins' house, but then he stayed silent, staring out the window. As they drove up to the tower, Isla glanced back at him. The poor little fellow was suffering. His face was white and set, and large tears trembled on his lashes, about to spill. She laid her hand on Edmondo's arm, warning him to stay quiet, and turned to the boy.

"What's wrong, Adriano?"

"I thought...I thought you weren't coming back. I thought you fell into the hole and that was the end." His voice seemed to crack as he went on. "*Papà* said he'd get you back, but I didn't think he could."

"Because you saw the hole yourself when you were up in that room? And you realized how bad it could be?"

He nodded silently.

"But he did get me back."

She squeezed Edmondo's hand, and she continued, "I was lucky, you see, Adriano. Sometimes that happens. When I was down there, I thought about how dangerous it was, with all those rocks falling, so I made myself a good place to hide."

This aroused a scintilla of interest. He wiped his eyes with the back of his hand and said, "Where did you hide?"

"Under a table. I dragged it up against a wall, so that, when the stones fell, they didn't hit me. They hit the table instead."

"Under a table. That's cool."

Her heart was breaking. The poor child had imagined all sorts of horrors because he had understood the danger that they'd all been in. And he'd had to contemplate the thought that maybe his father was not able to work miracles, as he'd previously believed.

She leaned over the back of the seat and took the boy's hand. What she really wanted to do was to gather him in her arms and give him a cuddle, but she knew it wouldn't go down well.

"Come on, Adriano. I'm here. It's over now." It wasn't really. It would take a long time for the images to fade, but they had to help him to move on. "Let's go and see Signora Forni. Maybe she'll cook breakfast for us. What do you say, Edmondo?"

She'd been aware of him listening closely to the conversation with his son. He grinned now.

"So my breakfast isn't good enough for you, is it, Signorina Bruni? Now, you want someone else to do the cooking?"

"Your breakfast was the best breakfast I ever had—but you have been up all night. I don't think I want to risk it. You're so tired. Just think, you…you might fall into the omelet."

"You might splat the tomato sauce," said Adriano.

"You might drop the eggs," said Isla.

"You might step on the plates."

There was a note of hysteria in the boy's laugh now. It was getting silly, but it had cleared the atmosphere.

Edmondo laughed.

"Okay, I admit defeat. I already rang her. She's getting it ready now. She can't wait to see us."

Chapter 33

The weather had changed dramatically after the earthquake in Falesia began. The drizzle turned into a huge downpour just hours after Isla emerged from the sinkhole, and it hampered the rescue operation. She'd been lucky they'd found her before that started. The devastation was huge, and now a protracted clear-up was into its third week with no sign of a return to normal for those whose homes had been impacted. Those rescuers were miracle workers: two people had died and one of those from a heart attack and not from being trapped under a building. Everyone else had been pulled clear of the wreckage, and five remained in hospital with serious injuries.

Isla's shock and fear had worn off, but she still woke up at three or four in the morning, convinced she was buried and about to die. It would take longer than a few weeks for the trauma to end. Adriano on the other hand, seemed to have recovered. He spent a lot of time, in and out of school, with his little friend Marco, their shared experience binding them together.

This evening, Isla had finished work late and was now on her way through the driving rain to meet Edmondo, thinking that the weather hadn't improved much. The Trattoria Santarossa still wasn't visible through the murk. She hurried along the narrow, winding alley in Teramo, keeping an eye open for the restaurant, and she shuddered as the freezing rain trickled down her neck. It was later than she'd hoped, the new client having produced, almost at the last minute, a long list of things she wanted to discuss, but it had been worth the effort. She knew Tommaso was going to be happy that she'd taken the whole process through the preliminaries on her own. Tomorrow, she'd write a report for him. It was all good practice, considering what she had in mind. And she'd managed it all in her very basic Italian—or perhaps not so basic now, if she believed Eloisa.

The evenings were beginning to draw in, and tonight with the rain, she barely made out where she was going. Ah, finally! A welcoming glow at the corner marked the restaurant entrance. They'd eaten in this tiny place before. She picked up her pace as more freezing raindrops found their way down her neck. This was a fine time to have forgotten her umbrella.

She just made out the neon letters blurred by the streams of water, and now she scooted into the passageway, closing the door quickly behind her. A puddle immediately began to form around her feet. Damn, she really was wet. Her smart grey trousers were glued to her legs, and the snazzy, Italian shoes she'd spent so long choosing were probably ruined on their first outing, with all the water sloshing around. She transferred her laptop case to her left hand and pushed open the door into the main room. A wave of warm air swept over her, and she threaded her way between the tables.

A quiet meal with Edmondo. What could be nicer? Things had been very busy, and so much had happened. After they'd got back from Falesia and consumed a very large and wonderful breakfast, she'd found herself almost too tired to talk, and although he'd wanted her to stay, she'd insisted on going back to her flat. Toward midday, leaving Adriano with Signora Forni, Edmondo had driven her down into the town, with instructions to go to bed and stay there for twenty-four hours.

"I'll let Tommaso know you'll not be in the office tomorrow," he'd said. "I'm sure Leonardo won't be, either. Are you certain you're going to be all right? Ring me if there's a problem."

"I'm not going to have a problem, Edmondo. I'm going to sleep. Maybe I'll fit in a shower. That's it."

He got out of the car and came around to help her out. Tears had gathered at the corners of his eyes. He enveloped her in his arms and kissed her as if she were a precious piece of porcelain that he was afraid of breaking. "I must go. Sleep well."

A few minutes later, she'd entered the haven of the garden as he drove away. The autumn was well advanced, but still, the little courtyard was packed with greenery and quite a few flowers. Though she was desperately tired, the green oasis called to her, and she sank down on the old iron bench which the sun had just reached. She closed her eyes and enjoyed the warmth on her face.

She'd stay here for a few minutes, the strong, herby scents of the lavender and thyme helping to make this a special place. When she opened her eyes again, she felt different—still tired, but better. The dark images of the space under the rubble with the menacing void had been temporarily chased away. It wasn't only Adriano who had to recover.

Isla had lost her faith long ago, that day in the

churchyard. It wasn't surprising, given what had happened to her. So she didn't think she believed in God, nor in any religion. If there was a god, he was not the one she'd been brought up to worship. A cruel and indifferent god—yes, she could imagine that.

But from somewhere had come the necessary strength and determination to all those who had helped in the rescue of the earthquake victims, and in her case, it felt that it had come from somewhere outside herself. She shrugged. It was just the human spirit, she supposed. What did she know? Whatever it was, she was grateful for it.

She straightened and then stood up, knowing if she sat there much longer, she'd fall asleep on the spot. Forcing her aching limbs to move, she entered her building and began to climb the stairs.

****

So, on this wet and stormy Thursday night, she was longing to see Edmondo.

This was not intended to be a special meal, although every moment she was with him felt special. They'd formed the habit of meeting for dinner once a week in Teramo, usually when Isla had a client she needed to see or a site visit in the afternoon. Both agreed they'd like more time together, but there was the child to consider. So usually, after driving back to Fortezza, they'd spend an hour or two at Isla's flat, and then Edmondo would go home and relieve Signora Forni of her duties.

But Isla knew he didn't like it to be this way, that he felt he owed more time and attention to his son, or he'd be treating him much as his mother had done, putting his own needs first. So it was not a long-term solution. Soon, they'd have to work out something better.

It wasn't going to be a special meal, but she did want to talk about something important—a matter they had so far both avoided. Since her conversation with Susan, she'd given a lot of thought to what she was going to do in the new year. Christiano was coming back to Fortezza, so there were no vacancies at the studio. But this only meant she had to give more urgent attention to her plans, and she wanted to try them out with Edmondo and get his reaction.

He was sitting at a corner table at the back of the room, wearing the serious glasses and reading. It did appear that not everyone had stopped reading newspapers. She watched him for a moment, getting pleasure from his absorption in the article. Somehow, he sensed her presence and looked up, getting to his feet.

"You're absolutely soaking."

He bent to kiss her cold, wet lips and was already taking her jacket from her when the waiter hurried up.

"If the signorina would like to come with me, I can provide a towel."

Smiling apologetically to Edmondo, she hurried after the man. This was a family restaurant, and Edmondo was already known to the staff. How nice it was to be welcomed as a valued patron. Supplied with a large, white towel, she went into the *Bagno* and dried herself as best she could before peering into the mirror. Her hair looked like rats' tails, not a style she much admired. A comb, dragged through, smoothed it down, and she abandoned any further efforts, hoping it would dry quickly and bounce back into shape. Good, that was as much time as she was prepared to devote to her appearance.

She sat down. He'd ordered her a mysterious smoky beverage served in a dark glass.

"What is this?"

"Borgogno. Drink it. That's to warm you up. You're not driving, so you can drink what you want."

She took a sip. It was some kind of fortified wine, and it really hit the spot, leaving her instantly revived—and ravenously hungry.

They ordered, and she drank down a little more and slowly began to dry off.

He stretched across the table and took her hand. "What is it? I can see something's on your mind, and I don't think it's the weather—which, I must say, you seem to revel in. That wet hair look suits you, by the way. Something in your English genes, I expect."

She laughed. "I do quite like the rain—it feels cleansing after months of heat and dust, but I wouldn't expect anyone else to appreciate that.'"

"Three weeks of it is a bit of an exaggeration."

She drew on the fiery liquid, enjoying the warm glow as it traveled down. "Edmondo, you do know my exchange at the studio is only for six months, don't you?"

"I've been hoping you'd bring that up. I think we need to discuss the future."

"Well, obviously, it's been on my mind for a while. Before we say anything else, can I tell you what I'm thinking of doing?"

"This is very formal."

"Yes, but it will color everything I say afterward, so you need to hear it."

"What is it? If I can do something for you, just tell me."

"What would you say if I tell you I want to stay longer in Italy?"

"What do you think? I love you, Isla, and I want you to stay forever."

Love? He loved her. She fell silent, breathing deep breaths. They'd said all sorts of things to each other, but neither of them had actually said that in quite that way until now.

"I love you, too, Edmondo."

They looked at each other for a long moment.

"So do you have no confidence in me?" he continued. "What have I said or done that would make you doubt how I feel about you?"

"Absolutely nothing. I guess being abandoned by my father at a tender age means I lack trust. I can't quite believe I have someone like you, who makes me so happy—and I keep thinking it'll come to a sudden end."

"Please stay in Italy, in Fortezza, if you can find a way. Isla, I beg you. Please stay." He was gently stroking her hand, reminding her, if she needed a reminder, of just how she felt about him. "Are you under any contractual obligation to your firm?"

"I may have to go back for a month in January, but after that, no. You see, I was thinking of setting up in business for myself, even when I was still working in London. But I could do that here. Up to a point, it doesn't matter where I live. I could run it from my flat at the beginning."

He covered her hand with his own and squeezed. "Isla, that's a great idea, fantastic. There are lots of ways I could give you support."

"Thank you. You see, I realized when I was in London just how much I love living in Italy, how much I was missing it already, even after a couple of days." She grinned. "Something in my Italian genes, I suppose. I don't want to live in London anymore. And I'd miss you and Adriano so much. I can't bear the thought."

He pulled her toward him across the table and kissed her, taking his time, until they heard the elderly proprietor cough and steaming plates were set down in front of them, wafts of that wonderful tomato and garlic exciting their taste buds.

Edmondo leaned back and began to tackle his food. "I'm so relieved you're thinking like this. If you have to go back for a month, well, I guess we'll get through it, and then we'll be together again. You've convinced me this would be the right thing to do. I'll talk to Tommaso and get him to offer you a couple of clients to get started."

"No, Edmondo, please don't—I have to do this myself."

"I'm sorry. I'm not trying to push you in any particular direction."

"I did think of approaching him, but he might not want to—I'd become competition, after all."

"Right, of course." He thought for a moment or two. "Still, I think toward the end of the exchange, you should let him know. It's a big, established practice. Sometimes, there are small jobs he can't make any money from. He's told me that before."

She'd forgotten the two men knew each other.

"But he always finds it hard to turn people down,

especially if they're recommendations. As a start-up, you wouldn't have the overheads. He could pass them to you, and they'd be getting a first-class designer at a much-reduced price."

"Do you really think he would?"

"It's possible. And this is a very satisfied client speaking, so take note."

The tower was approaching completion now, and Isla herself was delighted with it. It had come together so well, and she was pleased with some of the riskier decisions she'd taken, like the display wall in the upper tower room. It was one of those things that had to be finely judged and could have fallen flat or just looked kitschy, but she did feel she'd got it right. Composed of many ancient pieces of pottery, it was an artifact in its own right and looked fabulous, as did the skis, now displayed over the chimney breast of the fireplace they'd installed.

Much later, she'd discussed the idea of a large, colorful canvas with Edmondo and suggested using one of the few drawings Adriano had done which were in color; she'd had it blown up to ten times the original size and printed on canvas. Edmondo loved this, and Adriano had told anyone who would listen that he had a "real" painting on the wall in the tower. That had definitely paid off.

"It's nice to know my client is happy."

Isla swallowed a mouthful of *pasta puttanesca*, Santarossa-style. Each time they came here, she tried a different dish, and each time, she went away feeling very full but still looking forward to the next occasion. They hadn't let her down, either. It was delicious.

"So you don't think what I'm proposing is a bad

idea?"

"Definitely not. In fact, I think I'll introduce you to my cousin."

"What…!"

"Not *that* cousin. My cousin on my mother's side, Sofía."

"I didn't know you had any other cousins. Tell me about her. Why does she need an interior designer?"

"Sofía is a very clever person. She's something of a math genius and now works in London for a British bank, where she earns huge sums of money. Bit of a contrast to Giacomo."

"So how do I fit into this?"

"I know she's in the process of buying a flat in Rome. It's in a great place, but she said it needs refurbishing."

"Sounds interesting."

"I think you'll find it is. I'm glad I thought of it because Sofía always hires people to do things. She just hasn't the time to see to it herself."

"So if you mention you have a friend who could help—"

"Exactly. But you'll still have to persuade her to take you on—she won't just do it on my say-so. I'll have a chat with her tomorrow. I'm almost sure she hasn't anyone on board yet. She may expect you to get on with it immediately, though."

"That's all right. I don't mind hard work."

"Too much work isn't a good idea, Isla." He was smiling. "You have to leave time for the other important things in life—like me."

"Says the man who works late at his business several days a week."

"I know. Both you and Adriano need more of my time. I'm going to change that. In fact, I already have—I've asked Maria to find an assistant for me. That will free up quite a lot of my time in the long term. Pietro handles the factory side, but I could do with someone to meet with new clients and so on."

"I was only teasing. I feel just as passionate about my own work, so I do understand when you have to work."

"That's a good thing because Adriano does have to come first, and with what's happened at Falesia, I am extremely busy. But it's not always going to be like that, I promise you." The whole area had been impacted by the disaster, and people were helping where they could. "But I do want to spend more time with you, so let's go back to Fortezza now."

When the plates were cleared, they ordered coffee and asked for the bill.

****

The town square was silent, a dimly lit space full of shadows, when the car purred to a halt.

"Are you coming up?"

"If you invite me."

"I invite you."

Moments later, they were climbing the staircase to Isla's flat. She opened the door, and they entered the tiny hallway, where there was scarcely room for the two of them at the same time, but it wasn't really a problem since they clung together as one. He led her into the next room, which was marginally bigger—but only just. She put out a hand and flicked a switch, and a small standard lamp sprang to life and then burned dimly, with just enough light for them to see each other.

His kisses were capable of sending her to a space where everything was sensation and emotion, while all else dropped away. Tonight was no exception, but suddenly, he stopped and put his hands on her shoulders, holding her off a little so he could look into her eyes.

"Isla, I meant what I said. I love you. I love being with you and making love to you. But why don't we make things easier for ourselves? We're both very busy people. Come to live with me. Come to my home."

"But what about Adriano—and Signora Forni?"

"Adriano already likes and admires you enormously. He might well even be a little in love with you, too." He kissed her again. "Like his father," he added, taking his time to make sure she understood that point. "And I really don't think Signora Forni has any say in the matter, much as I appreciate her. She's an employee, so she'll accept what I say, or she'll leave. It's as simple as that."

"You know you couldn't last five minutes without her, not now you've got Adriano at home. You'll have to take her into consideration." She thought for a moment and added, "I do love you, Edmondo, very much, but I need time."

"Time to…?"

"Time to accept I'll be giving up my independence. We *have* just talked about my setting up a business, Edmondo. I'm an independent woman, and I need to do this my own way and not lean on you to make it happen—or give up on it."

He frowned. "Even successful businesswomen have private lives and people who love them and whom they love. I'm not trying to force you down a particular path or take anything away from your achievements. But I do know a lot about business, and you've fired up all sorts of exciting ideas. Please let me help."

She leant across and kissed his cheek. "I know. I'm very touchy. It's just that it's been my dream since I started training, and well, I have to do it."

"I won't stop you. And just think about how much time we could spend together if we lived in the same house—with so much more opportunity to talk about things, as well.

"But that's for another day. Just now, I have about one hour before I need to get back. And brilliant ideas about what to do with that hour. I do know how you like to use your time productively, Signorina Bruni, so I'm sure I can persuade you to share it with me."

Isla simply couldn't fault his argument. "You are a man of many good ideas," she said and pulled him close again.

Chapter 34

"That's great news," said Isla when her mother rang a few days later. "I'm sure Tai-Lu is glad to see you back at home."

"Probably, but only because I respond to her every whim—and she's a creature of many whims. Poor Gillian down the hall had a few other things to think about while she was looking after her, so I don't think the queen of felines got quite the same service as she's used to."

"Are you planning your visit? Because I ought to tell you I'm thinking of staying here, in Italy, long-term. Or did I tell you that already? Anyway, that leaves you much more choice about when you come."

"Oh, you have decided, then? You didn't say much while you were here, except that you'd found someone to love. Which gives me a great sense of relief."

"I think we had other things to talk about, didn't we, but the idea has been growing for some time. Anyway, for your holiday, maybe you could choose a time when it's cold and miserable in England, like February or March. I'll check for you what the weather's like here at that time of year, see what the locals think."

It was great that her mother was already feeling so much better that she was thinking about a holiday. Isla could hardly remember the last time she'd gone outside of London. Maybe they could find a small hotel down on the coast, and she'd spend a few days there with the two friends, and Mum could get her strength back.

"We'll work something out and let you know. You are all right, aren't you, Isla? After all that's happened?"

"I'm fine, Mum. I've completely recovered, although I can't claim to have forgotten what it felt like, down there underground. Not yet anyway."

Her mother was silent for a moment, and Isla wondered what was going on.

"I'm glad to hear you're better." She paused again and then said, "But actually, that wasn't what I was ringing about."

"Oh, what is it then?"

"I've heard from your father."

Isla literally stumbled backward and fell into a chair, dazed. Had her mother really said what she thought she had? It couldn't be.

"You've what? But I thought—"

"I understand now that he must always have known where we were, Isla—through Father Ignatius, although the Father never said anything to me. I know you and I didn't really talk about him after he left because I was so angry with him and still coping with grief. And then later, I tried, and you wouldn't let me. You would never talk about him. Every time I started the conversation, you'd just say you didn't want to hear and walk out."

A moment of guilt at what her mother's suffering must have been evaporated as heat filled her chest and invaded her head, making her feel dizzy. How could he? She was astonished at how much this affected her, even now, so many years later. It just confirmed what she'd always thought of him. To contact her mother at this point, after all this time! Unbelievable.

"He knew where we were, but he didn't want anything to do with us, is that it? Yes, I get it—we just weren't important enough in his life."

"Isla, you've always hated him, and I understand that, but I could never feel like that about my own husband, however hurt I was. I understood too much about his reasons."

"Yes, I hated him. I do hate him, because of what he did to you, to us, abandoning us like that." She couldn't find the words to express what she felt about this. "And if you like, it's selfish as well, and I do feel I lost out. Maybe that's childish, but I can't help it."

She stopped before she said something she'd really regret, and then added more quietly, "Okay, you see him, Mum, if you must, but don't involve me."

She hit the red "end call" button with such force, she thought she'd broken her new phone. As adrenaline surged, her heart banged like a sledgehammer and threatened to lay her out. How dared he? The weaselly bastard! Isla rarely used a swear word stronger than "damn," but this was the description that came into her mind, and it was perfectly fitting.

How dared he? She could see it all. Now he was getting older, he was looking for Mum to take him back, wanted to have someone to look after him in his old age. Well, she wasn't going to be a part of that. Mum would have to make her own decisions.

She remained in her chair, fuming, scenes from the past filling her mind.

Then it occurred to her that, instead of shouting at her mother, she ought to offer her some support, give her the strength she would need to get rid of him. She knew her mother too well, knew how easily he might make her feel guilty. So, maybe she should ring her back. It cost her a great deal, but finally, she stretched out her hand to pick up her phone.

At that moment, it rang, and "Mum" popped up on the screen.

"Sorry, Mum. I'm really sorry to be so horrible. I shouldn't have shouted. I was just about to call you back. Please forgive me."

"I'm sorry, too. I should have prepared you better for a shock like that."

Her mother had been crying, and Isla felt bad that she was the cause of it. It wasn't Mum's fault, and she should have known better. She'd be finding things difficult anyway, without adding in her daughter's selfishness. God, what a horrible person she was, only ever thinking of things from her own point of view.

"Have you time to talk, Isla?"

"Yes. I've just got home. I was trying to work out what to have for supper when you rang."

"Okay, listen. I think I told you Father Ignatius came to see me in hospital. Well, it seems that afterward, he got in touch with your dad to let him know what had happened, and in the course of the conversation he told Gianni about the earthquake—and you. I hadn't told the Father, but he'd seen your photo in the paper, or maybe on the news."

"How? Oh, you mean about the two little boys. Surely that wasn't international news? I don't even remember anyone taking a photo."

But then, she did remember, when they'd got her out of the collapsed building, there'd been a news van from a regional TV station parked at the end of the street.

"There was a tiny article on the BBC news site, 'English climber in earthquake rescue,' or something like that. That was all, but then Father Ignatius explained to Gianni what had happened. You can access the BBC pretty much anywhere. Your dad is living in Italy now, but he'd have been able to follow up after he was given the news."

"He's living in Italy? Where? What's he doing?"

Immediately, she imagined a big Italian family, lots of children, in some Neapolitan suburb. She felt like spitting. Some of his relatives had lived in Naples; the rest came from somewhere down in the south.

"Well, you know, he was completely traumatized by your brother's death."

"Was he? I'm not surprised. It was his fault."

"He couldn't function at all immediately after," said her mother, ignoring Isla's comment, "and I didn't help matters. We were all grieving. I blamed him. I accused him of—"

"Why are you trying to blame yourself for his selfishness? And what do you mean about not being able to function? Is there something you don't want to tell me? Did he go insane? Has he been living in some mental institution? Come on, Mum, you don't have to protect me. Just say it."

Her voice had risen, and then again, she realized the effect her hard words would be having on her mother. She took a couple of deep breaths and said, "Sorry, Mum, I'll try to calm down."

"He returned to Italy and became a monk."

There was complete silence while Isla digested

this. She swallowed. "A monk. You're saying he's a monk? He lives in a monastery?"

"Yes. I blamed him for what happened, but he blamed himself even more. He was on a downward spiral. He started to drink, and I spent all of my time trying to hide what was happening from you. He was never violent, but it wasn't good for a child to witness his...disintegration, and he knew that. It seemed hopeless and he felt...total despair. He left because of you. He left out of love for you."

Isla was trying to process this. It wasn't the way she remembered things. Her memory was that one day, soon after the funeral, he'd walked out and had never come back, and that her mother had cried for a very long time. From what her mother was saying it must have been months later that he'd gone. How had she never seen this? How had she no memory of it?

"I don't remember...," she began.

"You blocked it out, sweetheart. You were grieving, too. You loved Jack as much as we did. And you loved your father too, whatever you may think now. But you needed someone to blame for what was happening. It was your way of coping."

They were silent for a moment, and then her mother continued, "For a time, after the death, he was good for nothing. He couldn't work anymore, and we lost the house. He told me several times he wanted to commit suicide, but he'd grown up a Catholic, was still practicing. Taking his own life was something he could never contemplate, so he decided to devote the rest of his time to the good of others. And to the glory of God."

"What about us, Mum. What about our good?" She

wanted to rage and scream, but she was managing to keep her voice quiet and level now, though it took a big effort to do so. "I'm not sure this is any better than just walking out and abandoning us. In fact, it's exactly the same."

"I know, love. But I don't think he was strong enough to do it on his own—he needed the structure the church offered. We did have some hard times. But I would guess leaving was a lot better than if he'd stayed with us, in that terrible, depressed state. Mental illness like that...it affects everyone around you. And maybe he knew that. Things *were* hard for us, but at least your life wasn't ruined by his state of mind. And you gave meaning to my life. My whole focus was to get you launched, especially after...anyway, you helped me. It's taken time, but I have accepted what he did and I'm happy."

Isla was still reeling from the shock. She needed to come to terms with this new information but had no idea how she should handle it.

"And Father Ignatius has always known about this?"

"I believe so—but he would have been bound to secrecy and, no doubt, tasked with making sure we were all right."

Isla remembered the kindly, now elderly, parish priest whom she'd known all her life. There'd been times when he'd helped them, including right at the beginning with finding the flat where her mother lived.

"And my father has made this contact now because...?"

"Because he wants to meet you, if you're willing. I think he has a fair idea of how you feel, and he accepts that you may refuse, so it'll be up to you."

"So why now? Just because of the photo?"

"No." She sighed. "Isla, he's dying of cancer and has been given just a few weeks to live." She began to cry.

Isla didn't know what to say, how to comfort her mother on the other end of the telephone. Finally, the tears dried up, and she managed to end the conversation. "I'm going to ring off now, so that I can think about what you've told me. One more thing, Mum—are you going to see him?"

"I don't know, Isla. I really don't know. I'm still trying to make up my mind."

Chapter 35

"Are you free on Saturday?" asked Edmondo.

"Yes."

"What? No weekend work?"

Ah, he was wearing his provocative smile, just trying to get a rise out of her. What was he going to suggest?

"Not at the moment. Totally free."

"Then, let's drive down there to see your father," he said, looking serious again. "Adriano will be out at a sleepover. It's Marco's seventh birthday tomorrow, and his mother said she'd be happy to have him stay over. The cousin's house is a bit crowded, but she thinks it's good for them to be together, that it'll help them work through any issues caused by their experience."

"I think she's probably right, but—"

"I was going to suggest you come up to the house, but it's too good an opportunity to miss."

"But I haven't really decided yet, Edmondo. I—"

"Isla, you said he has only a few weeks to live. Either you do it straight away, or it will be too late. And this is a good weekend from my point of view, with Adriano being away. I'd prefer not to take him to visit a dying man."

She felt a flare of anger. Was it always going to be like this, with Edmondo making the important decisions? She was perfectly capable on her own. It was just that she wasn't quite ready yet. She'd do it in her own good time, when she'd sorted out how she felt.

"Isla?"

She sighed. She wouldn't sort out how she felt. She'd already let it drift after her mother's call, not wanting to confront the issue. Burying her head in the sand, her mother would have said. And of course, he wasn't taking over, he was taking care—of her, even if she didn't think she needed it. Left to her own devices, she would just let things go until her father died. And that would leave her with all sorts of unresolved problems. She recognized that.

"You really do think I should do this, don't you?"

"I do. If you don't, you'll have regrets later, and there'll be nothing you can do about it. What have you got to lose by going?"

It was a good question. My pride, she thought. My anger. My hatred. Which I've kept tight inside me. Put like that, a refusal to honor a dying man's request cast her in a very poor light. Did she really want to hang on to those negative emotions?

She looked away. Her head was pounding as she struggled to handle the anger she was now feeling toward Edmondo. How dared he try to push her into confronting the issue? It was her business alone. Why should she have to face up to something that was bound to be unpleasant, something that stirred up all sorts of painful memories? That was just stupid. Sensible people didn't do that to themselves. She wanted to push it all away, but it wasn't going to be possible because Edmondo wouldn't let her. She forced herself to calm down. He was right, so she had to deal with it.

"I don't know if Mum has decided to see him." She

was still avoiding his eye—and the answer to his question.

"It's you I'm worried about, not your mother. Hatred is corrosive, Isla. You're caring and sensitive. You do not want to hold a grudge that will never produce anything worthwhile."

She was quiet for a few moments, thinking. *I have to do this. I must do this. I must force myself.* What was she trying to put it off for? "Okay, we'll go."

There, she'd said it. And taking that first step did make it all feel possible.

"Where did you say it was?"

"A monastery, near Isernia."

He already had his phone out and was searching for the name. "That's about three hours by road if we take the Ferrari. Shall I pick you up at eight o'clock after I drop Adriano off?"

"I guess…should I ring to let them know?"

"That's a good idea—we don't know what his state of health is—or if they'd even let us in without being warned in advance."

Edmondo wouldn't say anything else on the subject—that wasn't his way. She had to handle this herself.

****

"You're very tense."

She was watching the long, straight road that seemed to vanish into the distant mountains as they sped southward. "Sorry. I can't help it. It probably shouldn't be so important—but it is."

"Of course it's important. And you've got used to being angry with him. The idea that the feeling may soon disappear probably feels uncomfortable."

"So when did you manage to fit in the psychology training?" she said and immediately regretted her waspish tone.

But all he said was, "It's just common sense. Anyway, we've got hours to go. Relax and enjoy the journey."

"I'll try."

It was not easy to do. She attempted to take in and appreciate some very beautiful scenery, but all the while, she was rehearsing what she would say to him. To the person whose actions had so affected her life. To her father.

She had to get rid of the anger; there was only one way to treat a dying man and that was with compassion. That's why she hadn't really wanted to come. Edmondo was right—it was hard to get used to the idea that he wasn't a monster and accept instead a flawed human being.

"You seem very at ease with all this monastery business," she said, after a long silence.

Isla had attended a Catholic high school, and going to church had occupied a part of every Sunday until she was thirteen, at which point she'd rejected all religion and refused ever to worship in a church again, despite her mother continuing to attend every Sunday. To her mind, many priests were deeply flawed, and monks were parasites, shutting themselves away, hiding from reality. She knew and liked Father Ignatius but believed him to be different from most members of the priesthood, a notable exception—but still deluded.

"Well, my sister is a nun, so I have a more detailed knowledge of how the church works than most people, I suppose."

"A nun? Your sister?" She took a moment to absorb the information and then asked, "Why is she a nun? I thought you had a good background, grew up in a loving family."

"We did—and it wasn't anything in her background that made her choose that path."

"So tell me."

"Okay." He was quiet for a moment and then went on. "Caterina is four years older than me. I was still a boy when she was already out socializing with her university friends, enjoying the scene. Then one night, when she was nineteen, already in her first year at law school but still living at home, she went to a party with some friends. My parents used to worry every time she went out—but not this time because the party was in someone's house, and the parents were supposed to be around."

"But they weren't?"

"No, it seems not. People were doing drugs, getting wasted. Probably Caterina was doing exactly the same herself. She never said. But her best friend took some drug and had a bad reaction, and by the next morning, she was dead. Caterina was devastated. When she got herself together again, she gave up her studies, and a few months later, she joined a religious order."

"But...isn't that just running away—like my father?"

"They live in Rome, Isla, and she's out every day on the back streets, in the drug dens, pulling the kids out, trying to get them rehabilitated. She's not running away. She's devoted her whole life to that. And I know she's happy because she feels she's doing something worthwhile. And this year, she restarted her studies.

She believes a law degree may be a help."

Isla didn't see why such work needed to be done under the cloak of religion.

"That's the way I saw it at first, too. I thought it was a waste of a beautiful, clever girl who had her whole life in front of her, my sister, and it made me angry."

He paused and then added, "But now I know more, I think it's so hard, doing what they do. Maybe they need the calm and peace of the convent to replenish the spirit, to keep them strong. So that they can go out there again and again. I've learned to accept it."

This seemed so strange. How hard it would be to do that work. His sister must lead a life that was completely different from anything she knew herself. A little while later, she said, "I'd like to meet her."

"You will. She's a lovely woman. You'll like her, Isla."

At some point during the morning, they stopped at a pretty little place called Pescocostanzo. It was a town for winter skiers, but no snow had fallen yet, and the place was deserted. The sky was a bright, hard blue with no cloud and the air noticeably colder. Despite her preoccupation, the town caught her interest.

"Maybe we could come back here some time, Edmondo. I'd love to look around."

"Definitely. I don't really know it myself."

****

"Okay, here we are."

A broad avenue behind iron gates led off to the left.

"Maybe I should get out here and walk up."

Edmondo put his hand onto her arm. "No, wait."

He got out and went up to the gate. Now that she

272

focused, she could see what looked like a sophisticated security system. He pressed a button and then appeared to speak. As he got behind the wheel again, the gates slowly opened.

"It's a good thing you didn't decide to walk," he said five minutes later, when they were still driving slowly along the well-made gravel road. Beyond the trees, which grew on both sides, fields that stretched into the distance were planted with dead-looking sticks which must be vines. Were the brothers producers of wine? Very likely.

As they drew closer, figures could be seen at work, more so as the old monastery itself came into view. Men in brown habits were tending the gardens. In the distance, a machine was running, and one of those peculiar, tall tractors rose steadily up a steep hill of vines, maybe clearing the paths between them.

They got out and walked slowly up to the massive front door, taking in the magnificent building which seemed, literally, to grow out of the living rock behind it. The mountain rose up almost vertically at that point, beautiful but rather terrifying at the same time. She just hadn't expected this. Really, she didn't know what she'd imagined.

"Do you want me to come in with you?"

"Please. I feel quite nervous."

They were admitted by another brown-robed figure who explained that they were an almost silent order. Only the person on the door and those who had to use the telephones to run the monastery's business were permitted to speak. This added yet another layer of strangeness.

"Please wait while I check that Fra Francisco is

ready to receive you."

Fra Francisco? Her father's name had been Gianni—Giovanni, really. Of course, they were probably given a saint's name when they entered holy orders. Or was this just one more instance of the extent to which he'd rejected his former life? And had he actually become a priest? Were all monks priests, able to conduct services like Father Ignatius? She didn't know how it all worked.

The monk's sandals slapped on the marble floor as he vanished through a door in the far corner of the cold, lofty hall in which they now waited. Two minutes later, he reappeared and beckoned to them. "*Venite, per favore.*"

They entered a broad corridor but soon turned off into a much narrower one, with doors along both sides. Her heart was beating too fast, almost as if it would choke her, and her mouth had gone dry.

"We're in the infirmary here," said their guide, turning to a door on the left-hand side. It swung open, revealing a tiny room, big enough for little other than a bed, over which hung a large wooden cross. A waist-high, shallow cupboard occupied the right-hand wall. The narrow window was uncurtained, and it let in a cold light. Two chairs had been placed close to the bed.

"I will be waiting here outside," the man said. "Come to the door if you need me."

Propped against pillows was a striking figure, his head crowned with a magnificent brush of white hair. This was all that was left of a tall and powerful man, now just bones with thin, almost translucent skin stretched across them, but Isla still knew him. And then came the familiar surge of fury. She pushed it away.

Somehow, she had to get through this. He smiled, but his skeletal fingers clutched the cover, the knuckles showing white. He began to push himself up the bed, a pathetic attempt which collapsed almost immediately. Isla couldn't stop herself hurrying over to help him. She would have done that for anyone.

"I'm Isla, your daughter," she said, speaking carefully, disguising her anger. "And this is Edmondo Benedetti, my friend, who drove me here today."

"Ah, the father of one of the boys."

So, he *had* informed himself.

"*Grazie per essere venuti*," he went on. "I wanted so much to see you, but I didn't think—"

Here, his voice failed, and he spent a few moments struggling to find the strength to continue.

"I am so sorry for walking out on you and your mother after the accident. I regret so much doing that." He stopped as he tried to find his breath, an eerie wheeze emanating from his lungs. "It was the action of a weak man, of one who had never really had to consider before how his behavior might affect other people."

"You just left us as if we didn't matter. You didn't think we loved you? That I loved you?"

This was so difficult. Her emotions roiled wildly within her as she spoke those words. It was almost too much to take, but she could feel Edmondo's strong, comforting presence beside her. Now, he put his hand on her shoulder, just a light touch, giving her the strength to go on, guiding her in the right direction.

"I...I couldn't understand my own feelings—or deal with them," her father said. "I had done something terrible. Whatever way you look at it, I was the cause of your brother's death, although, God knows, it was never intended. But you were only a child. It must have been hard."

They were speaking Italian, and Isla wondered if he ever used English these days. It didn't sound as if they spoke much at all in this strange place. She thought about what he'd said and knew that nothing less than complete honesty would do.

"I lost my brother and my father, so I was very angry." Her voice was cold. "I've been very angry for most of my life."

He lay back on his pillows, watching her, and she was silent, hardly knowing how to continue. "Now, it seems as if all that was a waste of time."

"I hope you can leave it behind you. Those little boys...I was so proud of what you did. A soul like yours is bigger than resentment and hate," he said, echoing Edmondo's sentiments exactly. "Please forgive me, Isla."

His mention of the children made her think of them, and of all the good things in her life, and she knew he was right, that she should let it go. Yes, she should—could—forgive him.

They stayed for a little over half an hour and left when it became clear he could no longer talk. In the corridor, the monk said, "Thank you for coming. Now he can die in peace."

It was clear he had listened to every word of their conversation.

A few minutes later, they were back in their car, their guide having assured them that he would open the gates when they pressed the green button.

****

She didn't want to talk about it. Her mind was devoid of thoughts, and Edmondo seemed to understand that she had no words. Half an hour had passed, and they were driving slowly toward the town of Isernia. Both of them were cast down by the experience at the monastery and disinclined to hurry. As they approached the town, houses seemed to climb up two hills and then head for a mountain that could be glimpsed behind them.

"We'll stop a while."

Edmondo parked and they wandered the charming streets in the freezing air.

"Let's eat."

He bought two large wedges of pizza from a kiosk to stem their hunger, and they sat on a low stone balustrade outside the cathedral, where they munched slowly as they watched people buying their fruit and vegetables at the market stalls.

"We need a drink."

He was looking after her when she most needed it.

After a while, they found a bar overlooking a little square. There they drank cups of steaming coffee. The cold was penetrating.

"You were right," said Isla at last. "The anger's gone, and I don't hate him. What's the point of hating a pathetic old man? Things went terribly wrong for him, and he couldn't cope. That's human, not evil. If I feel anything, it's pity and sorrow."

"So you meant it when you said you'd forgive him?"

"Yes, I did," she said slowly. "Maybe other feelings will come later, but for the moment, that's all I can manage. Yes, I forgive him. And after all, his rejection probably fired me up to want to make something of my life. It's my mother who will have to decide whether she can forgive him."

"And do you think she will?"

"Yes, I do, even though his actions brought her nothing but misery. She's a much nicer person than I am."

"I'm certain that's not true, but think, Isla—she was married to him, and I assume until the accident, they had a happy marriage. You have to take that into account."

For the first time that day, she laughed, with a genuine open sound, and then she nestled up against him, nibbling at his ear. "I do love you, Edmondo. You're very good for me."

"I know. Being very good for you is everything I aim for." He smiled, evidently happy with this state of affairs. "So having got that settled, shall we take advantage of this journey and stay the night?"

"Adriano…"

"Remember, I told you he's doing a sleepover with Marco. Their adventures in Falesia seem to have made them inseparable. But I will check first with Marco's mother that all is well."

Chapter 36

They wandered around the Centro Storico, looking for a hotel, and finally found one in an old town house.

"What do you think?" said Edmondo.

"It's a lovely building." It was ancient, the lines gracious. "Let's stay here."

It had grown increasingly cold, and he needed to get them inside, somewhere to restore her circulation and stop the shivering which was beginning to worry him. But the hotel was better than expected, clean and bright with an acre of bed and a large bathroom. And a tub. Perfect.

The proprietor welcomed them warmly because it was that time of year, he told them, with few guests in residence, before the build-up to Christmas would begin.

"Next week, the hotel is fully booked," he said as they registered.

****

Isla sat on the bed and began to cry. Tears pushed out of her eyes and rolled down her cheeks, and she didn't seem able to stop them.

What was the matter? One minute, she was commenting happily on what a lovely room they'd managed to get, and now she was crying so hard, she couldn't even tell him what was wrong. He pulled her against his chest and wrapped his arms around her. He wasn't sure what he could say to ease her pain but holding her close should bring some comfort.

Gradually, the sobbing subsided, and she looked up at him. "I'm sorry."

She hiccoughed and produced a faint smile. That was better.

He stroked her hair. "You don't need to say sorry—all that emotion has to go somewhere."

"It's just that...I'll never see him again, really never see him again. I feel so sad. What a waste, Edmondo, all those years. What a waste. How could I be so stubborn, so selfish? My poor mother."

And she began to cry again.

Edmondo thought that maybe others also bore the blame but decided he wouldn't say that. She didn't need a dissertation on the way people behaved toward one another. He waited until she had calmed and said, "You didn't cause it to happen. You were a child, and two people you loved were torn from your life. And according to your logic, one of them didn't have to go. I'm not surprised you reacted that way."

A little while later, he began to peel off her outer clothes, hanging up her coat, pulling off her boots, massaging her freezing feet. "You should get into bed."

"Yes, you're right, but I'm going to have a bath. It'll relax me—and I can't resist the tub," she added.

That was a second smile. Her words were a little tremulous, but she was making an effort.

Edmondo decided to leave her to it, reasonably certain now that she'd cope. He thought about the bar they'd walked past on their way to the room. Maybe they'd go out to eat later, but he wasn't sure that would happen. For the moment, a whiskey would go down well, and he could order a panino. He tucked a book under his arm as he left and went downstairs.

When Edmondo had gone out, Isla entered the bathroom and opened the taps, waiting a long while before she turned them off. Then she sat down in the bath, trying hard not to look at her swollen, red eyes in the mirror glass that covered most of the walls. But it was fast misting over, and soon she no longer had to avoid looking at something that would really have depressed her. Exactly what had just happened to her, back there in the room? It felt as if she'd been hurtling through a wind tunnel for an incalculable amount of time, and now, bruised and battered, she'd been shot out of the other end.

But here, all was calm, and everything felt new and fresh, the anxious, insecure person that she'd been, replaced by a stronger, sleeker version.

Isla washed and then dried herself and got into bed, dimming the lights as far as they would go. She hadn't liked being needy, but she'd had no choice, and Edmondo had borne the brunt of her turbulent emotions. That's how it worked when you were with someone, a part of each other's lives. She was beginning to understand that now—it wasn't just enjoying each other's company; you depended on one another when things were tough. She closed her eyes, but this was no time for sleep.

She was instantly alert when the door clicked shut behind Edmondo, but she didn't move. He went into the bathroom, the toilet flushed, the shower ran, and then came the sound of him brushing his teeth. While he was busy with these things, she thought about him and the fact that he would be coming to her. And the fact that she wanted him to come to her. She waited.

Edmondo slipped beneath the covers. Did he know she was awake? She still didn't move. He waited.

"I'm okay," she said after a few moments. "I've got over it."

She felt him roll onto his side. After a moment or two, the sensation of being looked at forced her to open her eyes. He'd propped his head on his hand and was gazing down at her.

"Really?" he said. "You've really got over it?"

"Try me."

"Are you by any chance challenging me, *cara mia*?"

"Could be."

"Well." He bent his head to run the tip of his tongue in a neat circle around her right nipple. "I've never been one to let a challenge go by—especially not a difficult one."

She gasped. It wasn't a tongue at all, but a rasp, harsh and insistent, and it was leaving a trail of pinging nerve endings in its wake as it headed in a leisurely fashion toward the other breast.

She forced herself to stay completely still. Within, the trembling was growing. He'd reached the other side now and paused to suck gently at the second nipple. She drew in a shaky breath, but he ignored it and began a downward trajectory, the rasp back in action, scoring her soft skin, extending the path of fire. Every spot he touched began to ache, the craving building and building. How much longer could she keep going?

"Is there any chance of success, do you think?" he said, as she gasped.

"I don't know." She was mad. She couldn't take

any more and should tell him to stop. But she didn't. Instead, she added, "Perhaps, but it may take some time."

"Time is something I have."

He reached her navel, and now he abandoned the path and veered onto the soft skin of her stomach, covering it with little bites, nipping and then soothing, nipping again. A moan escaped her, and a giant hand took hold of the core of her being and squeezed, gently, harder, inexorably. The sensation grew, and she began to pant. She'd have to do something about it, now...now...

But then he resumed the trail. That had just been an interlude. The deep ache expanded, ballooning outward and upward. He had an end point in mind, but it was unreasonable of him, preposterous to think she could hold back any longer, that she could wait for him to get there. She tried to control her breathing. It was no good, she couldn't, but then a moment later, he'd reached his goal. She heaved up and arched her back.

"You won the challenge," she whispered, scarcely able to speak. Then she sank back down and moved to let him in.

Chapter 37

The following Tuesday, Isla arrived back at the office late.

"Sorry, Chiara. I took longer than I expected. They've set up roadworks at the bottom of the road coming out of Teramo. There's a long delay."

"No problem. I've put him in the atrium."

Isla glanced back through the plants. A man was seated with his back to her, leafing through a brochure.

"Give me two minutes, Chiara, and I'll be right back."

In the toilets, when she came out of the cubicle, she studied herself in the mirror and took a few deep breaths, preparing to meet her visitor. It was Michele. That was the Signor Verdino whose name Chiara had given her over the phone. But she'd been concentrating on driving, and it hadn't meant anything. She'd just assumed it was the new client who was due later in the afternoon.

What was Michele doing there? They'd talked a few times on the phone since their dinner in Ascoli, and on each occasion, she'd made clear that there was no point in a meeting, that she wasn't going to change her mind.

How was she going to play this? It was hard because she really liked him. He was kind, intelligent, very attractive—and in love with her. Very early on, she'd worked out they never could just remain friends, not on his side, anyway. Much as she would have liked that.

She dried her hands and smoothed down her hair. There was no point in hanging around any longer. Squaring her shoulders, she made her way out to the atrium.

"Michele."

He smiled and stood up but didn't offer a kiss or even a handshake.

"Shall we go across the square and get something to drink?" she said.

A stiff breeze was blowing, and it felt good to go inside, where the air was warm and laden with the pungent aroma of coffee. They sat at a corner table, and within seconds, Toni was taking their order. It was interesting how the skinny wraith had gained in confidence. The Albertos had already smoothed off his rough edges, though it would take a while before he was smiling at the customers. But she was putting off the start of the conversation. She turned to her companion.

"What is it, Michele?"

"I've come to say good-bye."

"Oh, but...where are you going?"

This was not what she'd expected. Just three weeks ago, he'd been trying to set up a theater date.

"Africa. More specifically, South Africa—one of the boss's many connections. I've already started work on designing a housing estate for the client—upmarket, gated. Houses for very rich people. You know the sort of thing?"

"That sounds wonderful...but why you?"

"Mainly because of my good English. But I did volunteer."

"Oh."

"Yes, why not? There's nothing to keep me here, Isla."

Toni, the teenaged waiter, returned at that moment with the coffee, taking time to place the cups carefully and managing to do so without spilling any of the contents. Michele immediately dropped three lumps of sugar into his cup and stirred the concoction for a while before taking a long drink. He raised his head.

"You've told me many times that there can be nothing between us, but…you could still come with me." He held up his hand as she opened her mouth to reply. "I know you don't love me, but I don't think you find me repulsive or anything like that. We could work something out. We complement one another, and I believe we'd be good together. And maybe, eventually, you'd come to care for me."

"I'm so sorry I have to say no, Michele. I do like you very much indeed—anyone would be lucky to have you as their partner. But I meant what I said when I told you I already have someone. Please don't ever think that's just an excuse. There's no way around it—I'm in love with him. I'm simply not free."

He sat back, a sad smile on his face. "I was sure you'd say that, but I had to ask. It's okay. I understand. I know what it feels like to love someone like that. At least, you are loved in return." He looked down into the remains of his coffee and sighed. "I'll have plenty to occupy me while I'm over there. It's a big commission, might stretch to two or three years, with supervising the builds."

"It's very exciting. I am pleased for you."

"Thank you."

He stood up and took her hand, pulling her to her feet. Then, he dropped a light kiss onto her lips. "Maybe we'll meet again one day."

"And when we do, you'll be a famous architect."

"I wish." He smiled. "*Arrivederci*, Isla. He's a very lucky man."

And he was gone.

Isla slumped back down onto her seat and slowly finished off her coffee. She didn't quite know what to do with the sense of loss, what to do next.

Chapter 38

Only Edmondo and Isla were in the house that Saturday afternoon, two weeks later. Signora Forni had left them a prepared lunch which they'd picked through in a leisurely fashion, talking about the opera they'd attended, and how Puccini might have reacted had he ever seen the unexpected effects the contemporary set designer had created.

"I want to take you to an outdoor opera in the summer. It's an experience you must have, and there's a place where they put them on, just up the coast."

"That sounds great," Isla said, thinking about the forest of umbrellas in the pouring rain at a performance of *The Taming of the Shrew* that she'd attended in Regent's Park.

"And no rain." Edmondo grinned at her, reading her mind. "It'll be a great experience."

They had driven Adriano to Paola's house in Rome the evening before. There was to be another party, this time for Adriano's cousin, Alessio, whose fourth birthday it was, and Adriano had been granted a day off school to attend it. This made it very special to him.

It had been such fun choosing a present, an activity which had occupied a good deal of everybody's time and effort, as Adriano could only contemplate getting presents that he liked himself. He found it difficult to imagine there were some things the younger child might not be able to do. Down in Teramo, they'd spent more than an hour in a toy shop, picking up and discarding all sorts of unsuitable items, before finally choosing an outdoor explorer kit. It did have a great magnifying glass and a bug booklet, but Isla still thought it was far too advanced for the younger boy.

As far as Adriano was concerned, no visit to town was complete without ice cream, so when they'd finally made their purchase, Edmondo led them to a *gelateria* in the center. At the door, he said, "I have to pick something up from a shop along the street, Isla. Could you get ice cream for us? Lemon for me."

"Any restrictions as far as Adriano is concerned?"

She'd already learned he had no limits if the choice was left to him.

"He can have whatever he wants but no more than two scoops in total. He'll have to make a decision—which means you'll probably still be at the counter when I get back."

But Adriano chose raspberry and chocolate quite quickly. It looked as if he was like her cousin's boy—at his most difficult with his parents.

They found a table in the window, and a few moments later, Edmondo arrived.

"This is for you, Isla. A small present."

"What is it? Can I see?" asked the boy.

"In a moment."

Isla opened the package and took out a long, dark blue box with the name of a jeweler engraved on the lid. Inside was a delicate silver necklace with a blue stone that looked like a topaz.

"I wanted to give you something to go with your blue dress. That color is so good on you."

"Oh, I don't know what to say. It's so beautiful. Thank you." She stood up and planted a kiss on his cheek.

"Here, let me."

He took it out as she sank back onto her chair and walked behind her. Then, draping the necklace around her neck, he fastened the clasp.

She could see her reflection in the mirror opposite and sat more upright to view it better. "It's beautiful, Edmondo. The loveliest piece of jewelry I've ever had. Thank you so much."

"You lend it your beauty. I'm glad you like it."

Adriano was gazing up at her. "Is it your birthday? Is that why you've got a present?"

"It will be very soon, Adriano. It's a good present, isn't it?"

"My pencils and sketchbook were better."

Isla and Edmondo looked at each other, smiling.

****

Adriano had arrived at his aunt's house clutching the large box with the present inside, and Isla wondered if his little cousin would ever get the chance to use it. The family only had a small garden. Would there be enough outdoor space for the four-year-old to practice his new hobby?

How much fun she'd had that day! She'd loved that precious time spent with the two of them, wandering around the shops and getting to know them both. If she moved in with Edmondo, there could be more excursions like that—family time, so much to gain. And would she really be giving up so much? She would still be able to run a business—there was enough space to fit several businesses into the rambling old house. And

Edmondo had made it clear that he would not stand in her way—indeed, he seemed keen to support her. A decision had to be made.

Now, with lunch over, she lounged beside Edmondo in front of a TV screen, watching an old black-and-white film—or, in her case, appearing to watch the film. She lay lengthwise along the sofa, her head in Edmondo's lap. The film credits began to roll, so at least an hour must have passed, but she had no idea of the story, her mind full of other things.

Edmondo clicked off with the remote and silence fell. Then, he pushed back her hair and kissed her forehead. "What is it, Isla? You're not very relaxed."

"It's nothing. I'm fine."

She smiled up at him, but she was indeed feeling tense, mulling over a dilemma.

Should she tell him or should she not? She really didn't want to talk about it and never even gave it any thought these days. Or hadn't, until she noticed what day it was and began to consider the deeper implications of her relationship with Edmondo. The event had marked her early teenage years, at a time when she'd barely come to terms with her brother's death, so it was important. But was there really any need for confession?

She pushed up off the couch and went to the window. Autumn was well advanced now, the trees lower down the mountain almost bare, and a wind stirred the few leaves that remained. Soon winter would come, and she'd be going back to London to spend Christmas with her mother. But maybe she had to sort out a few things first.

She'd heard that people often dug things out of the

past because they needed to relieve themselves of a secret, perhaps of guilt. But that was not so in her case. Surely, it should be left there, in the past, where it belonged.

She could almost convince herself this was true. She glanced behind her to where Edmondo sprawled, watching her. This man was not like Richard, who had never deserved access to her innermost thoughts. She frowned, pursuing the thought. Did anyone really? Did you need to lay bare your soul?

She turned, her back to the glass, watching him now through half-closed eyes. This was Edmondo, and they were contemplating spending at least some of their lives together. That was the difference. She'd never made that sort of commitment to Richard, even though they'd talked about getting married, and neither had he to her. The relationship had been convenient for both, often pleasant and occasionally fun—but not at all like this.

Edmondo got up, gathering the coffee things and piling them on the tray. Then he sat down again, folding his arms, waiting for her to speak.

Shouldn't she be open about things? Even if she felt this huge reluctance because telling him would be to risk everything? Because maybe he would change his mind about her. Because maybe he would no longer want her.

She sat back down beside him and blinked back a tear at this thought and then quickly wiped her eyes, but Edmondo had seen.

"Is it about your father?"

He had finally died two days earlier.

"No, I think I've dealt with that. It's been harder on

Mum than on me, because it happened so quickly, and she never got the chance to see him. I'm fine, Edmondo, just grateful you made me visit him."

"I persuaded you it was a good idea. You chose to go."

"It was a good idea."

She sat there a while longer, but suddenly, she got to her feet and said, "Let's go for a walk, shall we?"

Chapter 39

Maybe if they went out, the cold air would help clear her thoughts.

They pulled on jackets and walking shoes and left by the back door. Outside, it was still bright, and although everyone kept threatening terrible weather, recent days had been very pleasant. Edmondo led the way. He'd only lived in the area a few years, but it was impressive how he seemed to know the mountain paths like someone who'd been there the whole of his life, and they'd enjoyed quite a few walks. He'd made this place his own.

They were gaining height and could soon look down over the house and then over the tower. If they went much farther, the cold would begin to bite on the exposed surfaces of the mountain. The track doglegged sharply to the left, where the trees quickly grew thinner and were more windswept, finally disappearing altogether. So late in the year, the peaks were picked out in white, but at this level, there was still no frost or snow, and the path was quite easy to walk on. They came to a rare patch of green, with large boulders behind and a small overhang. It would shelter them from the wind.

"Let's sit here."

He dug in his backpack for a blanket which he spread on the grass, and they sat. Isla leaned against him, needing the contact, and she gazed down the mountain to the plain. From here, the town of Teramo was visible as a smudge on the horizon, and several tiny villages clung to the route.

Isla's eyes drank in the view, which was cold, still, and beautiful. Her recent experiences in Falesia had been traumatic, but she had no fear of these mountains. Instead, she felt at home in this harsh terrain. Sometimes, when she wanted to work something out, she walked in the rocky landscape, and it always made her feel stronger, more able to tackle even difficult things. Her heart slowed, and she allowed the deep calm of the mountain to steal over her.

But she hadn't come to think about her relationship to the mountains. The issue in her mind had grown and grown over the last few days, until it left room for little else, and she knew she couldn't continue like that. It was time to open up about it—when she could find the courage to do so.

"So," said Edmondo, lying back with his arms forming a pillow for his head. "Are you going to tell me now?"

She stiffened. He wouldn't let the moment pass. It looked as if she had no choice. A minute or so of silence went by, and then she lay down beside him, so she could talk without looking at him. She didn't want to look. She didn't want to see the rejection and disappointment there.

"I'm afraid."

"Afraid of me? What do you mean?"

"Not of you. Afraid of what you'll think and of what you'll do."

"Well, having got this far, I think you must tell me

what it is, *cara mia.* If you're holding something back and it's making you unhappy, that's no basis for our relationship. Maybe there's something I can do about it."

"There's nothing you or anyone can do, but I don't want to lose you, Edmondo."

"Can you not trust me?"

Still, she waited. Even now, she wanted nothing more than to run away. She'd spent a lot of her life not facing up to things. When she finally turned her head to look at him, she saw that his face was filled with love and concern for her, nothing else. Though she turned away again, it gave her courage.

"I have a child, Edmondo."

"A child? So, why is that a problem? I have a child also."

"You were married, and the relationship broke up. The circumstances are completely different."

"So, tell me."

Still not looking at him, she sat up, drew her knees to her chest, wrapping her arms around them. She couldn't bear to watch his reactions while she spoke. She had to get it all out before she ever looked at him again.

"When I was thirteen, I was attacked by two boys in my school and raped."

She'd never talked about it to anyone except her mother, had rarely even thought about it. Now, it was painful to articulate the words.

"I was walking home after a school trip. It was a visit to the V & A—that's a big London museum of design—for those of us in the art class who were really interested. I remember I loved every minute of it. We'd had a wonderful day, and it was about seven in the evening when we got back to school. Mum was working and couldn't pick me up, but my friend, Suzie, lived close by, and I was supposed to walk back with her and her mum. But then Suzie was ill that day and didn't go on the trip. I didn't even think about it. When we got off the coach, I started walking home. It wasn't far, and although it was dark, it wasn't particularly late, so I didn't worry. In fact, I'd always thought Mum made far too much fuss.

"The boys, Kyle and Stephen, followed me and attacked me by the churchyard. They dragged me in behind the gravestones. I remember fighting, scratching Kyle's face and drawing blood, but Stephen held me down and covered my mouth to stop me screaming and it was Kyle who raped me. Then they ran off, shouting and laughing. They just left me there on someone's grave."

Edmondo's hand found hers and squeezed gently. Then he turned toward her.

"Don't look at me, Edmondo. Just listen." But she kept a tight hold of his hand. "I was traumatized and in a lot of pain. I suppose I was a bit immature at that stage, hadn't really begun to think about things like sex, so what had happened was terribly shocking. But I did understand what it was—how could I not? I didn't know what to do, but eventually, I got up and struggled home. When I arrived, such a short time had passed that it seemed unreal. It had all happened so quickly. It wasn't even eight o'clock, and Mum wouldn't get in until nine.

"I didn't know about things like forensic evidence at the time. I was crying and shaking. All I wanted to do was to get rid of anything they'd left on me or in me, so I showered and scrubbed myself. Then I ran the bath, got in and stayed there until the water was cold.

"I thought I wouldn't tell Mum—she'd be so upset. I was in my pajamas when she came in and began asking what sort of day I'd had. But then she looked at me and knew straight away that something dreadful had happened. Gradually, she prized the story from me."

Isla was silent for such a long time, reliving the events in her mind, that Edmondo wondered if she was going to continue. He sat up and put his arms around her, but she shrugged him off.

"No, let me finish. We went to the police, but there was no evidence. They were two well-liked boys, a year ahead of me. The policeman who took the details didn't try to hide behind the system, not really. He said he'd follow it up, but that it was unlikely I'd be believed without evidence, and if by chance it did get to court, the resultant testimony and publicity could ruin my life. The truth was, there was no appetite to pursue a rape case against two fourteen-year-olds. Maybe there still wouldn't be.

"He said I might even get accused of encouraging them and then trying to draw back when it was too late, so they could claim it was consensual, just kids experimenting. I remember how mad Mum got when he said that. She shouted at him and said the system was no good if they could allow such things to pass without taking any action at all. But there were so many reasons not to pursue the case. So in the end, we left it there.

"Nine months later, I gave birth to a little boy. Today is the anniversary of his birth. I was just fourteen when he was born, and I never thought of him as my child. But I haven't forgotten the date."

"What happened to him?"

"He was legally adopted a few days later by a couple who couldn't have children. An abortion hadn't even been considered—all our family were Catholic, Mum included. It was out of the question.

"Afterward, I started at a different school—I'd only missed a few months, and no one knew the reason. My body had recovered quickly, and we told them I'd been suffering from ME, you know, that fatigue thing. God knows, that was true. I could hardly do anything for months, I was so devastated by what had happened. Few people were aware of the truth."

She slumped back onto the ground, her arm over her eyes.

Edmondo said nothing, trying to rein in the horror that had overcome him as he listened. Now, he lay back down beside her and drew her toward him. All that hurt and anguish—how had she coped? She was silent, but he kept his arms tight around her, wanting to infuse her with the love he felt. Of course, it made a difference to know this. A red-hot feeling rose in his body, and he had an overwhelming desire for violent action. For revenge. Then his mind cleared. Two kids? Twelve years ago? There was nothing he could do.

It didn't change the fact that he loved her.

How much she must have suffered to have this horrible thing happen on top of her brother's fatal car accident and being abandoned by her father. She'd still been a child herself when it occurred. It was amazing that she'd remained fundamentally sweet and caring, her instinctive response always to help others—even if she did have an acerbic tongue at times.

She'd been crying after all, her head turned away, the tears flowing silently down her cheeks as she'd told the story. Finally, she sat up, groping around blindly for a handkerchief. He found a tissue and handed it to her.

"Here—blow your nose. It'll make you feel much better." He smiled. "I remember saying that to you before." He waited and then took her hand. "You do know this makes no difference to our relationship, don't you? Not one iota. In fact, I have even more respect for you than before. How could you imagine I'd reject you?"

They were quiet for a long time until Isla said in a small voice, "I seem to have been doing a lot of confessing and crying recently. And I like to think of myself as a strong woman."

"You are a strong woman. And anyway, these things probably needed to happen for you to be truly free of the past, of the bad things in the past. What do you feel about the child now?"

"Nothing, really. He was like some alien life-form that had taken over my body, and it was a relief when he'd gone. I didn't think of him as a child, not like Adriano or my little cousin in London. I love them."

Hearing her refer to his son in this way gave Edmondo a warm feeling, a hope that they could build a family together. Adriano needed people to love him.

"So you're not against having other children—as a result of your experiences?"

"Oh, no. I'd love a child of my own—one I've chosen to have—but not right now, of course, not until I've built my business."

He smiled at the determination in her voice. "That's very good to hear."

"You don't think any less of me for…for what happened?"

"What do you think, you goose? I love you, and that's not going to change."

Edmondo stood up and held out his hand, and his heart was light, despite his sadness at what he had heard. This had been the suffering he'd sensed when he'd first met her, and it was a relief to have it out in the open.

"Come on, on your feet! It's almost dark. Let's go home."

Chapter 40

Isla lay on her side and watched Edmondo for a few moments. In his sleep, the small boy he once had been showed through. He looked completely relaxed and, at the same time, vulnerable. She moved a little, reawakening her desire, wanting to run her fingers over his bare chest. Maybe…oh, what time was it? Carefully, so as not to wake him, she turned to the bedside table and picked up her phone. What? Nearly eight o'clock! Unlike on other weekends when Adriano was visiting his cousins, there was no chance of a leisurely breakfast and its delightful prelude this Sunday morning. It was a pity, but that pleasure would have to be deferred.

Isla slid out of bed and went into the bathroom, where she turned on the shower and enjoyed the powerful spray. Faint noises reached her ears, which meant Edmondo must now be up. They would be driving to the capital to pick up Adriano in a little while, and then, they'd go on to see Edmondo's father, so they needed to arrive in Rome somewhat earlier than usual. His mother had died a couple of years earlier, but his father still lived in the quiet suburb of the city where he'd been brought up.

When she came out, the bedroom was empty, and water was running in the guest bathroom. She wandered over to the clothes she'd laid out on a chair. She'd thought about what to wear for the visit and brought everything she needed with her. It was important to make a good impression, to be welcomed in by Edmondo's father, not just accepted as the girlfriend. After all, this was his family.

It had taken a while to make up her mind, but conscious that it was a style that suited her, she'd decided on a clinging, white shift dress in a soft wool with its hem at mid-calf. And the new shoes, of course. Thank goodness they'd recovered from that downpour—she could hardly see any sign of it now. She stood in front of the long mirror and gazed at her reflection as she added the beautiful silver necklace. It was just as stunning with the white dress as with blue. Not bad! Yes, that would do.

It was such a relief to have told him her horrible story. The outcome was so much better than anything she'd imagined, and she knew it had been the right thing to do. She didn't want any secrets between them.

In the night, after their conversation on the mountainside, she'd dreamt for the first time in many years of the child she'd given birth to twelve years earlier. The process of revealing what she'd come to consider a terrible secret had been cathartic, sweeping away all the negativity, much of which had been caused by her fears—for herself, for their relationship, for the future. The habit of concealment had been bred into her by so many events in her past—it had always seemed better to remain quiet than to risk getting hurt. It had created a toxic mix, but now, thank God, all that had changed.

****

The birthday party had apparently been a great

success, and Adriano came away from his aunt's house with a present of his own—a battery-operated robot which, to his total delight, he could take apart and rebuild. As they drove to his grandfather's house, the car was filled with the grating tones of Robbie the Robot issuing various orders. If Isla shut her eyes, she could imagine it was Stephen Hawking whose voice she heard. They'd arrived. Isla took a deep breath and composed herself as they approached the front door.

Signor Benedetti was a man in his late sixties, not as tall as Edmondo, but nearly so, his once-dark hair liberally streaked with grey. The men hugged each other. Edmondo introduced Isla, and then the old man swung Adriano up onto his shoulders as they set off on a tour of the garden—not a long one at this time of year, he explained.

The grapevine that climbed a small pergola had died back, but there was an impressive kitchen garden area. He must be virtually self-sufficient with winter vegetables. The shady terrace he'd built at the back of the house was perfect—it would be heavenly in the summer, but Isla was relieved that he considered it too cold for al fresco eating today. They entered the house.

"Get any heavier and I won't be able to do that," he said to his grandson as he set him down. "What can I get you two to drink? Wine? I've got something special for you, Adriano."

They'd worked their way through half a bottle of red wine and a great deal of conversation, and Adriano was polishing off a carton of mango juice, when Signor Benedetti said he'd get lunch ready.

"Can I help?" asked Isla.

"Could you stay here with Adriano?" Edmondo

showed her where the cutlery and plates were. "Would you mind showing him how to lay the table? He needs to learn. I'll help in the kitchen."

"Okay." She'd spotted some brightly colored paper napkins. "Here, let's make it look extra special," she added to the boy, handing them to him. "I'll show you how to fold them into butterflies."

She guessed Edmondo wanted to talk to his father whom he hadn't seen much in recent months, which was a pity. Her advent on the scene was probably partly responsible for that situation.

The lunch was simple and practical. After a short interval, they brought in a massive slab of lasagne bubbling in an earthenware oven dish, followed by an enormous salad.

"I'm no cook," said the older man, when complimented. "I buy this stuff prepared—there's a *gastronomia* down the street. And it doesn't take much to put a salad together. Even I can manage that. But thank you."

As the afternoon progressed, he engaged her in conversation but kept away from personal topics, except to mention that he knew she'd rescued his grandson and was grateful. At this point, Edmondo, who was listening in, said he wanted to propose a toast to a brave and wonderful woman: Isla Bruni. Adriano demanded more mango juice so that he could join in. Isla looked around at the smiling faces of this little family, bathed in their warmth and love, and knew at that moment that her decision was made.

Chapter 41

On Wednesday, Isla put on a crisp, white blouse tied at the neck and donned the navy business suit she hadn't worn for several months, not since the Milan conference, in fact. Aiming for a professional look, she pulled back her hair in a loose chignon. It felt as if she were attending a formal interview, and in a way, although she was only going to see Tommaso, that's exactly what it was. She needed him to understand that she was capable of presenting herself properly when talking with prospective clients.

Time was rushing past, with less than three weeks left before her exchange came to an end, so she'd requested a slot in his busy timetable to discuss the future. He'd looked a little surprised when she'd said this, perhaps because he was expecting her to return to London at the end of her stay, but he'd said he'd prefer an early morning meeting, and they'd booked it in.

She drank coffee and forced down a piece of dry toast, her stomach rebelling at the thought of food. Her phone was open in front of her while she ran through the list of matters she wanted to discuss. When she'd finished, she took a few deep breaths. It was strange to feel quite so nervous, but the conversation they were going to have was important. If her boss were willing to help, it would make the difference between a long, slow build-up to the business and the flying start she hoped for.

Of course, Tommaso would run the meeting according to his own needs, whatever was in his best interest. Working in his office for five months, she'd learned a lot about him. The main thing was that he always got what he wanted, so she couldn't expect it to be easy. His was an expansive personality, and he could make you feel as if a steamroller had run over you when he set out to have things his way.

As she walked into the studio, she drew back her shoulders and steeled herself; she had questions of her own and would seek the answers. If she'd learned anything from him about running a business, it was that you had to have a clear vision and be prepared to stick to it. It was no use just being nice.

There was Leonardo, early as usual. She gave him a wave but didn't pause, heading straight to Tommaso's sanctum. Half past seven, he'd said. She was a minute early.

"Come in, Isla, come in."

He was dapper this morning, striped grey and white blazer, white collarless shirt, pink-cheeked, and with freshly coiffed hair. His smile was welcoming, though, and that was a good thing.

"I'm so sorry we're losing you," he said. "I would've been very happy to keep you, but we haven't quite enough work to take on another member of staff. Anyway, I'm sure you're keen to get back to your London base."

So Edmondo had said nothing to him about their conversation. That was good. Tommaso pointed to the chair facing his desk and she sat down.

"Now, tell me how I can help."

"I've had a wonderful time here and learned a great deal so, first, I want to say thank you," she began. The man was susceptible to flattery, and she might as well use all the weapons she had at her disposal. "And that's due to the opportunity you and Susan created for me. I'm so grateful." Was she overdoing it?

No, probably not—his smile had broadened. "I believe both offices will have benefited, as I'm sure you'll find on your return. We certainly have."

"Thank you. I've loved the work here, Tommaso, and I've decided I'm not going back to London. I'm staying here, in Italy. And I'm going to set up my own studio."

He sat back, apparently startled. "Well...this is very sudden."

"Not for me, I assure you. I've been thinking about it for a long time, since well before I left London. I know I'm going to have to make my own way and work part-time for other people. I wondered if you would bear that in mind?" She threw him a confident smile. "If you had a rush of work or an illness, perhaps I could temp for you."

He was silent for the moment. As was his wont, he was taking the time to think before replying. "Interesting, interesting. Let's talk further about this. Maybe I can find something for you, come up with a proposition."

After an hour of intense discussion, she was completely exhausted. She'd done it! He really was willing to help—but not in quite the way she'd envisaged. She closed the door quietly behind her and went to sit at her workstation.

He thought he could push one or two jobs her way,

but consummate businessman and marketeer that he was, he insisted that every such job would bear the "In partnership with Abruzzo Design" logo that he would now design—even if she was pocketing the fees. It was actually an excellent idea. Clearly, he did value her work and was happy to have the things she did extend his reach, potentially bringing in more projects. And from her point of view, the studio was well-regarded, and the association could do her no harm. Although this would necessarily have to be short term.

It would help, of course, to decide on the name of her own studio. She gazed into the distance, seeing nothing while she played about with different combinations of words. Until she had a name, there was no business. A name, a bank account, a website, an email address—the list was endless.

Already she had a meeting scheduled with her bank for the following week, and Edmondo was putting her in touch with his own website designer who she thought was fabulous; he'd managed to make plastics look sexy, so he must have something above the ordinary. Sizzling with excitement at the thought of this entity she was creating, she had no illusions about how much work it would mean. She couldn't help smiling as she drew herself up and turned on the computer. The sooner she started, the better.

Leonardo strolled across from the tiny kitchen area, placed two coffees on her desk, and rolled a chair over. "What's up with you, Isla? You look like the cat that got the cream. To say nothing of the smart suit."

"I am that cat. I've just been telling Tommaso I'm staying on in Italy."

"So has he offered you a job? That would be

great." He took a sip of coffee. "You know, we've worked well together. I'd have been happy to have you in on a design like the tower at an earlier stage. I liked your ideas."

"Thank you, Leonardo. That means a lot to me. But no, I'm setting up on my own. I just wanted to know if he'd be willing to help with things."

"That's fantastic, Isla. We were all just saying how sad it was you'd soon be going. So where will you work?"

"Tommaso asked whether I would like to hire office space at advantageous rates. I said I'd think about it, but I won't be taking up the offer," she said.

To her mind, anything other than a straightforward, professional relationship with the studio was of advantage only to Tommaso. If she rented workspace there, she would probably become a sort of office dogsbody, and she didn't want that. Besides, she was going to live with Edmondo, and he would sort out a workroom for her.

"Yeah, I think you're better keeping it formal, set up your own thing, and work as a contractor. He has used contractors on the architecture side before, when we've had too much on, and I haven't heard any complaints."

She'd already decided that any work she did for the studio would be charged formally at her hourly or daily rate—when she'd worked out what that was to be. It was true she'd need a place for meetings, but initially she could simply visit the client. After all, with interior design, you definitely want to see the building under discussion.

The whole business of setting up her own studio

had a deeply romantic element. The truth was that 90 percent of the work would be a hard slog—talking to contractors, scheduling meetings, responding to emails. Getting the money in. She knew this, but she couldn't help enjoying the moment. She sat there, thinking it all through, reluctant to start on the mundane tasks that awaited her, knowing there'd be a lot more of them when she was running her own thing.

"Well," he said, getting up. "I'll leave you to it. I wish you luck, Isla. Let me know any time you think I can help."

"Thank you, Leonardo."

She'd be eating with Edmondo and Adriano this evening. Edmondo would want to know how the meeting had gone, and she was keen to pass on the information, to see if she'd missed anything important—or worse, if she'd misconstrued anything.

But first, she should check her computer. Ah, there already was the file for the small job Tommaso had mentioned. Perhaps it would be the very first project of her fledgling company. She hovered the cursor over the file—this was a special moment. With mounting excitement, she opened it up.

Chapter 42

Refusing an invitation to join her colleagues for a drink, Isla returned quickly to her flat to change.

They'd agreed that she would continue living at the flat until the lease ended in two weeks. She really didn't want to wait, but this seemed the simplest way to wind things up. Her flat was almost next door to the studio, and it didn't make sense to do anything else. It cut down on wasted time, especially in the morning, but still, she was spending more and more time at Edmondo's place and had already begun to move some of her possessions, bringing something with her each time she drove up the mountain.

Now, she turned into the courtyard and parked close to the tower. She hauled a box of books out of the boot of the car, hurried through the rain, and tapped lightly on the front door of the main house, but there was no reply. Where was everyone? She pushed it open. The main hallway was quiet after the wild weather outside, but she could hear murmuring from the sitting room and then Adriano's high-pitched treble. She placed the box on the hall table and closed the front door. Warmth enveloped her as she listened for a moment, before noticing that the door to Edmondo's study stood open. He had his back to her, bending over plans on his desk.

"Edmondo."

He stood upright, his face breaking into a smile of welcome, and he came over to kiss her. "*Cara mia*. You are early."

"Yes, I was so restless after this morning's meeting, I left as soon as I could. The others are at the bar in the square."

"Oh, you should have gone with them."

"What—and drive up here in this weather afterward? Certainly not. Anyway, it wasn't anything in particular, just social." She heard the voices again. "Has Adriano got Marco visiting? I can hear him talking."

"Ah—no, he's talking with his mother. I'd like to leave him to it, because on the last two occasions, they had to finish rather quickly when Basilio arrived home with friends. It's good for them to talk. And mostly, I think, better if I'm not present."

He laid down his pen. "I want to go over to the tower, so tell me what happened as we go."

He took her hand, led her out into the hall, and pushed open the door into the glass corridor that linked the house to the tower. The interior work on this was now complete, and they strolled along while the wind blew hard outside, and rain lashed at the triple-glazed panels. The temperature was perfect, with the tiles she'd seen on her first visit now laid over an effective underfloor heating system.

"I love this, the way you feel as if you've gone outside, but in here it's warm and calm."

"That's how Leonardo sold it to me," he said, grinning.

They stopped in the middle, gazing out on the mist and rain, and Isla filled him in on the morning's conversation. When she told him about doing work under the office logo, he looked rueful and said, "Well, that's certainly Tommaso's style. It's obvious he very much values what you do—otherwise, he would have turned you down flat, make no mistake about that. But he never loses an opportunity for business. Is it going to matter to you?"

"Probably not—and he will be doing me a favor. I expect I'll just not do that much work for him. It'll make me strive harder because I will need to find my own clients and build my own brand. But it is a start, and I appreciate it. He already sent me some information on a small job this morning after the meeting. It's a tiny *gastronomia* with a limited budget, just the part visible to the public, but he says he has something a bit bigger I can look at tomorrow, to see if it's the kind of thing I had in mind."

"That's good. He won't exploit you unless you let him, I'd say. Just don't be too generous with your time, or you won't have the opportunity to develop your own business. How's it going with Sofía?"

She turned to face him. It was a pleasure to talk about this—an ideal project. And come to think of it, *this* might be the first true project of her company. If only it happened.

"Really well. I'm so grateful for the introduction. I went to Rome yesterday afternoon, to meet her and walk around the apartment, and she likes the ideas I've put forward. Obviously, they were just ideas, first impressions of how it could work, so I'm going to have a lot to do, getting it all together—if we go ahead, that is. Apparently, the purchase goes through on Friday. There's not much point in doing any more work on it until she confirms that."

Edmondo pushed open the door of the tower. Now they'd opened this covered way, they were able to enter into the side of the building—no need for the giant key.

"Remember I said I had some ideas for your business?" he said, pausing in the entrance.

"Oh yes, of course. You were going to tell me the next day, but I think other things got in the way."

They walked into the building, and he flicked a light switch. Although the upper floors were now completed, down to the last detail and article of furniture, the ground floor area remained one large, impressive space. The lighting down here was necessarily basic, waiting for the final design. It would be great to begin work on this part, once he'd made up his mind how he wanted to use it. The room was open to the sturdy but elegant oak staircase they had finally settled on, which matched perfectly with the strong, solid look of the building. During the day, the whole place was flooded with light, as a number of windows had been set into the side walls, the front remaining exactly as it had been previously.

Inevitably, the massive fireplace on the right-hand side of the main entrance dominated. Isla looked around her wondering what he had in mind. It looked like a fabulous opportunity waiting for the right ideas. You could certainly divide the room up. The fireplace was so big, it might be a mistake to do that, but on the other hand, it could form a whole wall to a room in the front part of the building. After all, the idea wasn't to make it look in any way domestic down here. It would be more a feature, and a dramatic one at that. She shook her head, bringing her wandering thoughts back to the matter in hand.

"What were you going to show me?"

"Well…"

"Yes?"

"I thought we could divide up this space and put your business in here—and also my work room. What do you say?"

She took a deep breath, hardly able to believe what he was offering her.

"It's a fabulous idea, but you can't. This is your home!"

"This is our home. Remember?—you've agreed to share it with me. And what am I going to use it for otherwise? Reconstructing this tower has been a huge piece of self-indulgence, but it has to have a practical use—apart from that fabulous living space and the guest bedrooms upstairs. I can't think of anything better than turning the ground floor over to your new business."

"I don't know. I don't know. Oh, you're right—this would make a great workspace for both of us—and a lovely meeting room, with the focal point of the fireplace. Or we could just divide the room in two unequal parts—keep the rear part for both of us to work in, and a smaller area here around the fireplace as a sort of reception and meeting room."

She looked up and caught his eyes on her. Slightly embarrassed by her own enthusiasm, she suddenly understood the pleasure he was taking in being able to do this for her. How wonderful he had the means.

"I can see either of those ideas working well," she continued more quietly. "Or have you other thoughts?"

"I incline to that second idea—it sounds more companionable. But it's up to you."

She hugged him. "Do you really mean it?"

"I do. Those plans I was looking at when you came in—I got Leonardo to draw them up for me, without telling him it was your business I envisaged putting in here, of course. He suggested both the ideas you've just mentioned, so that means, as an architect, he can see either one working without damaging the integrity of the building. That was his primary concern, of course. Now the choice is yours.'

"Ours. We need to talk it through."

Plans didn't materialize overnight. He must have arranged this with Leonardo weeks ago. She continued to think about this and then said, "You were very sure of me, to get plans done!"

"Isla, I'm never sure of you. I keep wondering if you'll decide your business has to be in Rome or something. Or worse, that it's more important to you than I am, and you've decided not to move in after all."

"Oh, how could you think—"

"And then we'll spend all our time on the road, trying to snatch a moment to see each other. Instead of doing what really matters." He turned her to face him. "Things like this."

His kiss was light and sweet but lingering and promised things for later. Her heart began to pound. She wanted him now, not in some undefined future. Living with him had been a concept, an ideal, but no longer; he'd become a necessary part of her life. How could he imagine she might change her mind?

"And this." He placed his hands around her waist, pushing her gently toward the staircase.

"The furniture has arrived, and there's a lovely, long sofa in the top room. Want to inspect it now?—or maybe a little later on, when…?"

"*Papà! Papà, dove stai?*"

"Damn!" he whispered. "Definitely later."

He released her and walked to the door.

"Here we are, Adriano," he called. "Have you finished talking to your mother?"

"*Sì, Papà.* Dinner is ready."

Chapter 43

Sofía confirmed the purchase of her apartment in Rome at the end of the week—a mere 1.1 million euros, apparently. It seemed that was nothing for her. Isla's first real job for her new business was about to start, and that was massively exciting. She read and reread the notes she'd made when visiting the flat and, subsequently, when talking with Sofía.

It was a lovely place in Trastevere, on the second floor of a Renaissance-style building, with a lift and a concierge. That terrace with its sweeping views was a huge asset, even if it was shared with three other flats. But there was generous space, and one of the owners, presumably valuing privacy, had created tasteful screening with small trees in very large tubs. At one side was the River Tiber and the Ponte Sisto, visible from the large windows of the sitting room. Perfect, big-city living. And those double-height ceilings in all parts of the flat were fabulous, opening up so many possibilities.

Sofía had spotted the potential of that and had pointed it out to Isla on her visit.

"I know we haven't completed on the purchase yet, but I've engaged an architect to design a mezzanine, to add a second bedroom. The design work's ready, and we're assuming the legal completion is just a formality, so the builders are due to begin on Monday. It should all be finished before the Christmas holidays, when everything shuts down."

Cynically, Isla didn't believe it would happen quite that fast, but she knew money could turn anything around quickly. They'd soon find out.

"I've seen what you've done for Edmondo, Isla— he emailed me a whole lot of photos and I love it. Would you do a scheme for me?"

"Of course, but you'll need to give me a little of your time to discuss your budget and preferences."

"Can we do this right away?"

An hour into the conversation, having settled on an overall color scheme and how they would divide up the kitchen and living space, the woman pronounced herself satisfied that Isla could make the decisions.

"I know I can trust you since you come recommended by Edmondo."

This was both gratifying and worrying, but Susan had taught her well. "I'll need you to sign a contract to confirm exactly what the brief is and the sum of money under discussion." She showed her new client a basic contract she'd brought with her and now explained what would be necessary. "Can you get it back to me tomorrow, if possible? Email a copy and then put it in the post. Later, there'll be a detailed scheme of works, which you can query."

"Of course. Would it help if I make a down payment, just to start things moving?"

That was going to be very useful, since Isla didn't have a track record with any contractors and might well have to pay certain things upfront. Probably she had Edmondo to thank for that thoughtful gesture. As she left, they agreed to be in close contact by email.

The next day, the contract, signed and witnessed, duly arrived in her inbox, along with the original plans. She had the job—provided the purchase went through.

The perfect first project: the flat was in very good condition but had not been updated in at least twenty years. That was exciting because things had changed so much in that time and the apartment would look very different when she'd finished. The work required respect for the historic building coupled with a modern, streamlined effect.

That evening, Isla opened her laptop, started the video she'd made, and "walked" through the rooms. Apart from the new bedroom, the main change would be in the kitchen. It was hard to understand how anyone could ever have thought the heavy farmhouse-style cabinets were suited to a sophisticated home in the capital. And all that under-used floor space! It didn't look as if much thought had gone into the original design. Now she called up the plans Sofía had emailed and got down to work.

Ten minutes later, her phone rang. It was Edmondo.

"I'm sorry, Isla, I'm not going to be able to make it this evening."

"Oh, that's a pity." She was immediately aware of gnawing disappointment. "Can't you put off whatever it is until tomorrow? I went shopping for groceries today. I was going to cook something special for us. Or are you having to work late?"

"No, I'm going to see Giacomo. Stephano the investigator has finally found out where he is."

"Your cousin? Oh, be careful, Edmondo. That man is dangerous."

She hadn't met him—at least, not face to face—but there was every chance he was the one who'd hit her on the head. Certainly dangerous.

"It's okay. I'll have Stephano with me. He's agreed to give me backup."

"Darling, don't you think…"

"I'm not going to do anything risky, Isla, I promise you. I just want to find out what the problem is."

"And solve the matter without involving the police?"

"That's right. Look, he'll be picking me up at seven. It's only about twenty minutes away from the factory, at Torricelli, but I don't know how long it'll take to talk to him—an hour, maybe."

She sighed. He wasn't going to change his mind. Well, she had plenty to keep her occupied and stop her thinking over all the ways things could go wrong.

"Okay. I'm working on Sofia's plans. But ring me when you're safely away from there."

Isla worked for a good hour and then cooked herself some supper—just an omelet and a tomato salad, in the end—she had no heart for the new recipe she'd found on the internet and had intended to try. Lamb. He loved lamb. Well, it would have to wait.

He still hadn't telephoned when she'd finished and washed up. She eyed the phone lying silently on the worktop. Come on! Come on! But it was no use hanging around waiting, much better to return to the design. Suppressing the niggling worries, she picked up her pen, and soon she was deep in making notes, immersed in the changes she wanted to make. When she finally checked the time, it was a surprise to find it was already half past nine. He was supposed to be ringing her. What was keeping him?

She got up and paced around the confined space. She made a cup of tea. Still no call. When she tried ringing, his phone appeared to be shut down. Surely, there couldn't be a problem, not with Stephano there. Just how dangerous was this man?

Edmondo had made it sound as if the threat was nothing much, especially as he had backup, but Isla didn't see it that way. He was needlessly exposing himself to danger. She rubbed the spot on her head where the cut had now healed. She could still feel a faint trace of the scar with the tips of her fingers—proof, if needed, that the man was aggressive and vicious.

Twice more she rang. No answer. She breathed deeply, tamping down on her anxiety, but the longer she waited, the more worried she became. No, she couldn't lose him now, not after all that had happened. But that was stupid—he'd only gone to see his slightly wayward cousin, hadn't he? His slightly wayward, *violent* cousin.

It was five minutes past ten when the phone finally rang, and she snatched it up, her heart beating uncomfortably fast. She was convinced that something serious had happened.

"Isla, I'm fine. Don't worry. I—"

"Edmondo?" Relief flooded her whole being as she heard his voice. Relief, closely followed by anger. "You mean something has happened and you're fine now."

How badly hurt was he?

"It's nothing. Look, I'll see you tomorrow, and we'll talk about it. I promise you I'm all right."

"But you have come away from there now? You're on your way home?"

"Yes, there's nothing to worry about."

After a while, they said good night, but Isla still felt anxious—and put out that he wouldn't tell her anything. Whatever he said, something had definitely happened.

Chapter 44

"So, you see, we sorted it all out—once we'd calmed him down and he'd returned to something like normality, that is."

They were eating the lamb stew with mashed potato and buttered carrots sprinkled with parsley in Isla's tiny living room, a space so small that she had to sit on the kitchen bench and Edmondo perched on the single chair with the narrow table between them. It was the night after the confrontation with Giacomo and she'd had twenty-four hours to worry about what had happened—and worse, about how badly it could have gone.

She pushed the food around on her plate while she studied the deep cut above Edmondo's left eyebrow, on which a dark-red scab was forming. She felt sick. There was a quite dreadful bruise on his cheekbone—the other side from the one he'd got clearing rocks in the earthquake, the last traces of which had only recently disappeared. This one looked worse.

"Come on, eat up. This is delicious."

She hadn't said anything about it when he'd come in, overcome by the sight of his battered face.

"What did he hit you with?" she asked now, ignoring what he'd just said. "A lump of steel? You're lucky he didn't poke out your eye."

He'd taken far too big a risk, and it didn't sound as

if Stephano was quite the bodyguard he'd suggested. She heaved a huge sigh. Men could be so stupid with their conviction that they knew what was best. She hadn't realized just how angry she was with him.

But that wasn't fair, because Edmondo wasn't like that. He really had wanted to sort things out without involving the law. Not that risking himself like that was a sensible way to go about it. She suppressed her irritation and said quietly, "You should just have gone to the police. They wouldn't put a mentally ill man in jail, especially if you didn't press charges."

"Maybe not. But it needed a more personal touch. We talked to his mother. The poor woman's worn down and looks ten years older than her age. His father left years ago, when Giacomo was still at school, and she's looked after him ever since. I don't think she can continue to do that. Apparently, he's been working in a bakery in the town—some of the time. But he's absent from the job for days on end when it hits him. From what I can tell, his employer's been more than understanding. I'll need to speak to him, see if he can be persuaded to keep the job open while Giacco gets himself sorted out."

Well, at least he was here in front of her and not lying in a pool of blood somewhere. Maybe she was hungry after all. She mashed a little of the potato into the gravy and forked it into her mouth. Edmondo had almost cleared his plate, despite doing most of the talking.

"What is *it*? What's wrong with him?"

"I think the problem is about taking the right medicines—or, in his case, not wanting to take any at all, when he should be doing so. We've sorted out a hospital placement for him. Mind you, he's not just accepting this without protest. He won't admit there's anything wrong. We had a big row about it."

"I can see that from the state of your face! So, what happens if he absconds and turns up here?"

"*Se scappa dall'ospedale? Non lo farà.* No, he won't. We drove him there, and they accepted him into a facility immediately. He's not restrained, but he won't be able to wander out again. They'll keep an eye on him."

"Okay. That's a bit more reassuring."

"It won't have to be for long, just until they get the medical side properly balanced."

They were quiet for a moment, thinking through how these events might play out.

"Why didn't you ring me earlier, Edmondo? I had to wait all that time, and I was really worried."

"I am so sorry. I was about to call when he hit me. It surprised us all, and it took quite a while to calm him down. He has delusions, and unfortunately, I figure in them in a big way. It's a good thing Stephano was there. He literally had to drag Giacomo off me."

"He's delusional—about you?"

"Yeah—maybe he's schizophrenic or something like that, but I don't know much about these things. Let's hope they can sort him out. He exaggerates a lot and definitely doesn't let reality get in the way of his beliefs."

She sprang up and flung her arms around him, almost knocking the dishes to the floor.

"Oh, Edmondo, that was so dangerous. When you didn't ring, I thought something terrible had happened—and it sounds as if it did. I was so afraid. I thought I'd lost you."

"Now, who's exaggerating, *cara mia*?" He stood up and taking her chin in his fingers, he looked deep into her eyes and then kissed her gently. "Stephano was there. You haven't met him but…*è un tipo grosso.*"

"A big bloke?"

"*Sì*—like Pietro, only larger and fiercer. There was never any real danger."

She looked at his battered face. How could that be true?

They sat back down and swallowed the last forkfuls of stew. Now he came around and cuddled up to her. Of course, he was seeking to distract her and calm her fears, but she needed him there beside her. She leaned into him.

"That was totally delicious," he said. "Not only are you beautiful, clever, *and* brave, but a wonderful cook as well."

Isla felt her face growing hot. Really, blushing? She was totally useless, behaving like that. But it was lovely to be appreciated.

"Honestly, Edmondo, stew is one of only three dishes I ever cook. This was a new version—I've never used lamb before, so I'm glad you enjoyed it. My mother, now, is a different matter. Her cooking is a real experience."

"While you're in England over Christmas, I'll fly out to London for a couple of days so I can meet your mother—and sample her cooking."

"That would be great. It will cheer me up a lot. Although I'm keen to see Mum, I don't want to be away from here. I don't want to be away from you."

He kissed her again and said, "And I don't want

you to be away from me either."

He was quiet for a moment, pouring another glass of wine for her and water for himself since he'd be driving home later. "Isla, I'm so sorry about all the worry. I want to make it up to you. What about if I pick you up tomorrow evening around six, and we'll go somewhere nice."

"The fish restaurant?"

"Well, I didn't think I should mention it at this stage. Do you know how many times we've planned to go there? And usually, something bad happens to prevent us."

She laughed. This would actually be the fourth time they'd planned to dine there.

"That's true. Let's just wait and see. But yes—I'd like to go out tomorrow evening."

Chapter 45

"I'm not so sure about this excursion, now I've seen what the weather's like," Isla said.

"Don't worry. It's not far, and I know the route."

Well, if he thought it was okay, who was she to say differently? She glanced at him. She didn't feel that confident but said nothing, remembering how good a driver he was. But now they were on the way, the wind seemed intent on throwing the car across the road, with gusts that were far in excess of what had been forecast. It was so unpredictable and very scary, and she found herself gripping her seat despite her determination not to show her fear.

Suddenly, they arrived at the cliff top. The road began to descend steeply through dwellings that clung higgledy-piggledy to the slope heading down into the port and looked as if one big gust of wind could sweep them all off. Glimpses of the rain-lashed sea appeared between buildings. But here, finally, was the carpark close to the center of the little coastal town—and thank goodness for that!

As night was falling, he turned off the ignition, and they sat a moment as the engine sound died, and the cacophony of the storm rushed in to fill their ears.

"How do we get there?"

"You'll see. I hope that coat is warm."

They set out to walk along the beach. A sharp tang

330

of seaweed filled the air, and although no rain fell, it was another wild evening. The waves pounded along the shore, sending towers of spray into the air, and there was an extraordinary amount of noise. The beach was very flat at this point, and Isla leapt out of the way as the tide rushed up and threatened to cover her feet. As the freezing spray hit them again, they turned away toward a set of concrete steps leading to the promenade and then staggered up onto the firm surface.

This was hardly any better. The wind howled, icy blasts cut through the thick wool of her coat, and Isla felt even colder. She pulled off her gloves and rubbed her fingers together but couldn't get any warmth into them.

She was terrified, yes, but it was great being out here, struggling together against the elements.

"I like this," she said, grabbing his arm. "Especially when I know we'll soon be inside."

Edmondo was carrying a small, leather overnight bag containing clothes for them. This seemed like a really strange place. The restaurant they were going to had a tiny hotel halfway up the cliff behind it, but nowhere to park, so they would have to walk to it up steps cut into the rock. With the temperature dropping so fast, their thick, woolen coats hardly seemed adequate, and Isla increased her pace to stop shivering. Ah, at last! The promenade came suddenly to an end, and then they were crunching on sand and pebbles again. A spatter of icy drops made them put on a spurt, but already, the pinpricks of light were resolving themselves into golden globes, and moments later, they entered the warm lobby of the restaurant.

"So, we finally got to the fish restaurant," said Isla.

"I was beginning to wonder if we ever would."

Given the dark, cold evening and the time of year, the place was surprisingly full, which probably showed just how good the food was. The establishment had an excellent reputation in the area. They hung their coats on a stand and spoke to the waiter. A table had been reserved for them at the back of the room. It was the sort of place where they spread your napkin on your knees—as if you wouldn't be able to do it for yourself. It always made Isla smile, and she looked up to see Edmondo sharing her thought.

This waiter was an elderly man and very formal. With a bow, he handed them the menus. Isla scanned hers, impressed by its range.

"There's so much on here, and it's all fish. I'm not sure I know how to choose."

"Well, Italians eat almost everything that comes out of the sea. There are some things you won't be able to have because we'd have had to order it in advance—and some things you probably wouldn't want—but that still leaves plenty of choice."

"It's my first visit to this part of the coast," she said.

"One day, we'll go to a fish market. There's one about fifteen minutes away, just past the point. I guarantee you can find an unimaginable number of different fish—and it's a fascinating place."

"Oh, this sounds good," said Isla, spotting something she thought she knew. "It looks like their own version of baked sea bass."

"We'd better both have it, then. They do it here with a strong garlic sauce—very antisocial if the other person isn't eating garlic." He grinned at her. "Go on, choose whatever you want."

"No, you choose. I'm a complete novice where fish is concerned, and I ought to try something I haven't had before. I've only ever eaten one or two varieties—but I do like fish."

"I've heard that's typical of English people, and a bit strange. You live on an island surrounded by waters that are rich in varieties of fish and you sell most of it to other countries. Bizarre."

A long time passed, and they found plenty to talk about. Eventually, they got onto the subject of the Christmas holiday.

"I'm going to leave my car in Fortezza because I don't intend to be gone for long, so I've booked a flight to London next Friday." Isla laid her hand on Edmondo's arm. "I...it's going to be so difficult to leave, even for such a short a time. I didn't know how much I was going to mind that."

"I hate for us to be parted."

He leaned across to kiss her, but she pushed him away.

"We'll embarrass people," she said.

"Not in Italy." He pulled her back towards him. "They are probably watching us out of the corner of their eyes and wondering when we are going to get together. Mmm...I can see I shall have to fill in the gap between your sketchy Latin education and the very proper English miss you are."

"I really am not."

"You really are...but I can see the ice already melting."

His mouth came down on hers, and she managed to forget all her worries about correct behavior in a restaurant. Finally, they drew apart and ate a little more of the main course, but emotion filled her entire being. Her stomach was churning and soon, she had to stop.

"My mum was hoping to meet you over Christmas. And I won't be able to wait for you to arrive, I can tell you. It's going to be difficult. If it wasn't that I want to see her and make sure she's properly recovered, I wouldn't go."

The waiter came to clear the main course and went discreetly away again.

"Isla, I've got something to say to you, and I'm feeling nervous about it."

What did he mean? He didn't look like a man who was about to give her bad news but that didn't mean he wasn't. Oh, no, he'd just remembered some obligation and was going to say he couldn't make it to London after all. Disappointment was crushing her. She leant forward, picking an imaginary piece of fluff off her sleeve, in the hope of hiding her expression. How much she wanted him to be there, just for a day or two over the Christmas season.

She'd pictured her mother returning from church on Christmas morning, while she oversaw the dinner. Then her cousin Sally and her husband Rob would arrive with their six-year-old. He'd always been her favorite—until Adriano had come into her life. And Penny, of course. She'd seen Edmondo right there with the rest of them. Now it wasn't going to happen.

She'd been silly. Of course, he would want to be with Adriano, to celebrate with Paola and her family. How could it be otherwise? She shrugged. It had been such a lovely idea—and now, it wasn't going to happen. The thought was deeply painful.

He leant across the table and took both her hands, pulling her toward him, but she looked away.

"Where did you go just then? What was in your mind?"

"Oh, it's all right. I was thinking about what you said. I do understand that Adriano has to come first."

"What are you talking about, Isla?"

She looked up then, and his expression of bewilderment confused her.

"You," she said, "not being able to make it for Christmas. I was just feeling a bit sad about it—but we can meet after the holiday, of course. It's not a—"

"Isla, you've completely misunderstood."

Her heart seemed to stand still and then picked up its steady beat again, while a slow flush worked its way up her neck and into her face.

The way he was looking at her—it meant something important, but she wasn't sure what.

"You know, when I first met you, I had to fight against the feelings you evoked in me. Do you remember that first time, in the bar in Milan? We didn't even speak. But I was overcome by the idea that something momentous had happened. Then, there you were in my home. I couldn't believe it and tried to remind myself there were many reasons why I should walk away."

She was paying attention now. This so exactly mirrored what had happened to her. So he had felt this as well?

"At the house, as we discussed the work to the tower, I considered asking Tommaso to find someone else."

Isla drew in a sharp breath, terrified now she knew

how it had all hung in the balance.

"And do you know why?"

Her mouth was dry, and for a moment, she couldn't speak at all. "Why?" she whispered at last.

"Because there was that one moment when I knew I was already smitten. When I knew I couldn't fight it if I kept on seeing you." He was still holding her eyes with his gaze. Her hands were trembling in his. "There was just that moment when I might have been able to turn my back. Not get away unscathed, oh, no—the damage had already been done—but maybe I could have moved on at that point. And then it was gone. Do you love me, Isla?"

"You know I do."

"No, I mean really love me. I'm in love with you. I know what that feels like—it's fantastic and I believe it's the same for you. We're good for one another on all sorts of levels. But I meant real love. What would it feel like if we decided to split up so you could pursue your career, for instance? How would you feel?"

Her heart was beating so fast, it threatened to choke her. Was he suggesting they part after all? How could she possibly face the future without him? She hadn't done anything to move the situation along because she'd loved him from the very first moment, and it had never occurred to her to make sure that he'd stay, that they'd form a couple and be like that forever. And now he was asking her what she thought. She couldn't begin to imagine life without him.

And suddenly, she knew what the answer was.

"I would die, Edmondo. Maybe not literally, but I'd be less than I am, unable to function. I'd die."

"So, it's the same for me."

And gazing into her eyes, he brought his hand down over hers, where it now lay on the table, and squeezed gently. It stayed there, warm and comforting.

"It's the same for me, and I do have a solution, but this was the point I was worried about, that you might not agree to it."

"The only thing possible," she said, "would be for us to spend our lives together."

"I truly believe there's no other option, Isla."

He slid out of his seat and was suddenly down on his knees in front of her. "*Cara mia*, will you marry me? Please say you will. *Sono innamorato di te. Ti amo*. And you've told me you love me—and you've said you'll move in with me. What's to stop us taking this final step?"

"Absolutely nothing at all. I do want to marry you, Edmondo."

Isla's heart was thumping hard, making it difficult to breathe. All the sounds in the restaurant had receded into the background, and they were enclosed in their own bubble.

He pulled a small box from his pocket and inside was a ring, a diamond on a simple, white-gold band.

"I think this should fit," he said, "but we can get it altered if it doesn't."

He took her hand and slipped it onto her finger.

"This is so beautiful, Edmondo, truly a symbol of what we have together."

She was light-headed with the rush of joy that threatened to overwhelm her. She had thought it didn't matter to her that they be married, but now that he'd proposed, she saw it differently, and it was wonderful. The fact he wanted this meant so much to her. He sat down and slid along the banquette into the corner and kissed her in a way that left her gasping for air. Even his kisses now tasted different, as if she drank champagne from his mouth. And they made her think of the night to come, every inch of her body responding to that thought. But a moment later, they had to draw back, as the waiter came up with an ice bucket. It appeared he'd been warned of the possibility of a celebration and had been keeping his eye on the table.

"Your champagne, sir."

"Thank you."

They leaned back in their seats as, with not even the glimmer of a smile, the man poured them each a glass and placed the bottle back in the ice.

Edmondo picked up his glass, and looking into her eyes, he said, "*Al nostro futuro, cara mia.* To our future together."

"To our future together."

The glasses chinked, and they each took a sip.

Then, Isla looked down at the lovely diamond, winking in the candlelight. "It fits perfectly."

"I told the jeweler that you had long, slim fingers, and he's got it just right."

A little while later, he took her hand and pulled her to her feet. "Come on. It's time to seal our promises."

A word about the author…

Mary Georgina de Grey lives on the beautiful English Riviera in the UK with her artist husband. Having lived and worked in several countries in Europe and South America, she sets out to infuse her books with the language, culture, and atmosphere of the country in which the story is set.

With interests that range from European cooking to designing and making haute couture clothing, there are plenty of sources for ideas.

Mary Georgina swims every day and often walks on the dramatic cliffs of this stunning coast.

Visit Mary Georgina at her website:
www.marygeorginadegreyauthor.com
or on Facebook:
https://www.facebook.com/profile.php?id=1000864241
98194

Thank you for purchasing
this publication of The Wild Rose Press, Inc.

For questions or more information
contact us at
info@thewildrosepress.com.

The Wild Rose Press, Inc.
www.thewildrosepress.com